ONE LITTLE LIE

THE TRUTH COULD COST HER EVERYTHING...

Kate had high hopes when she moved to her husband's hometown, but her domestic bliss was short-lived. Blindsided by her spouse's public affair with his high school sweetheart, Kate's determined to hold onto custody of her kids and pull herself together. When Kate's struck in the head by a drone at her son's soccer game and face-plants in the grass, it's more than her self-esteem that's shattered. The drone's footage reveals that someone is stalking her. And though the handsome detective she's falling for vows to protect her, Kate knows to be wary of any man making vows.

With things spiraling out of control, she tells a lie. It was only *One Little Lie*, but a lie is a welcome mat for the devil, and with the one she told, Kate just rolled out the red carpet. Everything she worked for begins to unravel, along with her sanity. Confused, alone, and afraid, can Kate untangle the web of lies and unmask her stalker, or will she lose everything—including her life?

One Little Lie is a riveting suspense novel power-packed with love, greed, and betrayal, set in an idyllic town where money talks, gossip flows, and the court of public opinion rules. From multi-award-winning Wall Street Journal bestselling author Christopher Greyson comes this spellbinding tale with jaw-dropping secrets and a female protagonist you'll root for from the first page to the last.

Also by Christopher Greyson:

The Girl Who Lived

And Then She Was Gone

Girl Jacked

Jack Knifed

Jacks Are Wild

Jack and the Giant Killer

Data Jack

Jack of Hearts

Jack Frost

Jack of Diamonds

Pure of Heart

The Adventure's of Finn and Annie

ONE LITTLE LIE

WALL STREET JOURNAL BESTSELLING AUTHOR
CHRISTOPHER GREYSON

GREYSON MEDIA

ONE LITTLE LIE
Copyright © Greyson Media 2021

The right of Christopher Greyson to be identified as author of this Work has been asserted by him in accordance with sections 77 and 78 of the Copyright, Designs and Patents Act 1988.

All rights reserved. No part of this publication may be reproduced, distributed, or transmitted in any form or by any means, including photocopying, recording, or other electronic or mechanical methods, without the prior written permission of the publisher.

Any references to historical events, real people, or real places are used fictitiously. Names, characters, and places are products of the author's imagination.
www.ChristopherGreyson.com.

ISBN: 1-68399-332-2
ISBN-13: 978-1-68399-332-2
ONE LITTLE LIE V 1.0 4-28-21

This book is dedicated to Anne Cherry. Her help, guidance and friendship have enriched my work and my life.

The clock on the therapist's desk tolled three times, signaling the end of another toxic session. Kate swayed as she rose from her chair and retreated to the door.

"Kate." Dr. Sprouse motioned in vain for her to sit back down.

Tugging her jacket over her sweat-soaked shirt, now clinging to her back, Kate seized the doorknob.

Dr. Sprouse remained seated but pointed to the prescription clutched in Kate's hand. "Since we've increased your dosage, please call me immediately if you experience any serious side effects."

"I will." Kate plastered on a smile as she ripped open the door. "Thank you, Doctor."

She hurried through the empty waiting room and burst out the exit, finally gulping in air and releasing it. Another "successful" session. At least she still hadn't ever cried in front of him. That was success in her book. She stumbled on the stairs in her haste and paused to calm herself, removing her glasses and pressing her thumb and index finger against her eyes. The cloudy October sky dulled both the sun's light and its warmth. She shivered, but not because of the chilly fall wind. This cold came from someplace deep within.

Rejection. Humiliation. Fear. They all swirled together in a tornado of emotions.

"It's perfectly natural to feel this way, Kate," the good doctor had told her again and again in his calm and objective voice. *"It's part of the grieving process."*

Kate wanted no more of it. She zipped her jacket and turned the collar up. With the prescription to increase the dosage of her antianxiety medicine in hand, she headed for the pharmacy across the street, eager to dull the pain.

The medicine's side effects concerned the doctor, but Kate didn't care as long as it worked. Suicidal thoughts, memory loss, and bloating—she was already suffering two out of the three. If she developed memory loss, maybe she could forget Scott. That alone made it worth the risk.

"Scott." She said his name out loud.

As if in reply, the mellow melody of an old favorite song wafted through the air. She traced the sound to a young man playing guitar for money on the corner. His sandy blond hair hung over his eyes in a style that made her want to brush it back out of his face. Dressed in jeans and a blue T-shirt, he couldn't be long out of his teens. Kate stopped beside the light pole as he finished his cover of the Rolling Stones song. The light changed, and the two people watching the guitarist walked away without even looking at the empty coffee tin at the musician's feet. He closed his eyes and muttered something under his breath. When he opened them again, they watered.

Kate reached into her handbag and pulled out two dollars, the only money she had in her purse. She approached the busker, dropped the cash into the tin, and turned to cross the street before the light changed.

Behind her, she heard, "Thanks a lot. It's for tuition."

Kate looked back. The young man looked a lot like Scott. She glanced at the paltry two dollars, knowing it wouldn't even buy him a good cup of coffee. "May I offer you a little advice?"

Disappointment and worry shone behind his brown eyes. He gave a one-shouldered shrug, the guitar strap rising up on his chest. "If you're gonna tell me to get a real job, no offense, but my parents beat you to it."

"No." Kate shook her head. "It's just... If it were me, I wouldn't use the coffee can for tips. You want to make it as clear as possible you'd like their help. The can is small; they won't see it. I'd use your guitar case."

"That's smart." He bent over, opened the wide case, and put Kate's two dollars on top of the red velvet.

"And your sign needs a little work." Kate picked up the large piece of cardboard, which had the word TIPS scrawled across it. "Do you mind?"

"Not at all."

She dug around in her purse until she found one of the two markers her four-year-old daughter, Ava, had been using as drumsticks. She flipped the sign over and wrote on the other side: WORKING MY WAY THROUGH COLLEGE. THANK YOU!

"That's sweet!" He took the sign from Kate and propped it against the guitar case. "Is that what you do? Advertising?"

"Kinda." A familiar pang of longing stabbed her chest. "But yes, I have a marketing degree."

He nodded.

"One last thing, now that you've got me going…" She motioned to the pickup trucks and men wearing cowboy boots. "You need to think about your target market. Do you know any country music?"

"A little Johnny Cash."

"Around here that'll sell better than the Stones."

"Thanks, lady." He flashed her a wide grin as he started to play "I Walk the Line."

The pedestrians bunched up along the curb, waiting for the signal to cross the busy intersection, shifted closer to listen.

Kate exhaled. Today wasn't a total disaster. She slipped to the back of the crowd and stood beside the light pole. The young man had a nice voice, and his unassuming smile grew as people started dropping change into his guitar case.

She pictured Andy and Ava in the living room having one of their pretend concerts. Ava always provided the vocals, belting out a Disney song on her karaoke machine, while Andy played his air guitar or used pots from the kitchen as a drum set. Maybe she could talk them into a show tonight after Andy's soccer game? She could order pizza.

As a parade of cars sped by, the crowd on the sidewalk continued to grow. Kate faced the street. A massive dump trunk's engine rumbled louder as it raced to beat the yellow light.

Faintly and far away, as if carried on the breeze, she thought she heard her sister whisper her name—"Kate."

But that was impossible. As she turned toward the voice, something shoved against Kate's back. Her arms windmilled. Her right hand grabbed at the light pole, her fingers tightening around the walk button. But she lost her grip. The momentum carried her body forward and she arced into the street, directly into the path of the truck barreling toward the intersection.

Her world slowed to a stop. The truck was so close. Her green eyes, wide with terror, filled the side mirror as it passed an inch away from her nose. The blast of cold air from the speeding truck slapped her in the face, turning her head and blowing her hair into her mouth. She gasped and stumbled back onto the curb. Her skin prickled with sweat and she trembled like a newborn deer, unsteady on her legs.

With everyone watching the musician, the only people who seemed to have noticed Kate's brush with death were an elderly couple.

"You okay?" the old man asked. "Another step and you woulda been a hood ornament."

His wife shook her head as she stepped closer and added, "You really have to wait for the light, dear. You were almost hit. People just won't stop nowadays."

Kate stood shaking on the sidewalk. "I'm fine," she blurted out.

The walk signal clicked on and the crowd began to move.

As she processed what had happened, she questioned herself. She hadn't tried to cross, had she? No, something had pushed against her—hard. Hard enough to shove her into the road.

Kate glanced around, but her fellow pedestrians were going on their way, including the old couple. She turned in circles, searching, but no one stood out and nobody looked directly at her.

Kate pulled the crumpled prescription from her pocket and stared at it in her trembling hand. Dr. Sprouse had doubled the dosage of her antianxiety medication because of this kind of paranoid thinking.

No one had pushed her. The sidewalk had just been crowded—it was an accident. After all, who would want to kill her?

Standing on the sideline of the soccer field watching her son's game, Kate waved as her free-spirited best friend, Donna, headed toward her. They were the same age, but their lives were polar opposites. As were their clothing choices. Donna usually looked like a cyclone had ripped through her closet and she'd put on whatever whirled out. Somehow, she always made it work. Of course, the mile-long legs, rich sepia complexion, and sweet face didn't hurt. Today it was distressed jeans, Doc Martens boots, and a black T-shirt layered with a plaid lumberjack shirt she'd customized with bleach. A black bowler hat with a purple flower in the band topped off her look. Beneath it spilled colorful braids with a rainbow of tiny, mismatched beads that clicked and jingled as her head rocked back and forth to her own internal soundtrack.

"How'd your appointment with the shrink go?" Donna asked.

Kate stepped close to her friend, embarrassed in case one of the other parents nearby had overheard. "He asked me if I were an object, what kind of object would I be?"

Donna raised an eyebrow, conveying in her own Donna-like way that she was mildly interested.

"I told him I'd be a lamp because I'm always shining bright and happy."

Donna doubled over, laughing. "What a load of BS."

"Shut up."

Donna let out a dramatic sigh. "If you want to get anything out of therapy, you have to tell him the truth."

"And what's that?"

"You, my friend, are a doormat."

Kate's jaw clenched.

"Oh, don't get all sensitive. I'm a doormat too. At least I was." Donna flashed a hundred-watt smile. "You helped me change that. I'm telling you, you should come to the codependent support group with me."

"I'm not codependent," Kate said as she fiddled with the remote control in her pocket.

"You're as codependent as they get. Daughter of an alcoholic—check! Recently divorced from an abusive husband—check! Low self-esteem—"

"Scott wasn't abusive."

Donna gave a signature eye roll. "Are we talking about the same guy who dragged you and your two kids clear across the country, had an affair, kicked you to the curb, and then tricked you into approving the least you can get in child support?"

Kate squirmed.

"He set you up with that stupid prenup, used you like an indentured servant to build his business, and threw you away like a used Dixie cup! How is that *not* abusive?"

Kate rubbed the empty spot her wedding ring had once occupied.

"I signed the prenup because he told me that his mother thought I was only interested in him for his money."

"And now you get no alimony."

"He's done a lot of rotten things, but he never laid a hand on me."

Donna's beads jingled as she shook her head. "Words and actions can cause the deepest scars."

Everything Donna said was true. Their marriage had been far from perfect. Scott's drive to build his law firm and step into politics had resulted in an absentee husband and father. Kate had fulfilled the role of dutiful wife, juggling everything life threw at them, while Scott focused on his goals. But… still she felt guilty.

Donna's eyes softened. "I love you, Kate. You're my best friend. And I hate to see someone with a big heart like yours get crushed under the weight that scumbag and his townies have heaped on you."

Kate's hand instinctively rubbed at her chest. Donna was right about the deep wounds she had faced over these last few months. But—

The referee's whistle brought their attention back to the game. Kate cheered her eleven-year-old son, Andy, as he charged down the soccer field, dribbling the ball with the fire only a child wanting to impress an idolized parent can summon. After his great play, he passed the ball and scanned the crowd, searching for his father. When his lip quivered and his head sagged until his chin touched his chest, it felt like someone had squeezed Kate's heart hard enough to crack it. Andy had only joined the team because Scott told stories of playing when he was Andy's age, and her son believed it was a way to win his dad's approval.

"How can Scott do this to our little boy?"

"Because he's a callous snot," Donna said frankly.

Kate shook her head, her brown hair touching her reddened cheeks. "It's Andy's last game of the season. Every week Scott promises he'll come, but it's been one excuse after another. He can't fit in one hour for his son? You're right, Donna. He is a callous snot, and I'm going to demand he shows some respect to the kids he fathered."

"You go, girl!"

Kate's shoulders slumped. What would be the point of confronting Scott? He'd say that a client needed this or a judge required that. He'd explain it away by saying he was providing for the family—financially. It wouldn't matter to him that he conducted most meetings while golfing with the aforementioned client or judge.

"So," Donna said, "are you ready to get back on the horse and ride a different cowboy?"

"If you're talking about speed dating again, no way. That was a disaster."

"You need to change how you look at things. You got to meet five guys you never would have had the chance to meet otherwise."

"All of whom I never want to see again."

"You need to kiss a lot of frogs before you find a prince."

"I'm done getting warts. Background checks from here on out."

They laughed.

Kate peered along the bleachers, searching for Ava. Her daughter had slept over at her friend's house and was watching the game with Stacy and her mother. Ava caught sight of Kate and waved with both of her hands lifted high overhead. Kate smiled when she saw her daughter's outfit. Dressed in an oversized hoodie and carrying a children's tablet, her theatrical daughter was playing dress-up and pretending to be the coach. Kate was glad to see her happy. Ava had put on a brave face since the divorce, but the night terrors and bedwetting were signs of deeper issues. Though Kate had promised she would never leave her, Ava believed anyone she loved could simply walk out of her life.

The referee blew his whistle, signaling halftime. Like a flock of birds, the boys swooped over to their benches squawking happily—all except one. Andy paid no attention to his teammates as he continued to scan the stands and the parking lot for his father. Desperate to encourage him, Kate waved and gave Andy two big thumbs up, but still his shoulders slumped.

"I gotta jet," Donna said, picking up her purse. "I'm meeting Louis."

"I thought you were seeing Tim."

"That was a different lying jerk."

"I'll walk you to the parking lot. I have to test a few more features of the drone before I can complete the review." Kate pulled out the drone's remote control from her pocket. "Then I can give it to Andy! That should cheer him up."

"He's going to freak out. I can't believe they're going to let you keep it when you're done, and you get paid for writing the review." Donna wiggled her shoulders. "This could be the start of a new career!"

"It's only one article, and I got the gig because I begged my sorority sister."

"Still, it's for a national magazine, and maybe it'll lead to more work. Have some faith!"

Kate doubted that would happen, but it would be great. Her temp job was ending soon, and so far, her job search had been fruitless.

Pushing aside her self-doubt for the moment, Kate followed Donna out to the parking lot. Kate kept looking over her shoulder as they went and her pace increased.

Donna stepped closer to her, her own gaze sweeping the parking lot. "Are you all right?"

Kate swallowed and nodded as they stopped beside Donna's bright-purple VW Bug. "Yeah, I just…" She closed her eyes and exhaled.

Donna placed a reassuring hand on her shoulder. "Relax. Remember, you aren't in the city; you're safe here in the burbs. The worst thing that could happen to you in Hartville is being bored to death, right?"

Donna's easy smile made Kate follow suit. "How do you never seem to worry?"

Donna held up her purse. "I have Harry!" She laughed, wrapped her arms around Kate, and gave her an enormous hug.

Kate tried not to make a face as Donna's purse tapped against her back. Kate could picture the gun inside, which Donna had affectionately named Harry, pointing at her spine.

"Thanks for coming to the game. I appreciate the support," Kate said.

Donna sat down in her car and another smile lit up her face. "Hey, remember how your shrink asked you what object you'd be? I just figured out what I'd be!" She playfully knocked the fuzzy gold dice hanging from her rearview mirror. "Dice! I'm unpredictable!"

They both laughed as she drove away.

Kate marched toward the far corner of the lot, whipping her phone out of her purse. She checked every possible method of modern communication again—text, voicemail, email… nothing from Scott. She clicked it off and stared at her darkened phone screen and into the reflected eyes of a worn-down, thirty-six-year-old woman she barely recognized. Like it or not, Scott wasn't her husband anymore and she couldn't tell him what to do.

She shoved the phone back into one of the pockets of her purse. Thanks to the crowd, she had been forced to park on the other side of the lot, next to the empty baseball field. When she reached her dark-blue minivan—boring but functional—she hid behind it. Glancing around to make sure no one was in sight, she adjusted the Spanx that was strangling her like a boa constrictor. As she pulled, twisted, and wriggled, she swore under her breath. She hated herself for the hours spent in front of the mirror trying to conceal each emerging wrinkle and the putrid smell of hair dye that had to be applied continually to cover the gray. But she submitted to the self-inflicted torture in the hopes of propping up her wilting self-esteem. Or perhaps there was another reason. A faint hope she clung to.

She adjusted the bulges beneath her green chambray shirtdress as she assessed her outfit in the reflection of the van window. It was the best Goodwill had to offer. Today, she'd gone so far as to match her seemingly new purse with brown leather ankle boots and a belt.

She smiled, but it quickly faded. She didn't want to admit it, but Scott's absence still hurt. The divorce had been finalized three months ago, and she had done everything in her power to save the marriage, but it was of no use. He'd moved on. Eventually, she'd have to too.

Climbing into the van, she reached down to pick up the surprise that was certain to put a smile back on her tech-loving son's face. The best part, even an eleven year old could fly it. The first couple of times Kate had tested the drone in the empty field near the house, it shot into the air at the touch of a single button. Her review would agree that the slogan on the box wasn't false advertising—a drone that flew itself!

She didn't have much time before the second half of the game started, and the baseball diamond next to the soccer field was the perfect spot. She'd have to jog between the bases to finish testing the drone and get back to the game before it started again.

Kate flicked the power switch, took out the remote control, and selected follow mode. The propellers hummed and the drone rose. She disliked getting her picture taken but needed some good pictures for the review. She waited until the drone was soaring high overhead before pressing record and shoving the remote into her pocket.

Each time she rounded home plate, Kate gazed toward the parking lot. Scott probably wouldn't see any of Andy's game. Even if he did come, he probably wouldn't arrive alone. *She* would come. His high school sweetheart. His affair. His dirty mistress. Actually, not his mistress anymore. From what little information Kate had gleaned from the kids, she knew that Tammi had moved into Scott's new house.

Less than a year earlier, when they moved to Hartville, Scott had picked out a small house that needed a lot of work. Kate had been grateful he was finally getting more financially prudent. How naïve. After the divorce, he'd bought a McMansion in the most expensive subdivision in town. Was he already planning on dumping Kate when they bought the little fixer-upper?

Did he know he'd never stay in it? Was that why he didn't care that it needed so much work?

The questions made Kate's head spin so severely, her eyes crossed. She was ruminating again—that's what Dr. Sprouse called it—but how could she not?

A branch snapped behind the third-base dugout. The cement dugout bordered the woods. The area was dense with trees and overgrown. Kate scanned the brush, but an elephant could have been hiding in there and she wouldn't have seen it.

"Kate!"

She spun around. Scott stood beside the first-base fence, holding a new soccer ball under one arm, a gift bag on the other, and propping the gate open with his foot. At thirty-six, he looked the same as the day she'd met him—the bright, handsome, go-getter lawyer with a thousand-watt smile. He gave her one of those grins now and warmth spread throughout her body. It still melted her, and it was even more dazzling because of his tan. *How'd he get a tan in October?* Scott burned faster than popcorn soaked in butter even with SPF 50.

"Hey, do you have a minute?" Scott waved her over.

Kate tried to get her breathing back to normal as she hurried over to him. "Did you see a dog or something at the other dugout?"

He craned his neck, then shook his head.

"I thought I heard something." She scurried through the gate and followed Scott as he started walking back toward the soccer field.

He shrugged. "Maybe a parent had to go to the bathroom. You probably embarrassed the hell out of them. The second half is going to start—you got a minute?"

"Sure. I'm so glad you're here," she said. "Andy's going to be over the moon!"

"You look great. New dress?"

Kate lifted up on her toes and forced herself to stay on the ground, thrilled that he had noticed. She nodded. "You look great too, so tan."

"Bahamas. Just a long weekend. I'm glad I didn't burn." Scott casually glanced at his arm, then held out the bag. "I picked up something for you and the kids."

Kate peeked. Inside was a stuffed dolphin for Ava and a box of Tortuga chocolate rum balls for her.

"There's something I'd like to talk to you about." He started snapping his fingers—his tell. He had an idea he wanted to sell her on. Whatever he needed to say, he was thinking of how to spin it.

"Hey, Dad!" Andy shouted from the sideline of the soccer field. "Dad!"

"Hold that thought." Scott flashed her an apologetic smile, then turned and jogged over to his son, who rushed to meet him. He tossed Andy the ball, and the boy eagerly dribbled it, showing off his skills.

Kate followed Scott over to the sideline. Ava and her friend came running over. Ava's ponytails bounced happily as she waved imaginary pompoms, cheering her brother on.

When Andy kicked the ball back to his father, Scott demonstrated his own tricks, putting on a performance that drew a crowd of envious spectators. Everyone stared as he effortlessly dribbled the ball, kicked it, spinning, high into the air, and caught it with precision in the crook of his ankle. Hartville's darling son was in his element, the star of the show wherever he went. That was one reason introverted Kate was drawn to him, along with his handsome, boy-next-door looks, swimmer's body, and gilded upbringing. Everyone in town loved the former high school president and homecoming king—including his ex-wife. They'd had their ups and downs as a couple, but she had always been proud to stand at his side.

Kate stopped short. The crowd shifted and Tammi strutted over to stand beside Scott. His leggy, buxom, blonde-in-a-bottle girlfriend was even more gorgeous with that deep tan that matched his.

Kate lifted her chin, trying not to think about her own pale complexion. In the store, she'd imagined her new outfit would turn heads, but it wasn't in the same league as Tammi's stylish, painted-on leggings with knee-high leather boots.

Kate forced a smile on her face.

A half-dozen soccer moms formed a semicircle behind Tammi. The dark coven, as Kate silently referred to them, moved as one—they crossed their arms, dipped their chins, and frowned, letting their displeasure at Kate's presence be known. Tammi's friends usually behaved one way in public, sociably chitchatting about nothing and smiling like they were advertising the Stepford wives' dental plan. But behind their gated fences and vacuous pretensions, they gossiped like preteens at a slumber party.

Kate heard the whispers now.

"She's not from Hartville. You'd think she'd have the decency to move back to wherever she came from. Why does she stay?"

My children, you vicious bunch of...

Scott whispered something in Tammi's ear that elicited a loud giggle. Her head tipped back and her perfect beach waves danced in the sun. The sound of her laugh made the coffee in Kate's stomach churn. Tammi attracted the envious gaze of all the males as she grabbed Scott's tie and reeled him in for a pouty-mouthed kiss. There they were, the notoriously happy couple on display for all the town to see. So public, so painful.

Blindsided by a sudden flood of emotion, Kate pushed her glasses up her nose, grateful for her transition lenses that darkened in the sun, hiding the pain in her eyes.

Scott motioned her over, but Kate clutched her purse and stayed rooted to the spot. Her phone made an odd, muffled beeping sound. She pulled it out. The timer for the drone filled the screen and blinked red. She silenced the alarm, but the beeping grew louder directly above her.

Puzzled, Kate glanced up, just as the drone came plummeting down. Ducking her chin, she let out an unbecoming yelp as the drone, drained of juice, slammed into the top of her head. The propellers buzzed to a stop as they tangled in her hair, plastic bits snapping off. Kate lurched sideways, her feet crossing over one another, and pitched forward. Her purse flew one way, her phone the other, and the gift bag tumbled from her hand. She slammed into the ground like a baseball player sliding into the home plate with her arms stretched forward, but her head hit the turf first.

"Mommy!" Ava cried.

Kate attempted to pull down her dress, which had hiked up on her hips, revealing her shapewear. Her stomach flipped and a nauseous warmth in her belly spread all the way to her throat. She clamped her eyes closed, but she sensed the crowd pressing in around her. She touched her head and winced; a bump was already growing beneath her fingers.

Scott raced over. "Kate! Are you all right?"

She opened her eyes to see him kneeling next to her, his blue eyes, rounded with worry, searching her face. His fingers on her arm were as warm as his breath on her cheek. Her heart thumped like a poorly loaded washing machine.

"Are you okay, Mom?" Andy's voice snapped her back to reality. His lip trembled. Ava raced to her other side, crying all the way.

"I'm okay. Mommy's fine," Kate said, trying to soothe her frightened children as she sat up. Ignoring her injury, she wrapped her arms around both of her children. The drone, its propeller still caught in her hair, dangled down her back.

"Take it slowly." Scott's voice soothed her throbbing head as he managed to free the blades from her hair.

Kate looked down at the mangled plastic mess now lying in a heap in front of her.

Tammi stepped into the fray. "What happened?"

"Mommy got a boo-boo!" Ava tried to comfort Kate as she held her hand.

"Let me take a look at that boo-boo," Scott said.

"I'm fine, really."

"You're definitely going to need some ice." He wrapped his arm around Kate's waist and helped her to stand. Kate leaned into him without hesitation.

"What hit her?" one of the soccer dads asked from the crowd.

"It's a drone!" Andy's voice cracked as he held up the quad helicopter. One of its rotors drooped down, connected now by broken plastic and stretched wire.

Kate winced. *I'm a moron. Now I've broken it...*

Scott took the drone from Andy and glared out at the crowd. "What idiot does this belong to?"

Everyone shook their heads and shrugged.

"It's illegal to film children," said one parent.

"Drones are not allowed on school grounds," another replied.

Disapproving murmurs rippled through the crowd as the dark coven flocked to the aluminum bleachers for a better view of the spectacle—buzzards eying the crowd for the owner, who would no doubt be the next target of their contempt.

"Whose thing is this?" Ava stamped her foot and yelled. "Whose toy hit my mommy?"

"Who does this belong to?!" Andy exclaimed.

Kate blinked back tears as Scott, Andy, and Ava defended her. For a moment, surrounded by the people who loved her, the hollow spot inside her stopped aching.

Then Tammi slunk over and crouched in front of Andy. "Hey, buddy, I don't know if anyone's going to be too eager to admit they were stupid enough to let their toy hurt somebody. We should let it go."

Kate, absolutely mortified, kept her mouth shut.

Tammi raised a well-groomed eyebrow toward her. "Are you okay, Katie?"

Kate fought down a snarl. She had repeatedly asked Tammi not to call her Katie, yet Tammi never missed an opportunity to do it.

"I'm okay." Kate nodded and paid the price as sharp pains bounced back and forth between the bump on her head and her eyes.

"I'm so glad!" The perpetually perky former cheerleader smiled without showing teeth.

Scott held out Kate's purse, phone, and the dropped gift bag.

"Thank you." Kate stared at her open purse. Maybe it had opened when it hit the ground? She stuffed her phone inside and zipped it shut.

Tammi stepped beside Scott, her hand moving to the small of his back as she stared at Kate. "Since you're obviously okay, we do need to get going and we wanted to take the children—"

"No." Ava wrapped both arms around Kate's leg and pressed her cheek against Kate's thigh. "I want to take care of Mommy."

"But, sweetie"—Tammi brushed back the little girl's bangs—"we were going to pick out some new shoes for you."

Ava shook her head again and squeezed Kate's leg even harder.

Scott skittered sideways as Tammi poked him in the side. He didn't meet Kate's eyes. Instead, he spoke to her feet. "If you're not up to having the kids... uh, with your head and all... it wouldn't be any trouble for us—"

"We're good." Kate, in no mood to play peacemaker, went for the jugular. "I'll order pizza."

"Pizza!" Andy and Ava cheered. Kate relished her victory as Andy and Ava did their happy pizza dance.

Tammi crossed her arms and fixed Kate with an accusatory stare. "Do you know whose drone it is?"

Taken aback by Tammi's seeming clairvoyance, Kate darted her gaze between the drone and Tammi, who pinned Kate with her icy blue eyes.

Kate's aversion to being humiliated in public overrode her conscience. "No. It appeared out of nowhere." She pictured Grandma Barnes standing at her little stove in the kitchen and wagging a foreboding finger in the air. "The Devil loves a good lie. Tell one, and he'll bite you with it." Ignoring both the wisdom of her grandmother and the growing knot in her own stomach, Kate pressed a hand against her breastbone and shrugged, hoping to sell her feigned innocence.

"Hey!" Andy's eyes lit up with excitement. "There's a camera on it!" He grabbed the drone back from his father.

Tammi held out her hand. "It doesn't belong to you, Andy. You can't just take it."

Kate's heart sped up as Tammi reached for the drone. Kate's grandmother was right: her lie was going to bite her on the butt hard if she didn't get the drone back. She ran down a mental list of reasons she should take it with her, but none made sense.

Andy stepped sideways, keeping the drone out of Tammi's grasp. His grin grew bigger. "Maybe I can figure out who it belongs to. Please, Dad? If I can find out who owns it, you can sue them!"

"Please? Please?" Ava joined in with her brother and tugged on Scott's jacket.

Scott kept his mouth closed, so Andy turned to his mother. Somewhere between *please* and *Mom*, Kate blurted out, "Yes! You can take it home."

"Thanks, Mom!"

The referee blew his whistle, signaling the end of halftime. As the other boys ran toward the soccer field, Andy's eyes ping-ponged between Kate and his coach.

In spite of her throbbing head, Kate smiled as she took the drone from Andy. "Get back in the game, honey! Go show your dad what you've got."

Andy balled his hands into fists and held them tightly against his chest. "Are you sure, Mom? Don't you need to go home?"

"No. I'm fine. I'm going to watch the game with Ava."

"Yay!" Ava cheered.

"Dad? Are you going to stay?" Andy asked.

Scott pointed to the bleachers on the left side. "Are you kidding? I wouldn't miss it."

As Andy dashed back to his bench, Kate sat beside Ava on the bleachers and then tucked the mangled wreck under the seat beside the gift bag.

Ava's eyes lit up when she glanced inside.

"It's a gift from Daddy."

As Ava clutched her new toy dolphin to her chest, Kate lifted out the package of rum balls. She and Scott had planned a trip to Tortuga last year, but it had fallen through because of a big case he had been working on. Kate had researched every detail, from the airline they would take and the hotel they would stay in, to all the outdoor activities Scott wanted to do. As with all their vacations, she'd handled everything.

As Kate pictured Tammi and Scott walking down the beach hand in hand, she popped a rum ball into her mouth to keep herself from screaming. As soon as she'd swallowed the first, she gobbled another. Her lip curled. *I'm going to regret this in a couple of hours.*

Ava whooped and hollered as Andy played his heart out for the rest of the game. His team lost in a landslide, but it didn't seem to bother him as he rushed over to his father after the final whistle.

Carrying the remains of the drone in one hand and holding Ava's hand with the other, Kate got up and waited for him. "Why don't you run over and say goodbye to your father?" she said to Ava.

"Bye, Dad!" Ava shouted and waved, but she stayed at Kate's side.

Scott returned the gesture as Tammi scowled at Kate.

Andy came running back and held out his hands for the drone. "Are you feeling better, Mom? We lost. But it was close. I can't wait to find out who this belongs to. Did you see me out there? Dad said I was great."

Before Kate could answer, he was dashing for the van with Ava following.

"Hold your sister's hand in the parking lot!" Kate called after them. Her own raised voice sounded like a freight train in her ears. When the wave of nausea passed, she opened her eyes and her stomach soured again—Scott and Tammi were walking straight toward her.

Scott stopped a few feet away. He snapped his fingers and cleared his throat. "There's something I really need to talk to you about—in private."

Tammi had one arm coiled around Scott's waist. A victorious grin dawned across her painted lips. She raised her arm, placed it on Scott's shoulder, and bent her wrist. The diamond on Tammi's finger sparkled in the sunlight.

Kate's knees wobbled.

It's... it's only been three months.

"I really need to get going," Kate said as she backed toward the van.

"But, Kate..."

"Oh, um... I'll bring the kids by next week," Kate managed to say before turning on her heel and hurrying after the children.

Remarry? Already?

The realization punched Kate square in the face. She swayed like she was about to tumble to the ground again, blindsided by the painful wallop.

Kate stalked back to the van with her arms hanging limply at her sides. Her breath came in wheezing gulps. She hoped the numbness in her chest was from the bump on her head, but deep down she knew it wasn't. Part of her had still thought if she could only talk with Scott alone, without the lawyers, they would figure things out. If they spoke the way they had when they first met, endless conversations in her dorm room when they would stay up talking until dawn, juiced up on nothing but love, oblivious to the long day ahead—if they communicated like that, they'd pull their family back together and put this whole mess behind them.

That hope had just died.

Kate reached the van and opened the door. Andy sat in the back, cradling the damaged drone in his lap like he was holding a puppy. Ava gazed up at Kate as she buckled her into her booster seat.

"Do you feel better, Mommy?" Ava asked.

"Um… yes, a little. Thanks, sweetie."

"Was that man a friend of yours, Mommy?" Ava pointed out the window.

"What?"

"That man in the blue baseball hat." She pointed back toward the soccer field.

Kate spun around in her seat. "Tell me what you saw."

"He was watching you," Ava answered matter-of-factly. "Grammie says it's impolite to stare, but he was doing this…" She jutted her chin forward and opened her eyes as wide as she could. It was a terrifying look, even on a four year old's face.

Kate scanned the faces in the crowd. Every other man seemed to be wearing some type of hat, but nobody was staring.

"Everybody was looking at Mom when the drone hit her!" Andy chimed in.

"Was that it, Ava?" Kate asked.

"No. It was *after*." Ava shrugged and picked up her stuffed bunny, Mr. Fluffy Butt. "He's gone now."

The delicate hairs on the back of Kate's neck stood on end and her mouth suddenly went completely dry. She started the minivan and locked the doors.

Moist and sticky little elf-like hands cradled both sides of Kate's face. Warm breath wafted across her nose, carrying the aromas of pizza, chocolate, and a cotton candy lollipop.

"Are you awake, Mommy?" Ava lifted Kate's left eyelid.

After the soccer game disaster, all Kate wanted to do was come home, nurse her aching head and wounded heart, and have a good long cry, but as a mom, taking care of herself had to wait until the kids were in bed.

"I'm awake, sweetie." Kate's other eyelid cracked open. Ava loved playing dress-up, and right now she was wearing one of Kate's old white shirts as a convincing doctor's lab coat, along with a pair of Kate's sneakers and an old metallic skinny belt slung over the back of her neck as a stethoscope.

"Drink this." Ava hoisted a large glass of water from the table and held it unsteadily over Kate.

"Careful. Thank you." Kate took the water and drank three big gulps.

Ava thrust her hand up like a policeman halting traffic. "Small sips."

Kate smiled and followed her daughter's instruction before handing the glass back to her.

"Take your medicine, Mommy." Ava held out two partially melted M&Ms in her chocolate-stained hand.

After the slice of pizza, half a bag of potato chips, and two pain relievers Kate had downed to ease the pounding in her head, the thought of adding chocolate to her stomach's contents made her clamp her mouth closed.

Ava pressed her own lips together and stuck the candy under Kate's nose. "Listen to your doctor."

Despite the headache, Kate smiled. She plopped the M&Ms into her mouth and almost convulsed when Ava patted her sore head.

"And now, your shot." Ava raised a tube of Xtra Sour Lemon Goo and squeezed. Her ineffective aim splattered the neon-yellow stream on Kate's cheek and splashed her in the eye. One drop of the sugary candy burned like a cattle prod.

"Oopsie." Ava flashed an adorable sheepish grin.

Kate wiped at her face with her shirt, but the caustic liquid still burned a little.

"All better!" Ava announced, following up her verdict with a quick hug. With her dark eyes and hair, she already resembled Kate's former mother-in-law, Audrey, more than she did either Scott or Kate. In photos Kate had seen of Audrey in her youth, she'd looked like a siren from the Golden Age of Hollywood. Little Ava Gardner, so ambitiously named, stood a good chance of maturing into another raven-haired beauty. "I'm gonna see Andy. He's still at the 'puter."

From the second they'd gotten home, Andy had spent all his time fiddling with the drone and his computer. At least the project was distracting him.

Ava skipped and hopped upstairs and Kate settled back on the couch. She glanced at the chocolate smears Ava had left on her old shirt and shrugged. Since Kate had already adorned it with a blob of greasy tomato sauce while attempting to eat pizza lying down and dusted it with potato chip crumbs, a little chocolate wouldn't hurt anything. Her head throbbed even against the soft pillow. *Stupid drone. Stupid me.* Her head would recover, but the drone wouldn't. And what about the tech review gig? It would have provided a good source of income. She only hoped Michelle would understand. Kate hadn't seen her sorority sister for years, but when Kate was scrounging for work, Michelle had come through. It was supposed to be a simple job: put a drone through its paces and write a review. Best of all, Andy would get a drone. But she'd managed to screw up the first promising work that had come her way.

Kate picked up her phone and crafted an email to Michelle. She explained how she had accidentally crashed the drone and sprinkled in plenty of earnest, humble requests for another chance. She offered to write the review based on what she had learned so far, even though she hadn't tested all the features yet. She scanned the email for typos. As she hit send, she pictured the job disappearing into the ether, along with the email.

Kate pulled Andy's sleeping bag up to her chin. It smelled like bug spray and wood smoke. He had hauled it out of his closet and tucked it around her, a glimpse of his sweetness, which she hadn't seen for a long time.

Ava raced downstairs and over to the couch. Her eyes were wide and the corners of her mouth curled up. "I need to tell you something!"

"Let me tell her!" Andy shouted from upstairs. "I figured it out!"

Ava cupped her hand to her little mouth, leaned close enough to kiss Kate on the cheek, and whispered, "A giant's following you."

Kate laughed. She glanced around the room and pretended to shake. "Oh, no! What will I do?"

"I wanted to tell her!" Andy cried as he thundered down the stairs, his tablet clutched in his hand. "I'm the one who figured it out, Mom." Andy held up his tablet so she could see the screen. It blinked to life with the aerial video of Kate from the soccer game.

"Figured what out?" Kate asked.

"This was this morning." Andy shook with excitement as he waved his finger across the screen. "Here's another video. I don't know where it is, but that's you! And there are two more videos of you on the drone. Someone is stalking you, Mom!"

"A giant!" Ava shrieked, her hands going to both sides of her face.

Andy rolled his eyes. "Not a giant, doofus."

"But giants live up stalks."

"That's a beanstalk. It's not the same. A stalker is a creep."

"No one is stalking Mommy." Kate took a deep breath as she prepared to come clean. "The truth is—"

The doorbell rang, and Ava ran to the window and peered out. "Look, Mommy!" Ava clapped. "A police car. Can you ask them to turn the lights on?"

Kate couldn't help but smile. Ava thought the blue and white lights were so pretty. Wait—why were the police at her home? She sat up with a start, pushing Andy's sleeping bag off her legs, and hurried to the front door. A police cruiser was parked in her driveway. Two men in suits stood on the front porch. They made an odd pair. One was squat, middle-aged, heavy-set. He stood casually with a coffee cup in one hand. The other was tall, broad-shouldered and ruggedly handsome, and he stood at attention like a soldier on a mission.

Kate looked down at her frumpy outfit and cringed. Why did she have to be dressed like a couch potato every time someone came to the house?

Ava tugged on Kate's shirt just as she opened the door. "Mommy, I have to tinkle."

"You run right in. Mommy needs to talk to these men."

"But I need help!" Ava pulled aside her pretend lab coat, revealing overalls underneath.

Kate picked Ava up. "Can I help you?"

"Ms. Gardner?" the older man asked and she nodded. "I'm Detective Mark Tills and this is Detective Ryan Daley. We're here about the incident with the drone at Cushing School."

Kate blanched. "I didn't call the police."

"No. Your attorney, Scott Gardner, did."

My attorney? A rush of heat raced up her neck and her cheeks burned. A flock of swear words flew to mind.

Detective Tills took out a notepad. "We need to get a few details to file the report."

Ava tugged on Kate's sleeve. "Mommy, I've really gotta go."

"I'm so sorry, but we have a little bathroom emergency. Can you please wait in the living room for one minute?"

"Certainly, ma'am." The older man nodded.

Kate carried Ava straight to the bathroom and began trying to get her out of her clothes. The little girl had obviously dressed herself and the makeshift knots were impossible to untie. Kate pulled the apron and white shirt over Ava's head and got the overalls off just in time.

"One second!" Kate called out the door.

There was no response.

Kate covered her eyes with one hand. Her lie had gone nuclear. What was Scott thinking? Now she would have to confess, and since Audrey was the godmother of the sheriff, she would find out too. *What have I done?*

"Maybe I can make up some lie to tell Audrey?"

"No, Mommy!" Ava shouted as she jumped off the toilet. "Don't ever lie to Grammie!" Her eyes grew big.

Oh, no... "What did I say?" Had Kate said her thought aloud?

"You said you were gonna lie to Grammie! Grammie said people shouldn't lie, 'specially to her. She can tell."

"Don't worry, honey. Mommy would *never* do anything like that." Kate hugged her daughter. "And please don't tell Grammie what I said."

Ava nodded, but Kate's hopes sank. Her daughter loved to tell secrets.

"Wash your hands, sweetheart." Ava hopped up on her stool while Kate tried to think of something that would help Ava forget what she'd just heard. "I need to go speak with those policemen. After, would you rather play dress-up or read for a little while?"

"Play dress-up!" said Ava, twirling on her toes like a ballerina.

"Good choice. When I'm done, I'll come and play with you. How does that sound?"

Ava said, "Scrump-diddly-umptious," and skipped down the hall.

Kate walked toward the living room, each step causing her head to pound more. Getting caught in a lie was horrible. Confessing to one was far worse. Katagelophobia. She hadn't known that fear of embarrassment had a name, let alone one so similar to her own, before she started seeing Dr. Sprouse. Kate had an extreme case of it. But this had gone too far. And how could she tell her kids not to lie if she did? She had to come clean. She stopped in the doorway, her shoulders slumped and her head hanging forward. She could almost feel the hangman's noose around her neck.

"I'm so sorry. I need to tell you something."

The two men in suits turned around. The taller man, Detective Daley, held Andy's computer tablet in his hands. As Kate stepped into the living room, he squared his broad shoulders and stood at attention. His eyes were like milk chocolate and there was a deep intensity to his gaze. It had a mesmerizing effect and she found herself staring.

"Mom, you're not going to believe it!" Andy waved his hands, trying to get her attention.

"Do you have any idea who this man is?" Detective Daley's voice had a deep rumble to it and a slight Texas twang. He pointed at the tablet's screen.

"What? Who?" Kate stuttered. Her eyes widened as she stared at the screen. A video showing Kate in the park near the house was paused.

Detective Daley zoomed in on the tree line. Almost hidden by the shadows of the trees was a man in a blue baseball hat. Because of the hat and the overhead angle, his face was obscured, but from the direction of the brim, it was clear he was watching her. Detective Daley played the video at normal speed. The man was visible for only a moment before he faded into the shadows again.

Detective Daley swiped the screen and the video from this morning appeared. Kate's breath caught in her throat as his finger hovered over the play button. Would there be a shot revealing her launching the drone? Would it begin with a close-up of her face as she stared at the camera? She thought she had started recording after the drone was flying, but...

Detective Daley pressed play.

The video opened with the drone high over Kate's head. She let out her breath. On the screen, as Kate walked around the bases, the drone tracked her. Because of the drone's follow-me option, it was easy to see how someone would think she was being stalked. A pang of guilt washed over her, until Detective Daley paused the video again. He zoomed in. The same man in the blue baseball hat was hiding behind the dugout. As Kate rounded the bases, he peeked out, watching her.

"The branch snapping..." she said. "It wasn't an animal I heard. It was a man."

Her heart beat faster.

Detective Daley switched to another video. This one was taken in her own backyard, the first test she had done. Once again the video began with the drone high in the air. At first Kate thought Detective Daley was pointing to nothing more than a shadow among the trees, but then the angle of the drone changed and there was no question: a man in a blue baseball hat stood at the edge of the tree line, watching her.

Detective Tills pointed at the screen. "Look at his hands. He's holding something in each video. A knife?"

"It could be the remote to control the drone." Detective Daley shot his partner a sideways glance and tipped his head slightly towards Andy.

Kate's mouth was so dry, it was hard to breathe. Someone was stalking her. A flood of questions shot through her mind, but like a hundred bee stings, the shock was too much for her system.

Detective Daley placed a hand on her shoulder. "It's okay," he said. She thought his hand was shaking until she realized her whole body was trembling.

Ava ran into the living room wearing a plastic police hat and sheriff's star from Andy's Halloween costume a couple of years ago. "Hi!" she called out as she jumped to a stop, her cowboy boots banging off the wood floor, making Kate almost leap out of her skin.

"Why, hello." The older detective's lined face broke into a grandfatherly smile. "And who do we have here? A policewoman?"

Ava shook her head. "I'm the chief. Grammie always says you should be in charge."

"Your grammie sounds pretty smart," Detective Tills said.

"She is."

Andy was so excited his hands were a blur as he pointed at the screen. "Someone is stalking Mom!"

"The giant!" Ava's voice rose high.

Kate's protective instincts kicked into high gear. "Upstairs." She herded both Ava and Andy to the staircase. They begged and pleaded to be allowed to stay, but there was no way she was letting that happen. Someone had been watching the house—Kate had no idea who or why—and they could be doing it right now. "Upstairs to your rooms. No arguing. We'll talk as soon as I'm done."

"Did you recognize that man in the videos?" Detective Daley asked when she returned to the living room.

Kate shivered. "No. Why would he follow me?"

"We'll figure that out." Detective Daley said the words with conviction.

Detective Tills asked, "Can you think of anyone it could be? An old boyfriend?"

"I only had one boyfriend before my husband, back in high school. He was sweet, and he became a cop. In another state."

Detective Tills kept eye contact with her the whole time. "You're married?"

"Divorced." The word still sounded like a curse to her. "But he's definitely not the man in the videos."

"Why do you say that?" Detective Tills asked, then took a sip of his coffee.

"For one thing, if you keep playing the video at the soccer game, he's in it. He's also the man who called you."

"The divorce was amicable?" Detective Tills asked.

For him. Kate nodded.

Detective Tills looked out the front window and up and down the road. "Have you noticed anyone suspicious? Anyone unusual at work or in the area?"

Kate gasped. "One of those videos was taken in my backyard last night. He was here. He—" Her throat tightened and cut off her words.

"Show me." Detective Daley's brown eyes darkened.

Kate walked with the detectives to the back of the house and pointed across the backyard toward the line of trees, where the yard ended and the conservation woods began. The two detectives marched forward as she directed them to the edge of the cut grass and the base of a maple tree.

"That's where he was standing in the video."

The men stood gazing at the ground, dead leaves rustling about their feet. She didn't know exactly what they expected to find.

Detective Daley strode forward and squatted down like a golfer examining the run of the green. Detective Tills motioned for Kate to come over. She hesitantly walked across the yard and stopped beside him.

Kate didn't know what Detective Daley was searching for with his intense stare, but she was acutely aware of the power in his shoulders, the muscles bulging beneath his shirt. He looked like a cop. If he had a tattoo, she imagined it would say, *Serve and Protect*. At least in that moment, it made her feel secure.

"That's a real man," Kate said.

"Excuse me?" Detective Tills asked.

Oh, no. She must have said her thought aloud again. She pretended to cough. "That's where the man stood." She pointed.

Detective Daley took a pen out of his pocket and flipped several leaves off the spot, revealing an impression where someone's foot had mashed three cigarette butts into the soft dirt.

"Do you smoke?" Detective Tills's voice in her ear startled her.

"No."

"Anyone you know smoke?"

"No, I don't think so."

Kate's shoes sank into the spongy ground. She took a step back onto firmer soil. Her legs tensed, ready to flee for the safety of the house. The idea that someone had hidden here, leering at her or the kids… She pictured the three of them gathered around the kitchen table at night while this monster lurked in the shadows of the trees, waiting for the moment to attack.

Kate's heart thumped.

Detective Daley stood and made eye contact with his partner and pointed at the ground. Like an old married couple, the pair seemed to have a short, unspoken conversation. The darkening of their expressions suggested it wasn't a happy one.

Detective Tills pointed to the house and the room over the deck. "Whose window is that?"

Kate's eyes widened as she noticed the raised shade and pulled-back drapes. She wrapped her arms around her chest, feeling naked and exposed. "Mine."

Detective Daley made a note as Detective Tills took an evidence bag out of his pocket.

Kate gazed back at the trees. Behind her house were acres of wooded conservation land. She loved walking the trails, but the forest now felt like a wild animal preserve with no fence. She took another step toward the house.

Detective Tills flipped back a few pages in his notebook. "Have you dated anyone since the divorce?"

"No, but... I did go on a round of speed dates," Kate stammered. "You know, they're not really dates. You sit down with someone for ten minutes, they ring a bell, and the men switch seats."

The older detective nodded. "I've heard of speed dating."

"How many men did you speak with?" Detective Daley asked.

The back of Kate's neck was getting impossibly hot. "Five."

"Did you have contact with any of them again?"

"No. They emailed but..." Kate cleared her throat and swallowed the words *but I was still carrying a torch for my ex-husband.* "I declined—politely. Everyone seemed nice about it." The sweat under her armpits was soaking into her shirt, so she held her arms close to her sides.

"Still, we should get their names," Detective Tills said.

"Sure. I'll have to go through my email. I don't throw anything away. Not like I'm a hoarder—I mean, I filed them. Not because I was going to call them back. I'm just organized. And rambling." Kate bit her lip. "I apologize; I'm flustered."

"It's going to be okay." Detective Daley touched her forearm lightly. "We'll get to the bottom of this, Ms. Gardner."

Maybe it was the words—or more likely the current of electricity that buzzed at the contact point of his hand and her bare arm—but she felt like he meant it. Like she mattered.

"Kate. Please call me Kate."

"I'm Ryan."

Detective Tills walked over. "In the meantime, we'll have them increase patrols in the neighborhood."

Ryan nodded. "We'll need to see the drone."

Kate swallowed. "Certainly."

While Detective Tills placed the cigarette butts into an evidence bag, Ryan followed Kate to the back deck. Andy and Ava were already there, their little faces pressed against the slider, fogging up the glass.

Kate opened the door and Ava stepped out onto the deck. "Andy, could you get me the drone, please?" Kate asked before sliding the door closed.

Andy turned and sprinted down the hallway.

Ava hid behind Kate's leg.

"Detective Daley, this is Ava."

"That's a pretty name." He squatted so he was on her eye level. "But maybe, since she's the chief and that makes her my boss, she should call me Ryan. Is that all right with you, Chief?"

Ava squeezed Kate's leg and nodded, her police hat almost falling off in the process. "Did Mommy tell you I saw the giant?"

Ryan gave Kate a puzzled glance.

"Ava thinks whoever is following me is a giant because Andy called him a stalker."

"Oh…" Ryan nodded understandingly. "And giants live up stalks!"

"Yes!" Ava flashed a triumphant smile.

"You think you saw him?" Ryan took out his notepad.

"No." Ava shook her head. "I did see him."

Ryan's lip curled up and the cleft in his chin deepened. "Where was that?"

"At Andy's soccer game. He was watching Mommy."

"What did he look like?"

"I didn't see his face too good. He was kinda far."

"What was he wearing?"

"He had a blue hat. And a tan jacket. Blue jeans and boots."

"You're very good at this."

The little girl smiled.

"Ava likes to play dress-up," Kate added.

"Did his hat say anything on it?"

"It had a circle thingy."

Ryan whispered to Kate, "Can she read?"

"I can hear," Ava said. "And Grammie's teaching me to read."

"I'm sorry. Did the hat have any words on it?"

"No."

Ryan made another note. "Did you see his hair?"

She shook her head.

"Was he thin? Or fat?"

Ava made a face. "That's not nice to say."

Ryan seemed a bit lost for words. Kate said, "Ryan's just trying to find the bad man who was staring at Mommy."

Ava nodded. "Not fat. But really big."

Ryan stood. With his height—at least six foot two, Kate thought—and his athletic build, he must have seemed like a giant to the little girl. "As big as me?"

Ava took a couple of steps back and squinted as she stared at Ryan. "You know what? He kinda looked like you."

Ryan drew his head back and blinked rapidly.

Detective Tills chuckled as he walked up. "That should make it easier for us to find him."

Kate jumped as the slider opened and Scott walked out of her house. "Excuse me," he said. He strode out onto the back porch and thrust out his hand to the older detective first. "Scott Gardner. I didn't expect you to get here so fast."

"Daddy!" Ava held up her arms and he hoisted her up on his hip.

Detective Tills shook Scott's hand. "When we mentioned your name to the sheriff, he *suggested* we come right away."

Ryan made a cutting motion with his hand. It was a slight gesture, but Kate picked up on it.

"I need a brief moment to speak with my client—in private," Scott said.

"That sounds like an excellent idea." Kate spun on her heel and marched into the house.

After shutting the door behind him, Scott set Ava on the floor. "Go play with Andy. Daddy and Mommy need to talk."

Ava frowned but obediently hurried down the hallway.

"Why would you file a police report without asking me?" Kate crossed her arms.

Scott took a step back and held up his hands. "Hey, I'm the one helping here. Do you realize how much money you could get from this?"

"What? When did you become an ambulance chaser?"

Scott bristled. "I'm only looking out for you. I saw the size of the lump on your head. You should've gone to the hospital. Have you?"

"No." Kate sagged. "I'm fine."

"You don't know that. You should get checked out at least. CAT scan. MRI. Those are expensive, and you shouldn't have to pay for them. The idiot who owns the drone should."

Fighting down all her fears about embarrassing herself, Kate sighed. "I'm the idiot."

"What?" Scott blinked like she'd poked him in the eye. "But you said you didn't know who owned it."

"I lied." The M&Ms in her stomach grumbled loudly. "Michelle Darling gave me a side job reviewing a drone. It was on follow mode and… I forgot about it."

Scott chuckled.

"It's not funny, Scott. Someone's following me."

Scott's laughter stopped. "What are you talking about?"

Kate explained everything: Andy downloading the videos, the detectives spotting a man watching her, the cigarette butts found in the backyard. The more she spoke, the tighter she wrapped her arms around her chest.

Scott ran his hand across his mouth. "And you don't know the guy?"

"I can't see his face in the videos, but I don't think so. Who would follow me? Why? It makes no sense."

Scott started snapping his fingers. "You can't tell the police you lied about the drone now. This really is serious. You need their help to catch this guy."

"I have to tell them the drone is mine."

"No. Don't do that."

"Why not?"

"You can't." Scott moved so she was staring into his eyes. "Listen to me. I deal with the police, prosecutors, the court all the time. You lie once, even one little lie, and they stop believing every word out of your mouth."

Kate bit her bottom lip.

Scott whispered, "You want them to find this guy, right?"

"Of course!"

"Then listen to me. Don't tell them about the drone. It doesn't matter now anyway. The important thing is that it recorded someone following you. Think about it. If you ask me, that drone hitting you on the head was a gift from God."

She stared at him. Everything he said made sense.

Scott placed his hands on her arms and peered into her eyes. "Let me handle it. Okay?"

Kate nodded, but the knot in her stomach continued to grow. She peered out the window toward the woods. A man had been stalking her for days. He'd followed her home, stood in her backyard, and watched her through her window. One question kept echoing in her mind: was he coming back?

Kate sat on the couch waiting for Scott to finish up talking to the police. Her head was spinning. Someone was following her. Why? Besides Tammi and her coven, she didn't have any enemies in town, and other than a failed round of speed dating, the closest she'd gotten to a date was the romance section of the library.

The front door opened and Scott strode through, a crooked smirk on his face.

Kate slid off the couch and caught sight of her reflection in the window. She froze. Scott had seen her at her worst a thousand times before—while fighting the flu, enduring wisdom teeth removal, and braving the indignity of birthing rooms. She had never felt self-conscious with him—until he added the dreaded two letters E and X to his title of husband. Now, standing there in her sweats, a tingling heat raced up her neck and across her cheeks. She wanted to dash away to her big, messy, empty bedroom and hide under the covers.

"Hey, Legal Eagle!" Kate's voice was unnaturally high.

Scott chuckled. "I'd apologize about filing the police report without speaking to you first, but"—his arms rose up and out—"it's a good thing I did. I just watched those videos. Someone is following you, Kate. Have you been seeing someone?"

She shook her head. "I tried this speed dating thing once. It didn't work out." She shuddered. "But I can't believe that one of those men would stalk me for not going out with them."

"What about someone from work?"

"My temp job? I don't talk to anyone. I'm stuck at the reception desk all day."

"The good thing is, the police are looking into it. They're going to see if they can enhance the video and make out any details about the guy. I'm sure they'll catch him. Who knows, he might just be a shy secret admirer."

"Shy I could handle. Hiding in the woods and spying on me—that's not an admirer. That's a full-fledged creep." Kate ran her trembling fingers through her hair and winced when she touched the bump on her head. She stared at her hand, now goopy with pain cream. "I need to take a shower."

Scott glanced at his watch. "Actually, I was hoping we could talk about something else. Tell you what, you take your shower, I'll put the kids to bed, and after that you give me fifteen minutes?"

Kate's heart pounded to the steady throb in her head as a flood of questions fought to escape her lips. *Why does he need to talk? Is it about the kids? Tammi? Him? Me? Us?*

"Sure," Kate said. "Sounds like a plan." But Scott's plans had a way of working out better for Scott than they did for her.

"Great. Take your time, okay?" He cupped his mouth to his hand. "Hey, kids!" he yelled upstairs.

Doors banged open and Andy and Ava thundered down the stairs. "Dad! Daddy!"

Scott swept Ava up with one arm and she squealed with delight. "How about I give this little princess a tuck-in?" He grabbed Andy around his shoulders. "Right after my genius son explains to me how he got that video off the drone!"

The kids cheered and began talking at the same time. Scott gave Kate a wink as he somehow managed to listen to them both.

"Thanks." Kate walked up the stairs and paused at the top to listen to the three of them laughing below. It seemed so familiar, so right. Shutting the door to her bedroom, she stripped off her stained clothes and grabbed an outfit—capri pants, a pair of high-top sneakers Andy had outgrown and Donna had deemed "funkalicious," and a worn-out, T-shirt that showed so much skin she'd only wear it around the house.

"Today's your day for a better tomorrow. Say goodbye to your past and hello to your future," she sang as she turned on the shower, mixing all the self-help slogans together. Giving her hair a rinse, she tried to stop the guessing game of what Scott wanted to talk about. She had no idea what was on Scott's mind, but she was so grateful he was spending time with the kids. They needed it. Especially Andy.

She dressed, carefully ran a brush through her hair, and dabbed on some perfume. Kate walked down the hallway to the next room, and stopped dead in her tracks.

Scott was sitting on the edge of Ava's bed reading *Jack and the Beanstalk* to her. Her little angel's eyes were closed. She was asleep. Scott gave Kate a quick wink but kept reading.

Kate rested her head against the doorframe, closing her eyes and listening to Scott's voice, which she had always loved.

How had everything gone so wrong? Was there anything she could say to fix things now?

When Scott said the most challenging part of the divorce was losing time with the kids, she believed that. The kids clung to him like barnacles. They loved and needed him.

Kate had given up torturing herself over why Scott had left her for the former homecoming queen. The long list of possibilities had cost too many visits to the therapist and bottles of wine to forget. Tammi wasn't the only reason Scott had left her. Their sex life had fizzled out before his affair. Kate was self-conscious because of her weight gain, and as the frequency of their lovemaking diminished, Scott's attempts to reignite a fire in the bedroom became more risqué. She went along with it at first, but the role playing and other things he asked her to try had the opposite effect. She wanted to make love to her husband, not act out some kinky fantasy. Then she'd found the lingerie in his briefcase. She so wanted to believe him when he said the red nightie was a surprise for her, but she knew it wasn't.

He confessed right away. The brilliant lawyer didn't even try a rebuttal. He laid it all bare. He admitted Tammi had reached out to him before he moved the family to Hartville, and the affair started within weeks of the first furniture being delivered. If written down, the list of reasons for his infidelity would have stretched further than Santa's scroll. He shouted each one of her faults at her as he ticked them off on his fingers. Her therapist said these were merely words used to try to justify the inexcusable, but each one of Scott's cuts had left a deep scar on her soul.

He'd apologized the next day when he handed her the divorce papers. He said he should have handled it differently. Kate agreed. Cheating and then blaming your spouse for your infidelity was no way to go. And yet she begged, pleaded, and did everything but wrap her arms around his legs and let him drag her down the street. In the end, he still left. There would be no attempt at reconciliation. No therapy. No couples counseling. Scott's verdict was final and his sentence swift.

Scott had stopped reading, and she opened her eyes. He gently tucked the blanket around Ava, turned off the light, and came to her side.

"Hey," Kate said.

"Are you okay?" He wrapped a protective arm around her waist and closed Ava's door.

"I'm fine." She let him lead her down the stairs.

"Andy's in bed too. Are you up for a talk?"

"Sure." She tried to act nonchalant, but the pit in her stomach was growing.

He led her over to the couch but didn't sit down himself. "I brought you a little boo-boo present. It's in the kitchen."

Wrapped in the warm glow of familiarity, Kate waited patiently, knowing that all too soon Scott would leave and the loneliness would return.

Scott bumped open the swinging kitchen door with his hip and came out with his hands full: a bottle of her favorite Cabernet Sauvignon and two glasses in one hand, and a plate of bruschetta with prosciutto, cream brie, and fig jam in the other. He must have stopped by the Italian bakery they loved on the way over.

"I thought you might need a little something before bed." He set the glasses down on the coffee table and held up a bottle of aspirin. "Found these in the medicine cabinet."

The thoughtful gesture meant more than flowers. Kate nodded and thanked him. Scott was right about her needing something, but... no, that was wrong. Or was it? He wasn't married yet. A chuckle escaped her. She was getting way ahead of herself. Scott was being nice, that was all. Any other fantasy rolling around in her mind was just that—a fantasy.

Flashing the smile that still made her weak at the knees, Scott handed her the aspirin and sat on the couch. "That was one heck of a soccer game." He deftly poured the wine. "And our son could be a star."

Kate popped three aspirin tablets in her mouth and reached out for the glass he offered. Her fingers touched his. His skin was warm. His index finger traced along the side of her hand.

He is flirting with me!

Kate recognized his signature technique, and so far it had worked every time, but she knew he was angling for something. She swallowed, and the chalky pills went halfway down her throat and stopped. The aspirin turned to a gloopy acidic paste in her throat. As hard as she fought it, she made a little gagging motion and her eyes bugged out. She pried the wineglass from Scott's grip.

"How's your head?"

The wine cleared the blockage, but it took three sips to get the foul paste out of the back of her throat.

"Sorry about that." Kate's face heated up and her cheeks flushed.

"Did the aspirin get stuck?"

Kate made a goofy disgusted face and nodded.

Scott tipped his head back and laughed at the ceiling. It was loud, big, and genuine. "That's what I miss about you, Kit." He patted her knee and drank his wine.

Kit. His old nickname for her.

Scott's hand moved to the back of the couch. "How are you doing these days?"

Kate stared into his blue eyes. A hundred desperate replies came to mind: lonely, hurt, sad, angry, sorry, miserable. But desperation wasn't a strategy—especially not with a negotiator as skilled as Scott. "I've been… adjusting."

"Good. Glad to hear it." Scott sat back. "So you, ah, haven't been seeing anyone?"

"No." She tucked her legs beneath her and settled back into the corner of the couch. "I still can't believe that someone is following me."

"The police will catch him," Scott said with a dismissive wave. "They'll blow up the videos and figure out who it is. I guarantee it's one of the men you met on the speed date."

"I don't think so. We only talked for ten minutes. All they got out of me was name, rank, and serial number."

Scott handed her a plate. "You've got to stop selling yourself short. A guy could talk to you for a minute and know what a great catch you would be. Either way, I wouldn't worry about it. I'm sure it's someone trying to work up the nerve to ask you out."

Kate felt her cheeks turning as red as the jam. Paired with the wine, the bruschetta was amazing. A mini picnic. She used to throw those for Scott when he was stuck at the office. This was a first for her.

Scott cleared his throat. "With all that's been happening, it got me thinking about you moving on. That hurt a bit, I admit. Though I'd be happy for you, you know, if you were seeing someone. All this change is a lot to get used to. Things are different. Really different."

You're the one who made everything *different.*

"So, I was wondering how you were handling it all," Scott continued. "How are you feeling? How are you doing?"

Yes, he was posing questions, seeming interested, but he just needed to get something off his chest. Like before, when he wanted to talk to her in the parking lot at the game, Scott was snapping his fingers. It was a habit he'd started in law school to psych himself up before launching into a presentation.

She took her glasses off and began to clean them. "Is everything okay with you?"

He finished off his wine and placed his feet flat on the floor. "Actually…" Scott began, then he backed up his complaint truck and dumped every little thing wrong with his life straight into her lap. "I don't know how you did it all those years, Kate, but this new ad campaign for the law office isn't doing the trick. If I'm going to run for DA next year, I need to up my exposure now. A bit of a pre-campaign. I've sunk a lot of cash into it, but I'm not getting anywhere near a return on the money spent."

Don't make a face. Kate thought about Scott's toothy photo plastered all across town on everything from buses to benches.

"You're making that face," Scott said. "You don't like the new ads, do you?"

"Grow Your Settlement! Call the Gardner!" She shrugged. "No, not a big fan."

Scott puffed out his cheeks and exhaled loudly. "You should have heard my mother. 'Are you a lawyer or a fertilizer salesman?'" His impression of Audrey was spot on. "My mother has psychic abilities. I'm sure of it. I never told her it was Tammi who came up with the idea, but she guessed." Scott launched into another Audrey impersonation. "'For Tammi, thinking is a Herculean endeavor, so although that insipid slogan must have taken but a moment of thought, she must be exhausted. Her skill set consists of spending your money, not making it. You are aware there are marketing agencies devoted to that craft, are you not?'"

Kate chuckled.

"The slogan is bad," Scott admitted, "but I got a quote from a marketing firm in town and it was outrageous."

"It's not just the slogan." Kate put her glass down. "You're all over the map on where your ads are running, and you're changing the campaigns up way too fast. What I'd do first is, use your story. The Gardner name is known and trusted."

"Everyone in town knows *my mother*," Scott grumbled.

"They also know Gardner Park, Gardner Library, Gardner—"

"But they don't know me." Scott brushed back an errant strand of his brown hair. It needed a trim, but he'd been wearing it longer since they moved to Hartville. Maybe Tammi preferred that style, but it softened his features too much.

Trying to put Tammi out of her mind, Kate continued to explain. "That's where the second part comes in. Selling yourself. People want a lawyer who gets results for them. You get results, but the only way they're going to know that is reading reviews and testimonials. We invested a lot of money in your website. You need to direct people there."

"Technology has forsaken this town." Scott took a long gulp. "I know that for a fact. No one is hitting the website."

"Because your ads suck. And you're directing them to www.growyoursettlementcallthegardner.com. Who would type all that in or even remember it? Use a QR code instead and add an offer for a free consultation. It's pretty simple stuff."

Kate continued to explain her ideas. They came effortlessly, and she enjoyed seeing how they impressed Scott.

When she was finished, Scott waved his hands around and the wine sloshed in his glass. "Yes! That's what I'm talking about. No one knows that whole marketing thing like you do. You're a genius at it. Brilliant. I can see now what your efforts did for getting clients." He refilled both their glasses.

A genius? Did he say that? Was he realizing only now how hard she'd worked on his marketing? She'd pored over copy, analyzed ROI, and studied markets in different cities to grow his firm—but he'd never thanked her before this moment.

"You don't want to talk about boring ad stuff tonight, right?" Scott suggested. He was as intoxicating as the wine. He handed her the glass, grazing her hand with his fingers again.

She tried to move away a couple of inches on the couch, but their combined weight made the cushions sag toward the middle.

"I need your help, Kit." He gazed over his wineglass at her.

Whatever he needed from her right now, she'd give it. "Sure."

"Great! Why don't you write up your thoughts about an ad campaign later and email me? Just what you talked about. The little ideas you've got and any slogans you think would be better." He shifted over on the couch so he faced her directly. "Sorry. I've done it again."

"What's that?"

"Rambled on about me. Me, me, me." He rubbed the place on her ring finger where her wedding band had once been. The lighter line had begun to merge with her skin tone—rosy and lightly freckled.

She pictured him standing there at the altar, in front of God, their family, and all their friends, swearing his undying love and binding it with the ring he slid onto her finger. When the minister said they were cleaved together, it sounded like a statue of lovers made from marble. No longer two but one. But the thing about cleaving is, the only way to end the union is to smash it. And she was the one who got broken. Somehow, Scott came free without so much as a crack, while Kate shattered into a million little pieces.

"It's just… with you I can talk about anything. And you listen." He shifted closer to her as if he were sharing a secret. "Do you know, Tammi doesn't even want me to talk about work? Nothing. It's taboo. Leave it at the office, she says."

Kate was about to let him know talking about Tammi was taboo too, but Scott interlaced his fingers with hers and leaned forward until their foreheads touched. His breath reeked of wine. He lifted his head and stared into her eyes. "Thank you," he said.

She didn't know what to say. She couldn't remember ever hearing those words when they were together—despite all she'd done for Scott. And now it was twice in one night.

"You're welcome."

A knock on the door made Kate jump.

"Were you expecting company?" Scott asked.

"No. And I can't think of anyone who would stop by this late."

Scott marched across the room and looked out the peephole. He shot Kate a puzzled glance. "It's a guy. Drives a white F-150?"

"It could be the stalker! Don't let him in!"

The man knocked again.

Scott chuckled and shook his head. "Stalkers don't come to the front door." He pulled back his shoulders, puffed out his chest, and opened the door.

Standing on the porch was a tall, middle-aged man in jeans and a sports coat over a black T-shirt. His eyes darted from Scott to Kate on the couch.

Kate shifted uncomfortably as she pulled the neck of her large T-shirt up to cover her shoulder.

"Can I help you?" Scott asked.

The man stepped back and glanced at the side of the house. "Oh, I'm sorry. I thought this was one hundred and forty-eight. My bad. Sorry again." He nodded to Scott, then again to Kate, before turning on his heel and hurrying down the steps.

"Do you know that guy?" Scott asked, shutting the door open.

Kate shook her head. "I've never seen him before." She tucked her legs beneath her and took a large swig of wine, hoping Scott would come back over to the couch. But what was that saying? If you love something, let it go, and if it doesn't come back to you…

"Hunt it down and kill it," Kate mumbled.

"Hunt what down?" Scott asked, clearly confused.

"Nothing. I was…" Kate's cheeks flushed as red as the wine. She must have been thinking aloud again. "Your new ad slogan. I'm gonna kill it."

"I know you will." Scott's confident smile made her flush again. "I should go, but there's one more thing. With me getting remarried, we need to talk about changing the custody agreement."

"What?" A fire ignited in her belly and made the bump on her head throb.

"Tammi and I talked it over. Of course, my mother is still freaking out about the whole marriage thing, but if you think it through"—he crossed back to stand next to the coffee table—"I'm sure you'll realize that switching the agreement is the best thing for everyone. Tammi and I will take the kids during the week, and you can spoil them rotten two weekends a month."

"Hold on. That's giving you full custody. I am not okay with this at all."

"It's different now. This can be a win-win. See, Tammi's always wanted to be a stay-at-home mom, and you always wanted a career."

"What did you just say?" Kate swayed as she rose to her feet. She felt dizzy and held onto the back of the couch for support. In the divorce, he had blamed her for not working. It was a lie. She had sacrificed her career because he asked her to. It gave her time to devote to her nearly full-time, unpaid role in building his law firm with her marketing skills and many other contributions. Still, Kate had never regretted longing to be a stay-at-home mother.

"Is that why you came here? All that business about being concerned, that was just to butter me up so you can take my children?"

Scott rolled his eyes. The practiced condescending look he used to eviscerate defendants in court was now directed at her. "Hold it right there. Don't twist this around."

"You're not changing the custody agreement because Tammi wants to play mommy with my kids."

Scott snapped his fingers as he worked on his rebuttal. "I'm trying to do what's best for everyone." He set his glass down so hard, wine sloshed over the side and spilled onto the table. "There's no talking to you when you're like this."

He stomped to the doorway, then spun back around. His jaw had the hard edge it got whenever they argued.

She braced herself. Scott never fought fair, and judging by the angry glint in his eyes, the knives were out, sharpened and ready for use.

"For the record, I was worried about you." His voice lowered dramatically. "I know today is always hard for you."

The warmth drained from her cheeks. October 13th. Emma. Like everything about her sister, she tried to bury the anniversary so deep she'd forget it.

"I know how you get on the anniversary," Scott continued. "That's why I wanted to take the kids. But what do I get for acting like a nice guy? You spit in my face. Take some advice: if you ever want to get another man, work on being a better woman." Scott spun on his heel, yanked the door open, and disappeared into the night.

Kate's lips quivered. She told herself not to cry, but her tears weren't listening. As she grabbed a napkin and mopped up the table, her tears mixed with the spilled wine. Kate tromped into the kitchen, threw the napkins away, and washed her hands. Of wine. Of Scott. Of everything.

It was over.

Anxiety's unseen fingers closed around her throat. Her hands grew cold and tingled. Her kids. She couldn't lose her kids. Gripping the window ledge, she forced herself to breathe. In, out, in, out. After a moment, she got her breath and peered through the kitchen window into the darkness, at the line of trees that marked the boundary between her yard and the woods beyond. The spotlights that illuminated her neighbor's backyard spilled across her grass, casting shadows across the trees. The boughs rolled back and forth at the edge of the woods like waves lapping against the shore.

Darkness. Crashing waves. Drowning. She was drowning in the darkness. What was she going to do? She didn't think she could fight Scott—again. She was trapped in a life that even in her nightmares she had never dreamed would be hers.

A shadow flickered at the base of the trees. Kate pressed her hand against the cold pane, her breath fogging the glass. She stared into the night until her eyes watered. Something moved near the trees.

Kate reached for her phone.

A huge raccoon scurried on top of her neighbor's compost pile, quickly followed by two babies.

Kate exhaled.

The raccoons' heads snapped up and they darted off the pile and raced toward her neighbor Neil's yard. His motion lights clicked on, and they changed direction again and disappeared into the darkness.

Kate pulled the shade closed with trembling hands. The glasses of wine were feeding her overactive imagination. It was just the "night creatures," as Grandma Barnes called them.

But what scared the raccoons off?

Kate hurried over and made certain the back door was locked.

Kate rolled over in bed, tugging the blanket up to her chin. The bump on her head grazed the headboard and sent pinpricks racing across her scalp. She swore into her pillow and gritted her teeth. The events of yesterday rushed back. Scott hurrying to her side, his eyes filled with concern. Scott reading to Ava and wrestling with Andy, the perfect picture of a family. Scott with his hand on her knee, laughing at her jokes. Those images were shoved aside by ones of Tammi and her giant engagement ring, the videos, the stalker, Scott demanding full custody, his easy laugh turning into snarls and threats, Emma...

"Focus on the now," Kate said with a glance at the self-help books piled next to her bed. "Leave the past in the past." She cast an eye at the smart clock and noted the flashing yellow exclamation point displayed on the screen. The Internet was out and her alarm had not gone off.

Kate was glad Ava wasn't there to hear the swear words spewing forth as she glared at the time: 8:07. It would be impossible to take a shower, drop Andy and Ava off, and make it to work in time. She shot out of bed, her foot sliding on one of the books on the floor—*You're the Only Thing Standing in Your Way!* Grabbing a hairbrush, she dashed to the bedroom door and called out, "Good morning! Everybody up!"

"I'm awake!" Andy yelled back.

"Me too!" Ava said.

"Great job! Grab yourselves a breakfast bar, please! And a juice box for the road!"

She scurried into the bathroom. Remembering she'd showered last night brought a wave of relief. She could make it on time if she hustled. She dressed like a marine before reveille, taking only a moment to assess the lump on her head as she gingerly smoothed her hair. It was smaller and less tender but still stung if she touched it. Another quick trip to the bathroom while brushing her teeth and she was out in the hall, rallying her troops.

"Andy, your lunch is in the fridge. Don't forget your jacket."

"Ma mère! Ma mère!" Ava came rushing down the hallway, her Snow White cape billowing out behind her. She had Andy's toy shield in one hand and a plastic sword stuffed into her belt.

Kate struggled to recall her middle-school French class. *My mother?* "And who are you, young lady?" she asked with a grin.

Ava pulled out the sword with a flourish and pointed it at the ceiling with a triumphant yell that made Kate wince. "I'm Joan of Arc! Grammie said she led a whole army of men when she was a little girl but bigger than me. Grammie says I can shape the world, so I better get busy."

"Well, get busy getting ready to see Grammie!" Kate's phone alarm blared. "Everyone to the car. Move it! Move it!"

"To my chariot!" Ava lifted her sword high and raced toward the garage. Andy rushed in front of her, eager to beat his sister in a foot race.

"Give her a head start, Andy! And don't hit your brother with that sword!" Kate called out as she grabbed a banana off the kitchen counter and shoved it in her purse. She checked that the back door was locked before heading to the garage herself.

Kate quickly buckled Ava's seatbelt and hopped in the driver's seat. She mashed the garage door button and drummed her fingers on the steering wheel as she waited for the door to rise. By the time they reached the end of the driveway, she was almost back on schedule.

"Looks like we'll make it!" Kate grinned as they zipped out onto the road.

"NO! Mommy, go back!" Ava wailed like Kate had run over her favorite stuffed animal.

Kate glanced at the backseat, but Ava's beloved toy, Mr. Fluffy Butt, was sitting next to her. "What? Why? I can't, honey."

"You have to, Mommy! I forgot my dress-up suitcase." Ava burst into tears.

"Don't cry. Please don't cry. You have plenty of dress-up clothes at Grammie's."

Ava tilted her head toward the ceiling and cried as if she really was Joan of Arc and she was on the pyre and Kate had just lit the match. Tears rolled down her face and she sobbed. There wasn't much that fazed her, but Ava needed that dress-up suitcase like she needed oxygen, and if Kate showed up at Audrey's without it…

Kate swore under her breath and turned the van around.

"Bad word!" Andy shouted. "That's a fifty-cent word too!"

"You're right. Sorry."

The car skidded to a stop, and she jumped out and ran for the house. There was no way she could drop Ava off having a full-blown meltdown. Audrey would get after Kate for not teaching her daughter self-control. And it was best not to anger Audrey; after all, she'd insisted on watching Ava on weekdays while Andy was at school. She probably had some ulterior motive, and if she saw Ava so distressed, she might show her true colors. It was so out of character for Audrey to lift a French-manicured finger to help. It had surprised Scott too. His mother, a wealthy widow, could have bought an entire daycare facility. Instead, she'd ordered everything Ava needed and set it all up in two rooms on the first floor of her mansion—that was the only appropriate term for it, as Kate assumed castles were reserved for royalty.

Kate grabbed the suitcase and raced back to the car.

Ava clapped and did a happy dance in her seat as Kate shoved the suitcase inside.

Now running seven and a half minutes late, Kate resisted the urge to pin the gas pedal to the floor as she zipped across town on the back roads to Andy's school. In the morning, she avoided the half-mile drop-off line by letting Andy out at his friend's house. She skidded to a stop. As Andy jogged away, Ava blew kisses and Kate waved with one hand while typing "ON WAY SRRY" with the other, even though it would garner her little mercy.

Kate put the van into gear, pulled back out, and made a beeline for Audrey's estate. Traffic was heading the other way, so she made great time but was still running five minutes behind. The minivan chugged up the hill and around the circular driveway, complete with a fountain in the middle. She parked outside the mansion.

After Audrey's third husband had died on a trip to the Swiss Alps five years ago, she'd had the home completely renovated. Not because it needed it, but because she could. Though she was probably tripping over bags of cash, up until the divorce Audrey had almost nothing to do with Scott and, later, his "brood," as she referred to Andy and Ava. Her rule had always been that you had to make your own way in this world. But something had changed in Audrey after the divorce. She still looked down her nose at Kate, but she warmed to the children and her role in their lives. Andy and Ava slept over there so often now that they considered this their third home.

Kate slid the van door back, scooped Ava into her arms, grabbed her dress-up suitcase, and ran down the brick walkway toward the ostentatious mahogany front door.

It swung open silently as she approached.

"I'm so sorry I'm late," Kate said breathlessly as she set Ava down.

Audrey's eyes met Kate's. The older woman studied her with an expression of disappointment and pity, and the slight curl of her lip added a dash of loathing. Having divined whatever she was searching for, Audrey turned her attention to Ava.

"And who is my little angel today?"

Ava ripped her fake sword out of her scabbard. "Joan of Arc! Liba… Liber…"

"Liberator?" Kate guessed.

With a withering scowl, Audrey silenced Kate. To Ava, she said, "Please tell Grammie."

"Liberator of France!"

"Magnifique." Audrey's eyes gleamed. "I have something special planned for us this morning."

"What is it?" Ava prepared to jump over the threshold, but Audrey shook her head ever so slightly. The little girl stopped, tucked her sword back into her belt, and waited.

How Audrey influenced Ava's behavior, Kate could only guess. The woman radiated an air of control that left Kate feeling like a babbling fool in her presence. Audrey possessed some magical ability to bend people, even children, to her will by merely raising an eyebrow or holding up a silencing finger.

Audrey folded her hands in front of herself. "This morning, I hoped you and I could craft a batch of your special pancakes. I would love to partake of them if you would be so kind."

A smile broke out across Ava's face. She clapped her hands together and seized her grandmother's hand. "I might need a little help."

"Grammie would be delighted to help you, darling." Audrey glanced at Kate, and all the warmth and love she had shown for Ava vanished in an instant. "You're late for work as well." Audrey led Ava inside.

"Bye, Mommy," Ava said.

Kate bent in for a kiss, but the closing door blew back her hair, the wood stopping inches from her puckered lips.

Wicked, wicked woman. Imitating Audrey's well-bred, musical intonation, she muttered, "I should be delighted to partake of your pancakes, as soon as your feeble-minded mother leaves the premises." She kicked the welcome mat a few inches to the side and glared at the hypocritical phrase. "'Welcome?' I should buy her one that says 'SCRAM'!"

She only made it to the bottom of the steps before hurrying back up and straightening out the mat.

Why Audrey disliked her so much, she had no idea, but it had always been like that. After the divorce, Kate had hoped their shared experience would elicit some crumbs of sympathy—Audrey's first husband, Scott's father, had left her after an affair too. But Audrey's already-low opinion of Kate seemed to solidify instead.

Kate pictured Audrey sitting on a gilded throne, waving a dismissive hand at her. "You're late for work as well."

Oh, crap.

Kate made a mad dash for the van. Without the kids in the vehicle, she sped to make up for lost time. She was officially late now, but there was still a chance Mr. Berman wasn't in yet. Traffic wasn't heavy, and she caught a break on some lights, but by the time she arrived, the parking lot was full, forcing her to park at the far end.

Kate jogged for the front entrance. Each time she passed a parked car, she scanned the spot beside it. On top of all her other anxieties, she now had to deal with the fact that someone was following her. She covered the distance in record time and finally reached the safety of the front door. The phone rang in reception as she swiped her badge and jerked the door handle. The door thumped against the frame. The phone rang again. After three rings, the call would go to voicemail.

Please don't stop ringing.

Kate swiped again, opened the door, and bolted the seven feet to the front desk. Her stomach slammed into the counter as she snagged the phone from the cradle.

"Good morning, TRX Global," she panted. "Hello?"

A dial tone met her polite, if breathy, greeting. Too late! The call had gone to voicemail, and as a lowly temp, she didn't have the access code for the voicemail. Now she had to alert Mr. Berman.

She let fly a stream of muttered curses as she trudged around the counter and flopped into the chair. She grabbed a memo pad and pen.

Mr. Berman,

My apologies. I was arriving at the office and missed an incoming phone call. Would you please check the voicemail?

Thank you,

Kate

Her only job was to answer the reception phone. Well, that and sign for packages and keep the conference room and bathrooms tidy. She was certain the regular receptionist didn't have to scrub toilets, but Kate wanted to make a good impression and be a team player, so she'd agreed to the duty. Still, her only real purpose here was to answer the stupid phone.

And she had blown it.

It was only a temp job—the regular receptionist was out on maternity leave for at least another month—but Kate had hoped she could show them what she had to offer and get a different position in the company.

Ha.

From the moment she was hired, she'd been exiled to the reception area, consisting of her desk, a conference room, the bathrooms, and Morris Berman's office. Kate had never seen the rest of the building. She couldn't even access the employee lunchroom—although judging by the state of the bathrooms, she wasn't sure she wanted to.

And she really didn't want to know what Berman would do after reading her note. She was only four minutes late, but Berman might make a huge deal out of it. Last month, she had been seven minutes late because Ava had fallen while getting out of the van. However, a hurt little girl didn't matter to Mr. Berman. He'd still given Kate a written warning before explaining the company's three-strike policy. He went on a red-faced rant as if she'd fallen asleep at her post and let the *Titanic* hit an iceberg. After that incident, she was so freaked out about missing calls that she held off going to the ladies' room for as long as possible—and her bladder rebelled with the worst infection of her life. Now here she was again.

"I took a call for you."

Kate jumped and dropped the note as Marshall Whitman walked out of the conference room. Marshall was the sales manager and used the conference room as his office when he wasn't on the road. Besides Mr. Berman and the IT guy, Marshall was the only employee who spoke to Kate. She wished he wouldn't. A tailored suit, spray tan, hair transplant—he was as fake as the plastic palm tree next to her desk.

He strutted over to her, his long legs quickly covering the distance. "I took a reception call for you." Marshall's usually raspy voice had a singsong lilt. "I even took the time to write it down." He was a very tall man, so when she stooped over to pick up the dropped note and he stepped even closer, his crotch was level with her face.

Kate stood up, instinctively using one hand to cover her cleavage as Marshall leered at her.

"From the way you rushed to get the phone"—he dangled the memo in front of his groin—"I've got a feeling this is a big deal to you."

Kate's fantasy of calling Human Resources and having Marshall dragged from the building was a pipe dream. He'd turn it around and say she had misinterpreted his intentions. Still, she needed that call sheet.

"Thank you, Marshall."

She held out her hand in front of her, but Marshall only grinned like a bra-snapping bully as he dangled the note suggestively in front of his crotch.

Middle school was a distant memory, but this encounter brought back the pain of being harassed. Kate's hand shot out as if she were going to punch him square in the groin. Marshall instinctively hunched forward, and Kate plucked the paper from his outstretched hand.

"Thanks." She hurried back to the reception desk.

Marshall cleared his throat and forced another salesman grin onto his face. "Not a problem. I figured I'd save you from another one of Berman's lectures."

She unfolded the memo Marshall had taken.

WRONG NUMBER!

Marshall laughed like the braying ass he was.

I should have punched him in the groin when I had the chance. Creeps like Marshall keep on creeping.

"A missed call is a missed call—am I right or am I right?" Marshall laughed again, then walked over to the mailboxes. His was empty. "I'm expecting a package. Have you seen one for me?"

The chaotic morning had aggravated the lump on her head and her eyebrows pulled together as the first signs of a migraine appeared. "I don't recall… but I put all the mail in the boxes. Unless it's too big; then it would go in the oversize bin."

"It would be small. A padded envelope," Marshall said, but he checked the oversize bin anyway. "Let me know when it comes in." He strode over to the interior door.

"I will."

"Page me. It's important." Marshall stopped at the door. "It would be a pity to have to tell Berman you were late, right?"

Kate stared at him in disbelief. Was he threatening to go to Berman over a package?

He swiped his badge and left.

Kate ran her hand down her forehead and over her eyes. *I have to find a better job.*

She spent the rest of the soul-sucking morning wiping down the reception desk for the hundredth time. She wasn't permitted to read or use her cell phone or do anything besides cleaning or sitting at the desk and waiting for the reception phone to ring.

It felt as if the clock were moving backward, though frequent checks revealed that noon was inching closer. She only had an unpaid half hour for lunch, but it was better than being chained to the desk, so when Donna's bright-purple VW Bug pulled up out front, Kate bolted for the door like a child at recess.

She scanned the parking lot for any sign of the man from the drone videos as she hurried to Donna's car.

"What's up, girlfriend?" Donna called through her open window, her colorful hair beads bobbing to the beat of the music streaming from the car radio.

"Donna, I am beyond glad to see you!"

Donna shoved the passenger door open. "Ditto! Pig and Fig?"

"Is that the new sandwich at Screamin' Beans?" Kate laughed, getting in. "I'll try it."

Donna's face lit up. "Your tastebuds will thank you. Trust me."

"How's the new job?"

"Great! I'm loving it." The Bug lurched forward. "Sorry. Still getting this manual shift thing down." Donna had been learning to drive a stick for the last month, but it was going about as well as her other endeavors. Still, Kate had to give Donna credit for her optimism.

Kate locked the door and sagged into the seat as the office faded in the distance behind her. She powered down the window and let the air cool her face.

"How'd the rest of Andy's game go?" Donna asked.

Kate filled her in on the drone, the engagement, the stalker, Scott coming over, and the custody battle. Even though she spoke quickly, she'd only touched on everything by the time they reached Screamin' Beans.

"That's crazy scary!" Donna checked her rearview mirror as she pulled into the parking lot. "You have no idea who the guy following you is?"

"No. You can't see his face clearly in the videos. But the police are going to try to enhance them."

"I knew I shouldn't have left!"

"Hey, you were great to show up. You saw more of Andy's games this season than Scott did," Kate reassured her friend as they got out and headed across the parking lot.

Donna gave Kate a side hug as she held the door to the bistro open. "You're gonna flip out over the Pig and Fig. It's the best sandwich I've ever had. I had one yesterday. Ham, fig, goat cheese, and arugula on pressed sourdough!" Donna smacked her lips for emphasis. "It's a mouthgasm. Hey, I, ah, I'm a little strapped for cash. Is there any way…"

"On me."

"Louis took me to dinner last night and he forgot his wallet—again."

Kate exhaled with relief when she saw there was no line. Her lunch break was only thirty minutes and a couple of indecisive patrons could chew up most of it.

"Afternoon, darlings." Grace, Kate's favorite barista, gave them a welcoming wave. "Whatcha havin'?"

"Two Pig and Figs, a large latte, and…" Kate turned to Donna.

"Sweet tea for me!"

Considering how hyper her friend was now, Kate doubted she needed the sugar, but who was she to judge? They made their way to a corner table and sat.

"The way I figure it," Donna said, "the creep following you has to be one of the guys you dated."

"Not necessarily—"

"It has to be. Who else could it be? I mean, seriously, you never go *anywhere*."

"Gee, thanks."

"I didn't mean it that way." Donna reached across the table and squeezed her hand. "You've always been there for me. I've got your back. What can I do?"

Kate smiled. "Nothing. The police are going to interview the guys I went on the speed dates with. I just want them to find the guy and tell him to leave me alone."

"Ugh, Scott. How long did he stay?" Donna asked.

"Till around eleven-thirty."

"Wait a second, did you two… do it?" Donna wiggled her eyebrows.

"Of course not! He just got engaged."

"There's no ring on his finger, so he's fair game, girl. You know what I think? You should have come downstairs as bare and beautiful as the good Lord made you."

"I was naked in front of Scott for years and he still left me for Tammi."

"How do you think she got him?"

"Well, I'm not a cheater."

"It's not cheating. If someone stole my dog, don't I have the right to take my dog back?"

"That's totally different."

"Seriously. If someone stole my dog, having possession of it wouldn't make it theirs. It's still my dog. If I chose to claim it, I'd be within my rights." Donna seemed pleased with her reasoning.

"You're right. Scott is a dog!"

The table shook as they howled with laughter, until Kate's phone alarm cut them off.

"Crud. Gotta go." Kate wrapped up her sandwich, grabbed her coffee, and speed-walked back to the car.

"If you are moving on"—Donna unlocked the car—"do you want me to see if Louis knows a good guy and we could double?"

Kate loved Donna, but the thought of her picking out a date for her made the Pig and Fig in her stomach squeal. "No thanks."

Donna punched it as they reached the main road.

"Scott has done a lot of rotten things, but I never thought he'd try to demote me to part-time mother of my own children."

"I bet that's all Tammi's idea. It's how she operates. She wants the kids so you don't have them. I guarantee that after a year or two, she'll ship them off to some boarding school."

There was bitterness in Donna's voice and her ever-present smile vanished. It seemed she would never get over how Tammi had bullied her through school. Donna had grown up as one of the only black kids in Hartville, and to hear her tell it, school had been twelve years of hell thanks to Tammi and her friends. Donna had shared some stories with Kate, but there must have been more tales that were harder to tell.

"I'm not going to agree to any changes to the custody agreement. Not a chance."

Donna pulled up in front of the office and gave Kate a sympathetic look. "Call me tonight and we'll come up with a combat plan. Thanks again for lunch!" Donna tooted her horn as she drove off.

Kate waved, then turned around to face her prison. The last bit of Donna's infectious enthusiasm died out when she saw Marshall waiting at her desk. She entered through the front door and he marched straight into her personal space.

"A package did come for me on Friday." His voice was clipped.

"I don't remember a—"

"You signed for it." He held up a page printed from the Internet. Her signature was visible at the bottom.

"If I did, I would've put the package in your mailbox."

"Well, you didn't. I've looked in every mailbox and it's not there. It was a white padded envelope. Did you take it?"

Kate's eyes narrowed as she forced down her indignation. She wouldn't yell. She wouldn't snap. *Use humor to defuse the situation.* She'd read that many times.

"You caught me, Marshall. I stole it."

Marshall's neck reddened and the veins in his temple throbbed.

"I'm kidding—of course," Kate blurted out as she hurried over to the bins. "I put all the mail we get in either the person's bin—"

"It's not there…" A mix of emotions washed across Marshall's face as he watched Kate go through the other packages. "Because you took it! You just admitted it!"

"I made a joke. Why would I take your package?"

Marshall's nostrils flared. His glare shifted from Kate to the mailboxes and then to Kate's desk. He'd taken two steps toward the reception desk when voices from the front of the building drew their attention. Mr. Berman was approaching the entrance, chatting away with the head of finance.

Marshall cast another glare at Kate and headed for the conference room. As he exited, the front door opened. Neither Berman nor the other man even glanced in Kate's direction before entering Berman's office and shutting the door behind them.

Alone once more, Kate set her purse down and sank into her seat. Men like Marshall had bothered her through her entire life. If Marshall had accused Donna of taking the mail, she would have stuffed him into the oversize mail bin. That would have ended it.

Kate must have signed for the envelope; it was her signature on the paper. But she had no memory of doing so. Maybe she had done something stupid, like the phone had rung and she'd put the package in her desk. With her heart thudding, Kate ripped open every drawer. It wasn't there. She must have put it in Marshall's bin. Anyone passing by could have taken it. Yes, that was it. Someone had to have taken it. Right? She hadn't done anything wrong. But the hammering in her chest didn't subside.

She looked up and her vision blurred a bit. Sweat beaded on her brow. She bent down and picked up her purse. Her fingers shook as she unzipped it and took out her medicine. Popping a little yellow pill into her mouth, Kate closed her eyes and took three deep, calming breaths. None of it helped.

Marshall wasn't going to let this stupid thing go. He wanted blood, and it was sure to be hers.

Kate shoved the office doors open. The fresh air filled her lungs and she lifted her head to the welcoming sun. She crossed to the other end of the parking lot and stopped short.

"What the—?"

Her breath came in halting puffs and she couldn't speak. The steel bands wrapping around her chest slowly constricted. Someone had scratched the word SLUT, in two-foot-tall letters, into the passenger side of her minivan. Kate scanned the parking lot for anyone suspicious, but no one stood out. Her fingers traced the gouges in the paint. They weren't very deep, but how much would this cost to fix? More importantly, who would do this to her minivan? Why?

Her head sagged forward, and her forehead bumped against the side of the van. She whimpered as pain shot down from the lump on her crown all the way to her toes.

Kate yanked out her phone and called the police. She expected them to send a cruiser, but ten minutes later, she was pleasantly surprised when a green sedan pulled into the parking lot and Detective Ryan Daley got out.

Ryan walked over to her, his notebook in his hand. "Kate." His dark-blue suit made his broad shoulders seem even larger.

She pointed to her van. "Someone—" Her voice cracked and she cleared her throat. "Did that."

"When did you notice the damage?"

"Ten minutes ago, when I came out of work."

"Did you see anybody in the parking lot or happen to notice anyone who matched the description of your stalker?"

Kate took a step closer to him. She'd assumed that whoever had defaced her van had done the deed and left, but had they stayed? Were they still here? "I didn't see anyone."

Ryan's gaze swept the parking lot and he pointed to the upper corner of the building. "They have security cameras. I'll request a copy of the footage."

Kate stared at the rusted camera and her hopes sank. Did it even work?

"I don't mean to alarm you, but this situation with whoever is following you has now escalated. You need to be extra vigilant about your surroundings. Don't get distracted by your cell phone. Remember to keep your car doors locked at all times, check underneath your car as you approach it, check the backseat before you get in, and don't park next to any vans."

She nodded rapidly as she inched closer to him.

"Sorry. I'm doing a fine job of calming your nerves." Ryan grimaced. "But you do need to stay alert." He took out his phone and began taking photographs of the damage to the van.

"I appreciate the suggestions."

Ryan put his phone in his pocket. "The lab is reviewing the drone footage. The techs think the man was remotely controlling the drone and then using a setting called follow mode to have it track you. It's why the device stayed directly over your head."

A wave of guilt washed over Kate, but she remembered Scott's advice. She needed the police to find this creep. If she admitted the drone was hers, they may stop looking.

"The lab said they're having a hard time estimating the man's height and weight because of the angle of the videos. We need that if we're going to put out a BOLO." At Kate's puzzled expression, Ryan said, "It's a 'be on the lookout' for someone. That way, we can alert patrols to keep their eyes open. I'm hoping the lab guys can work their magic, though."

"Me too."

"Would you like me to follow you home?"

Kate checked the time and frowned. She'd love for him to follow her, but he couldn't, not now. "No thank you. I have to pick up my kids."

Ryan handed her a business card. "My cell phone is on there. If you see anything out of the ordinary or think of anything else, please reach out."

Kate nodded, but she couldn't take her eyes off the word scrawled across the side of her van. How could she pick up Andy at school in this? What about Ava? What would Audrey say?

Cursing her day, she took back roads all the way to Audrey's, which added a few minutes to the ride but gave her some time to cool off a little and think of a way to hide the vandalism from Audrey.

When she reached the huge house, she drove around the large circular driveway counterclockwise, so that when she parked, the passenger side was blocked from sight. Now she had to make sure Ava entered on the driver's side.

She hurried up the granite steps. The large door swung open and Mary, Audrey's personal assistant, stood there smiling.

"Ms. Rochester is making a phone a call, but—"

Kate relaxed a little. "Oh, please don't disturb her."

"Mommy!" Ava came running down the hallway towing her suitcase. She wore an old apron, red beret, bright-blue scarf, and fluffy pink socks. She raised her spatula high and struck a pose. "The chef is ready!"

"So is your food truck! Let's go."

Ava giggled. "Let's make my van an ice cream truck! Bye-bye, Mary!" She waved and ran out the front door.

As Kate turned to go, Mary said, "Could you please wait for a moment? Ms. Rochester would like to speak with you before you leave."

Kate grabbed Ava's suitcase and kept moving. "Actually… I need to get Andy at school. I'll call her!"

She rushed down the driveway, but she was too late. Ava was standing on the passenger side, staring at the word etched into the side of the van.

"What's a slut?"

Kate hung her head. Audrey had been teaching her granddaughter how to read. Kate's lip trembled. *Not me!* she wanted to say, but she settled for, "It's a bad word." Her hands shook as she slid the suitcase into the back and buckled Ava into her car seat.

Ava frowned. "Why did you write it on my ice cream truck?"

Another little piece of Kate's heart broke off. "Mommy didn't write it. A bad person did. I'm sorry, honey. I'll get it fixed."

Ava crossed her arms and legs and glared at her feet.

Kate turned on the radio to fill the silence and drove back across town, trying to think of a way to hide the vandalism from Andy. But by the time she was approaching the school, she had no ideas. She pulled into the pickup line and braved the stares. Down the sidewalk, a group of women pointed and giggled. She knew most of them—Britney, Courtney, Haley. Like Tammi, they were all buffed and manicured; most had influential fathers or husbands, all had perfect children and beautiful houses. But Tammi had always been the queen bee. Kate imagined Tammi leading the cheer now—"Give me an S! Give me an L! Give me a U!..."

Kate swallowed as humiliation threatened to overtake her and she tried to turn the emotion into defiance. She would have to endure and do her best to shield her children. But those women were making it hard. And to think she had tried to befriend them. For Scott. All those pies she'd made for their idiotic bake sales.

"I can't believe I made twenty-seven of those stupid pies!"

"I like pie, Mommy."

Kate glanced into the backseat. Ava's eyebrows were knitted together into one, angry caterpillar and her shoulders were hunched to her ears. She pressed her lips into a thin line and glowered at her mother.

"What's wrong, honey?" Kate asked.

"You called pies stupid."

Kate looked at Ava as if she'd developed the power to read minds—before realizing she must have been thinking aloud. "Sorry, princess. Mommy's having a bad day."

"Grammie says, don't let the day rule you." Ava thrust her spatula-scepter high overhead. "You rule the day."

Of course, Her Majesty, Audrey the Great, could command the day and it would obey her decree. But Kate lacked that superpower, and right now, the day was kicking her butt.

She spotted a sea of curly-haired boys and Andy broke free from the crowd, his eyes wide.

"Did the stalker do that?" he asked, getting into the van. He clicked his seat belt and leaned forward, his eyes practically glowing.

"I think so." Kate pulled forward, eager to get out of the parking lot. "It happened at my work, but the police are making sure we're safe. Let's get home and have a nice afternoon."

Ava raised her hand. "I have to go pee-pee."

The line to get back into the school parking lot stretched down the block. "We'll be home in five minutes."

"That's a long time," Ava whined.

Kate had to agree. The way things were going, her migraine would be at DEFCON 5 by the time they pulled into the driveway. "Mommy will hurry."

As soon as the van crossed out of the school zone, Kate punched it.

"We dissected a worm today!" Andy proclaimed.

"What's dissected?"

"Cut up!"

Ava's mouth fell open. "Really?"

Andy nodded rapidly. Even though it made her stomach turn, Kate didn't interrupt him as he went into detail about slicing up a worm—his story was distracting Ava and that was a good thing.

Kate turned onto her road and barreled into the driveway. She put the van in park and Andy and Ava raced to the front door with Kate hot on their heels.

"Wait for me!" Kate called out as she scanned the yard for anything out of place.

"Open the door, Mommy!" Ava said, crossing her legs.

"I need to make sure the house is safe."

Kate opened the door and caught Ava as she tried to rush inside. Like a secret service agent protecting the president, she hurried Ava to the bathroom. Andy followed them, chatting away.

"I told my friends about the stalker. Tommy said it's probably an escaped prisoner they did experiments on and he went crazy, but Billy thinks he's just a serial killer."

Ava giggled. "You can't kill cereal. It's not real."

"Quiet down, both of you." Kate led Ava into the bathroom, shut the door, and turned to Andy. "The person following Mommy is not some crazed killer."

"How do you know?" Andy asked, his eyes rounding.

Kate stood there blinking. She didn't know. Not for certain, anyway. "The police are going to catch the man. I spoke with them today."

"Killed cereal." Ava laughed from behind the door.

"It's not cereal you eat, dufus!" Andy shouted.

"Bad word!" Ava called back.

"They call them serial killers because they kill so many people. Like pieces of cereal in a bowl, right, Mom?"

Kate held up her hands as Ava came out of the bathroom. "No more bad words or talk of bad people—period. What I need from both of you is for you to go play by yourselves until I get dinner started." She also needed to call the insurance company and see if any of the damage to the minivan was covered.

"What are we having?" they both asked.

"Pasta."

"Angel hair!" Andy blurted out like he was a contestant on a game show.

"Ziti!" Ava chimed in.

Kate held up both hands. "I pick elbow macaroni, and since the cook gets two votes, I win."

Both of them made a face, then they headed for their rooms. Kate trudged up the stairs after them. She may have gotten the kids to stop talking about serial killers, but every nerve in her system was on high alert. Someone was stalking her. He could be watching the house right now. Was there a chance Audrey would—

"The Internet isn't working!" Andy called out.

Kate swore. She turned on her computer and checked to see if her browser connected to the Web—nothing. Having dug out the cable number, she waited on hold for twenty minutes to speak with a customer service rep. The synthesized piano music had just about driven her insane by the time he picked up.

After she'd given the rep all her contact information, he said, "I'm sorry, ma'am, but your service was suspended for nonpayment."

Kate drummed her fingers on the desk. She couldn't handle the kids without the distraction of the Internet right now. "I'm certain I've already paid my bill, but I'll pay again now and sort it out later. Here's my card."

No sooner had she hung up than her phone buzzed, announcing the arrival of a text message from Donna. She'd brought her friend up to speed on the van vandalism and now Donna was insisting on helping.

I'M WORKING ON PLAN 2 CATCH STALKER.

Kate cringed. Knowing Donna, her plan could be anything—assuming a new identity, fleeing to a distant tropical island, hiring a hitman… Some actually seemed like good possibilities right now.

NO NEED, Kate texted her back. POLICE R ON IT.

RYAN? THE HOT 1?

YES.

Donna texted back fireworks emojis and a gif of a dancing cat in a tutu.

Kate switched over apps and checked her email. There was no message from Michelle about the freelance gig. Would her friend give her another chance? Or had the job crashed and burned like the drone?

Needing a break before dealing with the insurance company, she headed downstairs with Ava on her heels.

"Andy's boring. He won't talk to me because he's doing homework. So I'm coming with you, Mommy."

When they walked into the living room, Ava ran over to the karaoke machine that her grandmother had given her. "Do you want me to put on a concert for you, Mommy?"

Kate's hands trembled as she waved them back and forth, her throbbing head beating out a warning that any loud noises would be met with an even angrier migraine. Audrey must genuinely hate her. The karaoke machine was a far crueler gift than a drum set. The microphone worked and it had a very loud speaker. Ava was also able to record and upload her songs, belting out her personal rendition of every Disney classic over the relentless backing track. Then she would play them again and again as she danced around the room, until Kate, exhausted, announced it was bedtime and then lay sleepless, unable to stop the loop of jingles rattling around her head.

"How about I watch you play with your new house? Mommy would like that."

Ava clapped her hands together and sat down to play with her dollhouse. Kate had picked it up at Goodwill a few weeks ago and rehabbed every square inch with Donna on nights when the kids stayed with Scott. Ava didn't know it wasn't actually new and Kate wasn't going to tell her. Ava loved it, and Kate was proud of herself. Scott was another matter. Anything less than the best set him off and she didn't want to get into an argument with him because it wasn't brand new.

"Screw him," she mumbled as she picked up some pillows that had fallen off the couch.

Ava's head snapped up and she pointed an accusatory finger at her. "Bad word."

"I didn't swear. I said..." Kate racked her brain for something to say. She had single-handedly filled the swear jar and she didn't want to add to the pot. She'd come up with the idea for the jar when Andy started using words like "stupid" and "idiot" and Ava began using them too. But like the rest of Kate's plans lately, the swear jar had backfired, and it was now cutting into her meager coffee budget.

"You said, 'screw him.'" Ava clamped both hands over her mouth.

"No." Kate shook her head—and immediately regretted it as the pain made her eyes water. "I said, blue scrim."

"What?" Ava's button nose crinkled.

"Blue scrim," Kate repeated. "Scrim is like a fabric. I was thinking about... getting some curtains."

Ava hopped up and raised her hands over her head. She did a little happy dance, twirling like a helicopter until her belt-stethoscope flew off. "Blue curtains? Like from *Frozen*? Yay!" She launched into her version of the movie's theme song, "Let It Go."

Kate closed her eyes. *Oh, that's just great. Now I have to buy blue curtains!*

Ava, seemingly placated, raced upstairs. Andy was still in his room working on homework. Surprisingly, with everything going on, he seemed a little better today. In addition to the divorce, he faced all the angst that comes with starting middle school. He'd made friends over the last year, but he was still the new kid in town. On top of all that, Kate knew that the biggest problem was Tammi. Andy never said anything bad about his father's new girlfriend, but he was a little more subdued each time he came home from a weekend with them.

The front doorbell rang and Kate jumped.

"Door!" Ava yelled.

"Is it the police again?" Andy called down, his voice filled with excitement.

Kate hurried to the door, checked the peephole, and froze. Audrey—who had never been to the house, not when they moved in, not ever—stood on the front porch. Kate had invited her on countless occasions, but she had always been a no-show.

Audrey's stare fixed on the peephole. Kate's palms grew damp. Could Audrey sense Kate gawking on the other side?

Audrey's eyes narrowed.

Kate swung the door open and stepped aside as her mother-in-law swooped in. She stopped in the foyer, scanning the downstairs with one swivel of her head, and turned to face Kate. Audrey stood two inches shorter than her, but somehow Kate always felt diminished in her presence.

"Your front door was unlocked?"

"I don't lock it when the kids are playing and I'm home."

"In light of current circumstances, I would have expected that bad habit to have ceased."

Kate nodded. Of course Audrey knew.

Audrey's eyes shifted to the door and Kate double-locked it.

"To say I'm disappointed in your lackadaisical security would be a gross understatement." Audrey crossed her arms. "Why was I not informed of the situation?"

Kate cleared her throat. "You're right. I should have told you. The whole thing is so surreal. I mean, why would anyone stalk me?" The question tumbled from her mouth.

"Do try to set your low self-esteem aside for a moment and actually think about the question."

As Audrey stood awaiting her response, Kate mentally raced down the list of anyone who would have even the slightest reason to pursue her, but try as she might, no one came to mind. "I have no idea."

"You've been dating."

Audrey wasn't asking; she stated it as a fact, and that made Kate bristle. How had she gotten this information?

"No, I haven't."

Audrey's expression changed to one Kate had never seen on her face before. Hurt?

"I thought a bond we shared, besides the children, was honesty. Word travels fast in this town. Are you denying you attended one of those dating events?"

Kate cringed. It wasn't the thought of discussing her lack of a dating life with her former mother-in-law but the memory of the experience itself. "A friend signed me up for speed dating. They call it dating, but it was sitting down for ten minutes and trying to make conversation. It was horrible. It takes me more than ten minutes to pick out an entrée, let alone figure out if I want to date someone."

"I don't know what dismays me more, that you engaged in such lowbrow behavior or that you failed to realize how shallow the pool of suitable male candidates in Hartville is. But I accept your explanation. Is one of those men now following you?"

"I don't think so." Kate wanted to let her head roll back on her shoulders and swear at the ceiling, but whatever superpowers Audrey possessed made Kate stand straighter. "I sent each one a very nice rejection email."

"How quaint. Gather their names and send them to me."

"I already provided the detectives with them."

Audrey lifted her chin ever so slightly. The queen had made a demand, not a request.

Kate knew that telling Audrey to butt out would be as useful as setting herself on fire and throwing herself off a cliff. "I'll forward them to you."

Audrey nodded. "I know most of the families in town. I will make inquiries and see if any of those men have *issues*. I see that he also defaced your van."

"That's what the detectives think. They also found some cigarette butts next to a tree in the backyard."

Audrey's countenance darkened. "He was here? Outside my grandbabies' home?" She calmly opened her Chanel purse and removed her cell phone.

"They took a report," Kate said, but Audrey silenced any further comments with a lifted eyebrow.

"Timothy? It's Audrey." Audrey's heels clicked off the hardwood floor as she strode into the kitchen. "It is the lack of police presence now which concerns me." She headed straight to the back door and locked it with a loud click. Her slender fingers tightened into a fist. "Yes, and as an elected official, Sheriff, I'm certain you will correct this oversight. Excellent. Thank you, Timothy."

Kate stood there picturing the sheriff, quite a large man, scrambling out of his office like a scolded dog and barking orders at his staff. Even if she could only hear half the conversation, she'd picked up on the key phrase—elected official. And since Audrey was not only the sheriff's godmother but also his top donor with the deepest pockets, Kate wouldn't be surprised if a police helicopter showed up soon.

Audrey calmly tucked her phone into her purse. "There will be a police presence here tonight."

"Thank you." Kate covered her mouth with her hand. The muscles in her jaw tensed beneath her trembling fingers. "I have a favor to ask."

Audrey inclined her head.

"Whoever this stalker is, he's following *me*. The detective who came out to look at the van said his behavior has escalated."

"Obviously."

"It's not safe for the children here." Kate's stomach clenched. "It would be best if they stayed with you."

Audrey considered what Kate had said for a moment, her lips pressed together, and then she nodded. "Agreed. Gather the children."

Leaving her mother-in-law downstairs, Kate hurried to Ava's room. She was busy drawing, a bright sun hat perched atop her head.

"Hi, Mommy."

"Come here, sweetie."

Kate picked Ava up and sat on her bed. "So, how'd you like to sleep over at Grammie's house?"

Usually, Ava would have burst into a happy dance, but Kate's perceptive daughter frowned. "Because of the bad man?"

"Don't you worry, angel. You and Andy will be with Grammie."

"Okay. I like staying at Grammie's. But can you come too, Mommy?"

The words pierced Kate's heart, but she forced herself to put on a brave face. "That would be fun sometime," she said, dodging the question.

She bundled both of the kids up and helped them into Audrey's car.

"Is your Intanet working?" Ava asked Audrey.

"IntERnet," Audrey enunciated and Ava repeated the word. "Of course it is. Isn't yours?"

"Mom didn't pay the bill," Andy said, clicking his seat belt.

Heat rushed to Kate's cheeks. "I did pay it; the cable company must have made a mistake. They're restoring the service shortly."

Audrey rolled her eyes as she put the car into reverse. As she backed out of the driveway, she said, "On the way to Grammie's, let's discuss the phrase 'personal responsibility.'"

Kate wanted to throw her shoe at her, but instead, she smiled and waved with both arms high, a send-off tradition born out of necessity in the early days following the separation. Kate would do anything to ease her children's pain.

Andy's face appeared in the window. He cupped his hand to his mouth and yelled, "See you later, alligator!"

Kate's arms dropped to her sides. Her leg trembled as she pictured Emma waving and saying the same thing. Those were the last words Emma had said to her.

Audrey's car rounded the corner and Kate turned back to her house. Empty. No kids. No husband. A sudden profound loneliness swept over her. She was used to the kids leaving by now, but this was different. Would she see them again? It was ridiculous, but she couldn't shake the feeling that she may not.

Kate turned and headed inside. As she locked the door, she wiped away a tear. She felt more coming, like she was on the edge of a full-on meltdown. She took out her phone and called Donna, the one person who was sure to cheer her up.

"Okay, what's the plan, Stan?" Kate asked.

"I joined Speedy Dates and started to set up dates with all the guys you met."

"What? Donna, that's crazy!"

"Crazy smart! You emailed me all the guys you saw that night, so I sent each of them a photo they couldn't resist. Check out my profile pic."

Kate's phone buzzed. It was a photograph of Donna with her arms squished together, puffing out her chest and revealing way too much cleavage.

"Bait!" Donna laughed. "To quote my favorite Disney princess, 'Don't underestimate the importance of body language.'"

Still in shock, and even a little angry now, Kate replied in a monotone, "That was Ursula the Sea Witch."

"Are you sure?"

"*The Little Mermaid* is Ava's favorite movie. I must have watched it a hundred and seventy-four times."

"Whatever." Donna giggled. "The point is, I know I'll get dates with all of them. Then I'll have a quick chat with each one, deduce which is El

Creepo, and before you know it, you'll be sleeping like a baby again. Bada-bing-bada-boom!"

"No, Donna, no, please don't. This could be dangerous."

"Aw, don't worry, sweetheart, I've got this. We'll meet someplace public, and I'll get a read on 'em. Trust me, I have a built-in creep detector. When it goes off, I'll tell you, and you tell Detective Dreamboat. He does his thing, and whamo! No more creepo!"

"Seriously, Donna, let the police handle it."

"I'm telling you, my plan's going to work. Anyway, I gotta get going. Talk soon!"

Kate stared at her reflection in the darkened phone screen. The hairs on the back of her neck were standing on end. Donna might have thought her plan wasn't dangerous, but what would Kate's stalker do if Donna did catch him?

She scrolled back to the main message screen. She hadn't heard from Scott. She'd left messages and sent a couple of texts explaining that the kids were staying at his mother's and why, but all she'd gotten was radio silence. Why did she bother? Prince Charming wouldn't be galloping down her driveway to rescue her—unless he needed more free marketing advice.

Setting her phone down, Kate searched for her purse. She normally left it on the coffee table, but it wasn't there. Puzzled, she dashed around the house until she located it on the kitchen table. Her fingers shook as she unzipped the pocket and took out a little yellow pill. Besides making it difficult to focus, her happy pills weren't making her very happy, but the increased dosage was taking the edge off her panic attacks. Still, what was the deal with her thinking aloud lately? Hopefully, it wasn't a side effect she needed to be concerned about.

Kate didn't even want to think about going to bed. The sun had long set, but she was wired. During the last few hours, every horror movie she'd ever seen—plus the one starring her and the children and a stalker in a blue baseball cap—had been replaying behind her sore eyes. She headed to her office and logged onto her bank account. She pulled up Bill Pay and sat blinking at the screen. She hadn't paid the Internet bill. Or her therapist, for that matter. What was wrong with her? Maybe it was just stress. With a few keystrokes, she corrected the oversight and logged off.

Not able to sit still, she went around the house checking the locks on all the windows and doors, and finally ended up back in the kitchen. Her hands were shaking as she walked to the sink. Clasping them still, she stared at the knives. She should have a weapon, right? Maybe one in every room of the house. No, with these jittery hands, she'd end up stabbing herself.

She almost leaped out of her skin when a buzzing in her pocket announced a new text message. It was from a withheld number. It started out sounding like "The Piña Colada Song."

DO U LIKE WALKING ON THE BEACH + GETTING CAUGHT IN THE RAIN? WOULD U LIKE ME 2—

Kate stopped reading as the text turned pornographic. She clenched her stomach. She was about to block the number when she realized who it was—her stalker.

How had he got her number? Why wouldn't he leave her alone?

Kate's knees buckled and she gripped the edge of the counter to steady herself. Too afraid to fully let go of the counter, she used one hand to reach into her pocket, get Detective Ryan Daley's business card, and forward the text message to him along with an explanation.

She did yet another lap around the house, straightening up a little as she checked the locks for the umpteenth time. Doing anything to keep her hands from shaking, Kate pushed in all the dining room chairs and arranged the pillows on the couch. She picked up Ava's dropped spatula and brought it into the kitchen. Kate sniffled as she raised it high and proclaimed, "Today will be different," begrudgingly altering her self-help mantra to match Audrey's advice.

Hadn't the last book been called *Change Today for a New Tomorrow*? Even in her misery, she thought it was a little funny. She'd read the entire self-help section at the library and she snatched the new ones whenever they came in, hoping each time that the book might contain the secret formula for building a new life when all you want is the one you had. She could have written one herself at this point.

As she put the spatula in the dishwasher, her heart ached for the kids. Ava's antics and Andy's genius would surely have put her in a better mood. No, no, they wouldn't. If they were here, Kate would have been worried the whole time for their safety. They were safer at Grandma's. But the stalker had gotten Kate's number somehow; he could easily find out where the kids were. Her hand went to her mouth and she gasped. He was just targeting Kate, not them. *They're safer at Grandma's. They're safe, completely safe, at Grandma's. Safe. Safe.* Breathe. In, out.

Headlights flickered through the blinds. Kate pulled back the shade and watched a black SUV drive by. As it passed her neighbor's fence, the brake lights illuminated a car parked on the other side of the road. In the driver's seat was the unmistakable silhouette of a man. A tremor ran up Kate's legs and down her arms, and a gasp built in her throat.

Her phone rang, but this number wasn't blocked.

Ryan.

"Kate? It's Detective Daley."

"There's a car parked across the street from my house—"

"My apologies. That would be me and the reason for my call. I wanted you to know I'm here and keeping an eye on things."

Ryan was watching out for her. She almost broke into one of Ava's happy dances. Kate had expected at most a neighborhood patrol because of Audrey's phone call—she had never imagined Ryan himself would come.

The warm glow of safety wrapped around her like a Florida breeze.

"Oh, okay. Thank you." Kate slipped the phone in her pocket.

How long has he been out there?

Kate's nurturing instinct kicked in and she ran to the kitchen. It was late, almost nine. He must be hungry. She started a pot of coffee as she debated what to fix for him. Had he eaten already? He was fit, so she doubted he wanted something sugary. But maybe sugar would help on a stakeout.

She remembered she had some sliced chicken breast and decided to make a sandwich. Mustard, mayo, or chipotle sauce? She set out all the condiments in separate little saucers. While the coffee brewed, she headed to the front door with a heavily loaded tray she'd only used before to deliver breakfast to sick kids in bed.

Kate stopped. Maybe this was a stupid idea. Coffee and sandwiches? Would she come off like a Martha Stewart wannabe if she brought them out to Ryan?

Winners take chances. Her self-help mantra rang in her head. Or was it Ava quoting Audrey?

Kate opened her front door, marched forward, and froze on the front steps. The night sky was overcast and there were large sections of darkness between her house and Ryan's car. Feeling like a kid walking home alone at night, she sprinted across the street. As she got closer, she saw that

Detective Mark Tills was sitting next to Ryan. The older detective folded his arms across his chest and frowned. Ryan powered his window down as she approached.

"Hi," she said, holding out the tray as if it explained everything. "When you called… I wanted… I thought you might…" Kate forced a smile. "Would you like some coffee? I didn't know how you like it, so there's cream in the glass cup and whole milk in the purple plastic one. Skim's in the light blue." She glanced at the tray, grateful she'd brought two coffee cups, even though she'd thought one would be for her.

Her phone buzzed in her pocket. Friend or foe? She wasn't going to check now.

"Wow. I appreciate all this." Ryan smiled, but his eyes darted over her shoulder to the backyard.

"Oh, I'm an idiot. I've given away your position, right?"

Detective Tills nodded, but Ryan chuckled. "No, you're fine. It's nice of you to do this. Why don't you bring it around to the passenger side?"

Kate walked around the car, now trying to hunch over. From the heat in her cheeks, she was sure she was beet-red. Of course they didn't want anyone to know the police were watching her house. Ryan had been giving her a courtesy call. She might as well have put a spotlight on them.

Tills powered down his window and took the tray with a curt nod.

Ryan leaned over. "This is very thoughtful. Thank you."

Once again she had underestimated the mesmerizing effect of his eyes and mouth and found herself staring. "I'm sorry I loused things up. I wanted to thank you. For everything. I'll go now."

She crouched and hurried back across the street, scanning the tree line and shadows as she scurried to the safety of the house. She was halfway up the front porch steps when her phone buzzed again.

Another blocked number.

R U BUSY TONIGHT? R U NAKED? I AM.

The text made her skin crawl, but then she saw the picture and swallowed. His face was obscured and he was naked from the waist down. Her stalker had crossed another line.

Clutching her phone, Kate turned back and rushed over to the patrol car.

Tills swore as she ran up.

"I'm sorry! I'm sorry, but it's him again." Her whole arm shook as she held out her phone to Ryan.

He glanced at the picture, read the text, and said, "You forwarded me a message earlier. Do you mind if I see it?"

"Not at all. Just go back to the past messages."

Kate glanced over Ryan's shoulder as he swiped back to the main message screen. When she noticed the text from Donna, her shoulders curled forward and she thrust her hands deep into her pockets.

IS HOT COP SINGLE?

Praying Ryan wouldn't notice, she said, "It's the top one."

Detective Tills leaned over and took Kate's phone from Ryan. He used his own phone to take photos of Kate's screen. "We'll reach out to the phone company and try and trace these."

"I'm going to change my number."

Ryan handed the phone back to Kate. "You should hold off on doing that. It would make it more difficult to track him down. If he contacts you again, don't respond. Don't delete the texts. Just let us know."

Tills quickly added, "From a distance. Forward them to us. Okay?"

Kate nodded.

"Why don't I walk you home?" Ryan opened his door.

When the dome light clicked on, Tills exhaled and muttered something under his breath.

"I'm so sorry," Kate said.

"You've got nothing to apologize for." Ryan smiled and dimples appeared on both sides of his face, softening his expression.

She walked beside him as he escorted her across the street.

"Everyone gets nervous," Ryan continued. "It's normal. How are the kids holding up?"

"They're not here. I asked their grandmother to watch them."

"I think that's best in this situation."

"You said you think his behavior is escalating. How worried should I be?" She moved even closer to him.

"I need to be completely honest with you, Kate. I am concerned by the rapid change in his pattern. He's moved very quickly from following you to defacing your van and now contacting you. I think you made the right decision regarding your kids." Ryan's chocolate eyes filled with concern. "I can't imagine that sending them away was an easy choice."

When he stopped at the bottom of her steps, she did too. She didn't want him to leave and she didn't want to go into the house alone. Everything he'd said made her see how real the danger was.

"It wasn't an easy choice," Kate said. "But it was the right one." She trudged up the stairs and opened the front door. "Thanks again."

Ryan nodded politely and headed back across the street.

Kate stepped inside the house and watched him walk back to the car. Before getting in, he gave her a little wave. She waved back and closed the front door. All she could think was that the detectives couldn't keep a constant vigil. But whoever was stalking her already was. After all, he had followed her in broad daylight at Andy's soccer game, he'd vandalized her car at her work, and he'd boldly smoked in her backyard—waiting, watching. Was he hiding out in the darkness right now? She clamped her hand over her mouth, reducing her terrified scream to muffled sobs.

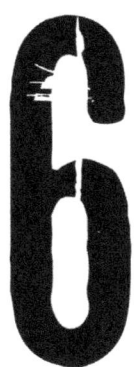

Kate's eyes snapped open. She lay in bed listening. Had someone really called her name? Inside her, a warning bell was going off. Something was wrong.

She slipped out from underneath the covers, careful not to wake Scott. He was fast asleep, the blanket pulled up high on his shoulder.

Kate tiptoed out of the room and down the hallway. A strange buzzing was coming from the other side of Andy's door. Pushing it open, she found Andy wide awake, sitting on his bed and flying Kate's drone around the room.

"Did you call me?"

"Nope!" he answered without taking his eyes off the drone circling around above him.

"Am I losing my mind?" Kate mumbled and moistened her lips. They felt heavy and coated, like she'd been drinking. She glanced up at the ceiling, but the roof above the house was missing. The sky was bright blue with white fluffy clouds.

She trudged down the hallway, placing one hand on the wall to steady herself as she went.

The door handle to Ava's room jiggled but wouldn't turn. Kate knocked.

"Come in," two voices called out. One was Ava's.

Confused, Kate tried the handle again. The door opened, but not into Ava's bedroom.

Ava was seated on a couch in Audrey's living room. Her little feet hung off the edge of the large couch. "I tried to warn you, Mommy." She nodded. "You should never lie to Grammie. She figured it out."

Kate stumbled backward. The back of her legs bumped into a chair and she sat down with a thump.

"Kate?" someone called out, clearly this time. But it couldn't be...

Emma.

Kate turned her head. Her sister was standing in front of a large elm tree.

"Kate, you need to get help."

Kate slowly rose to her feet. She wanted to wrap her arms around her sweet sister and never let go. "I don't need help, Em. I need you."

Her eyelids closed and darkness swept over her.

Kate's alarm sounded faint and far away. Her head rolled forward, and she sat up as a sharp pain shot through her neck. The room spun, and she tumbled from her home office chair and onto the carpet.

"What?!"

Kate sat on the floor of her office trying to get her bearings. How had she gotten here? She had fallen asleep in her bed, hadn't she? Had she gotten up...

Kate swallowed. Had she been sleepwalking? Not again. She stood up, grabbed the office chair, and sat back down. Her computer was on and her email was open. She had left it that way, right?

Muttering, she opened a new email:

Dear Dr. Sprouse,

I'm very concerned about the side effects I am experiencing since you increased the dosage of my antianxiety medication. I'm finding that I'm saying thoughts aloud unintentionally, I'm having vivid dreams and I sleepwalked last night. These same things happened when I had a bad reaction to Serofluxapine several years ago. I'm not sure if you want to switch to a new drug altogether, but I am cutting back to my prior dosage until I hear from you.

Thank you,

Kate Gardner

Her fingers shook as she sent the message. She hadn't sleepwalked since Andy was born, but she'd never forgotten the nightmare of those days. If things were getting that bad again, she didn't know if she had the strength to deal with it.

Kate managed to shower and get to work fifteen minutes early. The job was far from perfect, but it paid the bills. Just as important, being employed improved her prospects of getting another, hopefully better, position. Employers want a winner, and if you show up at an interview without a job, they wonder why you're on the market.

Maybe that was why her dating life was in the toilet too. Everyone wants a winner, and she was a loser at love. A wallflower at the school dance, standing alone on the fringe, praying someone would choose her. But no one was knocking down her door on the dating or job fronts.

Kate swiped her card, opened the front door, and swore under her breath. Taped to the side of her computer monitor was an envelope.

Please don't be another warning. Please…

She opened the envelope and removed the single typed page. Blinking back tears, she read the employee notice with VIOLATION: REPEATED TARDINESS emboldened. Two strikes. She'd only been four minutes late, but arguing would be futile. Now that she was on thin ice, one mistake away from getting fired, she'd better get another job and fast.

Stuffing her handbag under the desk, she flopped into the chair. Outside the front door, three parking spaces and the corner of the company sign were visible. The little view to the outside world was the only thing making the eight hours somewhat bearable. But even that small pleasure was now tainted because all she could think was that if she could see out, the stalker could see in. What if the mystery man from the video footage was hiding around the corner?

Shadows appeared on the sidewalk. Kate stared out the window, waiting.

Two men came into view, chatting amicably as they strolled by.

For the next twenty minutes, Kate watched the outside world. Every time someone walked past the front door, she jumped in her swivel chair. She scanned each passerby for a blue hat, like a sick "I Spy" game she didn't want to win.

Then another long shadow stretched across the concrete sidewalk and stopped. Kate couldn't see the person casting it, but judging by the size of the shadow, they were tall.

Seconds turned to minutes. Why hadn't they moved?

Her phone buzzed. Kate's gaze darted down to her lap, then back to the door. Maybe he had texted her just to distract her? If she looked at her phone, he would strike. She willed herself to keep her eyes on the window. Her phone buzzed again, and the glow was so bright, it illuminated the desk.

The shadow moved. A man stepped forward, a phone pressed to the side of his head.

Kate let out a chuckle that turned to tears. It was just the UPS driver. He glanced over his shoulder, gave her a wave, and hurried down the sidewalk.

As she struggled to catch her breath and pull herself together, she remembered her phone. Through blurred vision, she made out the name: Audrey. She'd never thought she would be happy to see her name. The kids were both doing splendidly and seizing the day. Kate exhaled. She'd spoken with them last night and they'd sounded like they were having a great time. Why wouldn't they? Audrey doted on them, and for that Kate was so grateful.

This was ridiculous. No one was calling the office; both Berman and Marshall were on the road this morning. She couldn't just sit here and drown in her imagination. She got up and vacuumed. Like a shark, if she didn't keep moving, she'd die.

Her eyelids drooped. She rubbed her eyes, her mascara flaking off beneath her fingertips. Kate was pretty confident that what began as slightly smoky eyeshadow had become an homage to Alice Cooper. Her belly rumbled. She'd forgotten to eat breakfast or to pack a lunch again.

"Try to look at the positives... I need to get back into my interview skirt." She kept her best outfit on a hook on the back of her closet door so she'd be ready for an interview at a moment's notice. The problem was, there hadn't been any calls. She was starting to believe Donna's conspiracy theory that somehow Kate was blacklisted in town. But it wasn't possible an entire town could be against her… was it?

Kate closed her eyes. That type of thinking was what had convinced Dr. Sprouse to put her on the yellow happy pills. To combat her growing paranoia, he'd suggested she list the people she knew were in her corner. She opened her eyes and counted them off on her fingers. She only used one hand and had fingers to spare. Team Kate had gotten pretty small.

The alarm on Kate's phone announced her release for time served and lunch. She raced out to the car. Lunchtime on a business day turned Main Street into a parking lot, but Kate knew a shortcut to Screamin' Beans. The truth was, she preferred the back roads even when it wasn't rush hour, but right now she didn't have a choice; with the word SLUT carved into her van, she needed to keep a low profile. The line for the drive-through snaked almost around the building, so she parked in the closest spot and hurried inside, ignoring the sidelong looks and snickers.

Grace, her favorite barista, was there and greeted Kate with a big smile. She was around Kate's age and her hair was pulled back into a messy bun. Even though she looked as busy as an ant at a picnic, she winked at Kate and called out, "You look like you could use an extra-leaded latte."

"Perfect. And a Pig and Fig to go, please."

"You got it!"

Kate paid and slipped a dollar into the empty tip jar. Grace gave her a grateful nod. There was something about the barista that had always teased Kate's curiosity. There was a story behind the way she enunciated her words and carried herself. Maybe she'd been a teacher? One of these days, she would have to work up the nerve to ask.

Kate moved over to the pickup area and glanced back at the line, which had exploded out the door. Wishing she'd left a bigger tip, she grabbed a stirrer and stepped even farther to the side to wait for her sandwich. Trying to keep her eyes off the dessert case, she let her gaze wander around the room. When she saw Tammi, holding court and laughing loudly at a table in the back, her heart sank.

Tammi saw her at the same time. Her blond curls stopped dancing and she put down her coffee cup. She locked eyes with Kate. A cheerleader grin rose on her face, but her eyes filled with pure venom.

Kate swallowed the bile in her throat and waved, cursing the limits of American nonverbal communication. There should be a gesture for what she wanted to say not involving the middle finger. Still, she figured her tiny, forced wave should help her avoid a conversation.

It didn't.

Tammi strolled over like a model on a catwalk who happened to be dressed for the gym. Her tight, low-cut T-shirt and vacuum-sealed yoga pants accentuated all her curves. Casting a quick glance at the table Tammi had left, Kate recognized five members of the dark coven still seated. Their chairs scraped the floor as they angled to get the best views of the upcoming show.

"Katie! Hi!" Tammi stopped a foot away, close but still out of Kate's personal space. "I'm glad I ran into you. How's the head?"

"It's fine, thank you."

"Good. Because I need to speak to you about something. Do you have a minute?" Tammi regally held her hand out toward the back of the room.

I'd rather cover myself in barbecue sauce and leap into a lion pit. "I'm sorry, I need to get back to work."

Tammi's smile crashed down. "Well, I didn't want to have to do this here."

"What's on your mind, Tammi?" Kate said in a low, even voice, so wishing Donna was with her.

"You need to stop trying to manipulate my fiancé!"

Heads turned. Tammi wanted a show, and like a carnival barker, she was drawing everyone's attention.

"Excuse me?"

Tammi crossed her arms, lifting her pert breasts even higher. "You need to get it through your head, Katie, you're divorced."

"I'm well aware of that. What I don't know is, what exactly you're talking about."

"You being stalked." Tammi fluttered her eyelids at the ceiling. It was a gesture Kate was certain she'd practiced a hundred times. "Scott and the children are worried, but you and I know the truth. It's all a pathetic ploy for attention. No one is stalking *you*."

Kate opened her mouth but then quickly closed it. As much as she wanted to give in to her anger, she wouldn't give this homewrecker any ammo. Anything she said could and would be used against her in the court of public opinion. "You think I did that to my own van?" Her hand shook as she pointed to the parking lot.

Tammi tipped back her sculpted chin and let loose a well-rehearsed laugh. "I thought you were advertising your services."

Snickers rose from the back of the room.

Feeling the pink rising in her cheeks, Kate held her head high, turned to the cackling shrews, and gave a thousand-watt smile, complete with a queen's wave. She turned back to Tammi, wanting to stab her with the coffee stirrer in her hand. "That was the best performance you've ever given, Tammi. Silly me, I thought your dreams of making it as an actress had died."

Tammi's eyes blazed, and Kate knew she'd made a direct hit.

At the coffee counter, a barista called out, "Kate! Order's ready!" Kate looked away from Tammi and grabbed the cup, desperate to make her getaway. But when she turned to say thank you, she realized it wasn't Grace handing her the sandwich; it was Ellen, owner of the Screamin' Beans and a close friend of Tammi's.

"Enjoy your meal." Ellen turned and winked at Tammi, whose grin widened.

Kate glanced at the bag in her hand like it was a snake. What had Ellen done to it? Wasn't there anywhere in this stupid town Kate could escape Tammi? She knew everyone, or they knew her. And now Kate could never return to this coffee shop without wondering what they might have put in her food.

Kate headed for the door, but Tammi stepped in front of her, blocking her exit.

"One more thing. I'm taking Ava shopping Saturday, and getting her ears pierced."

Kate's backbone stiffening brought her nose to nose with Tammi. "Not on your life. Ava is phobic about needles. She doesn't want to get her ears pierced."

"A good parent sometimes has to make difficult choices for their children. All the girls have their ears pierced, and you wouldn't want Ava to not fit in, would you? I mean, you know how painful that is, right, Katie?"

The mother bear in Kate was ready to charge into full attack-and-maul mode. It was all she could do to keep her claws to herself and not launch

Tammi over the counter. The image of the cheerleader tumbling through the air like a wayward astronaut brought a little smile to Kate's lips and a boost of confidence.

"Listen, Tammi. We're not talking about which summer camp is the best. We're talking about a permanent decision regarding Ava's body that only Ava should make when she is old enough to do so. So let me make this simple enough that even you can understand. If you touch my daughter's ears, I'll remove yours. That's a promise." Kate took a menacing step forward.

Tammi stepped back and bumped into the counter, crashing into the bottles of milk and cream and rattling the silverware.

Kate threw her coffee and sandwich into the trash, shoved the door open, and ran outside. All her bravado melted away as she dashed to her slutmobile, trying to get inside before she dissolved into tears.

The remaining four hours of work felt like twice that, but she made it through, eating a stale cereal bar she found in her purse. Home at last, Kate stood in the driveway staring at her minivan and the disgusting word scrawled on the side. It may be weeks before insurance would cover the repair, so what was she supposed to do in the meantime? She didn't have the cash to pay to get it fixed, either. She'd been counting on the money from the new side job but hadn't heard anything back from Michelle.

The sound of a loud muffler drew her attention to the street. An old blue Honda Civic with a mismatched red passenger door ambled down the road. The driver, a chubby man with big round glasses, slowed and watched Kate as he passed. Something about the way the man was leering at her made her skin crawl.

The car reached the end of the road and stopped.

White reverse lights glowed.

Kate's hands shook. She reached into the van and fumbled with the zipper on her purse before yanking out her phone.

The deep rumble of the broken muffler grew louder. The blue-and-red Civic turned around. The driver watched her. His left arm was hanging out his open window and he drummed his fingers against his door as he slowed, staring straight at her and smiling.

Kate swiped her phone, but the screen remained dark. *Oh, please, no.* She'd been checking her phone for text messages so often it had run out of power.

The car stopped at the end of her driveway. The man ran thick fingers through his shiny, dyed, jet-black hair, then gave her an open-palm wave.

Kate shook her head. She wanted to tell him to keep going and leave her alone, but the words wouldn't come. He hadn't done anything to her and he looked pretty harmless, like a portly school teacher, yet something about him made all her self-preservation instincts fire off.

Farther down the street, sparkling in the sun, Scott's new BMW turned onto her road. Her heart leaped in her chest at the sight of the prince on his silver steed.

When Scott slowed to turn into her driveway, the man in the Civic glared at Kate. Scott pulled alongside the man for a moment. The two spoke briefly before the Civic drove off, its muffler rumbling all the way down the street.

Scott parked behind her van. She was tempted to run up and thank him for scaring off the creep until she noticed the expression on his face. It was the neutral mask of a lawyer. She couldn't tell if he was smiling or frowning, or what he was thinking. But one thing was clear: Scott wasn't coming to rescue her. Kate squared her shoulders as she tried to prepare herself mentally for round two. She was surprised Scott had waited this long to contact her. Usually, a fight with him resulted in death by a thousand little cuts. Nasty text messages, abusive emails, and intimidating voicemails were his weapons of choice. He'd wear her down until she gave in, and he'd declare victory.

But not today.

Scott got out of the BMW with his hands high, like Kate was a cop and had pulled him over for a drug bust. He flashed one of his trademark grins and rotated his wrist. A small white box dangled from a string held in his left hand.

Uh-oh, pastries. Kate's Kryptonite.

"A peace offering." Scott walked forward and held out the box. "I want to apologize. I shouldn't have said those things when I was here the other night, and I'm sorry."

The full mea culpa caught Kate off guard. Scott's apologies always included some excuse, some twisted justification shifting blame for his behavior. But today, he actually seemed sincere.

"I heard about your van. Is there anything I can do?"

"Do you know the guy you passed pulling in?" Kate pointed to where the Civic had driven off.

"In the beater with the bad muffler? He was looking for Johnson's Nursery."

Kate shook her head. "He drove by the house twice. He stopped out front, and it freaked me out."

"I'm telling you, he was lost." Scott pressed his lips together. He took a deep breath before continuing. "I know there's a guy in the videos following you, but... you're sure you don't know who he is?"

"No. I have no idea."

"It's just... How come you didn't notice him following you?"

"He was hiding! He hid in the trees and behind the dugout. You were there. Did *you* see him?"

"Good point. Forget I asked." Scott held out the pastries again. "How about a little stress relief?"

Kate looked into the blue eyes she used to lose herself in, bit her lip, and took the box. He was the father of her children, after all. She had to take the high road and remain civil. "Thank you."

"My mother told me the police came by. After she chewed me out for abandoning my family again." He waved his hand dramatically. The similarities between Scott and his mother were striking.

Kate agreed with Audrey, but still, a tinge of sympathy for her ex rippled through her. Scott's rich, powerful father had been a hulking man, tall with broad shoulders. His son was the opposite, small and graceful but elegant like an old-time movie star. He was a great swimmer and a remarkable dancer—but those skills weren't manly according to Scott's father, a former football player who'd bullied and ridiculed his son incessantly. Kate was sure the abuse had left scars, the kind you can't see.

Scott's voice softened. "I'm worried about you. All the changes must be stressing you out. And I know how you get when that happens. I was there with you after Emma."

She grasped her chest. Like an icicle plunged into her breast, hearing her sister's name sliced open the old wound and memories spewed forth.

She had just found out she was pregnant with Andy and it was a particularly stressful time. She and Scott weren't married yet and neither of them had a job, so when Emma spiraled downward, Kate was too preoccupied to see the warning signs.

She glared at the sky. "It was my fault."

"That's why I'm so worried about you." Scott gently touched her arm. "You know how bad it got afterward. You didn't sleep for weeks. I didn't know what to do. I thought I was going to have to have you committed."

"What?" Kate took a step back.

"I didn't want to have you institutionalized, but I was afraid I might have to. You know how you were."

"My sister had just died, and I went into labor a month early. I nearly died in delivery and I had a premature baby requiring constant care. And then my mom died… My gosh, Scott, any woman would have postpartum depression after all that."

"You know yours wasn't typical. I had to lock up all the medicine and hide the knives."

"What are you trying to say? I was *not* suicidal."

"You thought about it. You even talked about it."

"Maybe in therapy or to you… because you were my husband. I never dwelled on it or made any attempts. The doctor said to want to be with the person who died was a normal part of the grieving process! Why are you bringing all this up? Seriously, I have enough going on."

"My point exactly, Kit. You're stressed out and you don't need more. That's all I'm saying. Take the van to the shop and get it fixed. I'll loan you the cash. I'm not going to have my kids driven around town in a van with the word SLUT on it. How does that make me look? A friend of mine owns a detail shop. I can give him a call."

It took all her self-control not to hit him with the pastry box. "And your friend is some high school buddy who'll charge me twice as much because I'm your ex-wife? Thanks, but no thanks. I got this."

Scott rolled his eyes. "You'll fix it?" he said, a singsong lilt to his voice, as he walked back to his BMW. "You're going to make it worse." He opened the door and stared her down. "Nicknames stick. Do you want to be known all over town as 'the slut'?"

"No." Kate winced. Scott's words had hit hard, but she wouldn't go down. "I wouldn't want to be confused with Tammi."

The cords in Scott's neck stood out. His cheeks flamed crimson and he grabbed the doorframe like he was holding himself back from charging her. "You have no right to call Tammi that."

"Actually, I'm the one person who does have a right to call her that, and you too for that matter."

"We'll see!" Scott stammered.

Kate had never known her ex-husband to be at a loss for words. She resisted flipping him off as he backed out of the driveway and instead allowed herself a little chuckle. She was going to fix the van—and not because that was what Scott wanted. She'd do it for herself, by herself. He might have the money and time to pay someone to do it, but Kate was tired of waiting for others to step in.

Winners don't wait for change; they make it happen.

She pulled out her phone, plugged it into the car charger, and googled "scratch removal." There were tons of videos on the subject. As she stood there watching a few, her confidence grew. Finding a video involving limited tools and supplies, she paused it and headed for the garage.

If Scott really was concerned for her, how did he expect her to heal from the affair with him and Tammi constantly pouring salt on the wound? She had been so wrong to trust Scott. How had she missed the signs? For months he'd been lying to her face, but she hadn't picked up on it.

A fresh tear ran down her cheek. Kate wiped it off, rolled up her sleeves, and shoved the garage doors open. Scott wasn't handy with tools, but the garage was still filled with all sorts of electrical devices, bottles and creams for cars, and different cloths for applying those things. They were so important to him he'd forgotten to take them when he moved out and still hadn't come back to get them. A fact she was now grateful for, as she found everything the video had recommended, along with a long extension cord. She brought it all outside.

A soft breeze tickled the back of her neck and the faint scent of lilies of the valley carried on the wind caught her off guard. Her knees buckled as images of Emma flooded her mind. *Don't think about Emma.* But the scent of lilies tickled her nose. They were Emma's favorite. Kate sniffed the air, but the scent was gone. It was far too late in the year for the actual flowers to bloom. She must have imagined it.

She turned back to the van. If the scratches weren't too deep, she could buff them out. She pulled up the video on her phone and got to work. The first step required a little elbow grease and some wet extra-fine sandpaper.

Her arm was starting to get tired when Ryan Daley's not-so-undercover police car pulled into her driveway. She waited for him to park, trying not to look like an awkward sixteen year old anticipating her date getting to the door. She crossed her hands in front of herself for a moment, shifted to a power pose with her hands on her hips, and then settled on a more demure look with her hands behind her back.

"Hi," Ryan said, getting out of the car. He wasn't dressed for detective work. He'd swapped his suit for blue jeans and an army-green shirt that hugged his muscular physique in all the right places. "I hope I'm not interrupting anything."

Kate held up the sandpaper and jokingly lowered her voice as she said, "Just a little bodywork."

Ryan chuckled. "I didn't peg you for the detailing type."

"I'm not, but the video I watched made it seem doable. I figured I couldn't make it worse."

A dimple appeared on his cheek. "Would you like some help?"

Kate's breathing hitched. She lifted the water bottle in her left hand and the drill with the fluffy spinning disk in her right. "Choose your weapon. Spray bottle or this thing?"

"I'll take the buffer."

"Step one." Kate turned back to her phone. "Double-check the instructions."

Ryan laughed. "You sound like me."

"I thought men didn't use directions."

"In my line of work, not following instructions can get you killed." He moved over and stood by Kate's side, giving her a nice view of the muscles rippling along his arm.

As they watched the video, she felt something she hadn't felt in a long, long time. Happy. They paused the video at the end of each step and talked about what they were going to do. Several times, he asked for her opinion. Again, the contrast with her ex-husband couldn't have been more complete. Scott would yell for her to hold a flashlight or hand him a tool. If she ever dared to have an opinion or tried to do something on her own, he'd act as if she'd shredded his man card. Ryan asked for her opinion and listened to what Kate said. He let her lead, and she was grateful for that. He also joked with her and made her feel part of a team. And for that she was even more grateful.

After they finished watching the video, they worked side by side, methodically sanding and buffing, and talking about the weather and what Andy was studying in school and whether they'd heard such-and-such new song—nothing about Kate's troubles. Little by little, the scratches became fainter and fainter, until it was impossible to tell what had been written there.

They stepped back to appraise their handiwork and Ryan's eyes sparkled. "Besides the door panel being shinier than the rest of the car, I can't see any traces of the vandalism, can you?"

"It's wonderful. I'd call this a complete success." She clasped her hands together and held them against her mouth. "I thought it was going to cost me a few hundred dollars."

"It was all you." Ryan tilted his head to the side and smiled. It was rich and real, the warmth rising to his eyes and making them bright. "I have to tell you, I admire someone who takes the initiative. Especially if it's something that needs to get done and they're unsure what to do. But you worked out a plan and you took the hill, Kate. Great job."

Kate felt like Superwoman—able to leap tall buildings in a single bound. But right now the only place she wanted to jump was into Ryan's arms.

"You too," she managed to say, although her voice sounded breathier than usual.

"And your idea to soak the sandpaper first was genius. The video didn't make that clear." Ryan glanced at his watch and the muscles in his jaw flexed. "I have to get going, but I need to speak with you about something first." His easygoing expression hardened. When he spoke next, even his voice was different—deeper and slower. "The technicians in the lab tried to enhance the videos from the drone."

Kate took a sip from her water bottle. Her hand was shaking.

"They weren't able to get enough detail for a description or even a height estimation. In all the shots, the man following you is obscured or hunching down. We're also hitting a stone wall with the phone company. There's been a lot of litigation as far as police versus personal liberties, and even with your permission, finding who's behind those blocked numbers will take some time. Are you still getting texts?"

"They're coming more often. About a dozen today. I was going to forward them to you in a batch." Kate gave him a one-shoulder shrug and tried to sound brave. "Guess all I can do is sit in the trap and wait for him to show up again."

Ryan bit his bottom lip. "About that." He pointed to the street in front of the house. "When we park across the street, we lose visibility of your backyard. And with the layout of your neighborhood, everyone can see our car from a mile off. Parking there draws too much attention."

"Not to mention my blowing your cover with my coffee delivery." The tips of Kate's ears burned, but Ryan shook his head and her embarrassment melted away.

"Tactically, it would be best if we're positioned inside the house. Would that be all right with you?"

"That would be great!" she said far too eagerly. She cleared her throat. "I mean, to make me feel safer."

"Wonderful. We'll be back tonight."

"Is there some way I can thank you? I mean, can I offer you, ah…" Her tongue mashed against her teeth as she tried to let her mind catch up to her mouth. "Dinner?"

"Can I take a rain check on that?"

"Sure." She lifted her chin and added, "I hope it rains soon."

He was surprised into a laugh but didn't make a comeback. Kate knew she must be coming off as a smitten schoolgirl, but she couldn't help it. The thought of him watching over her made her able to breathe again, as if a weight had been taken off her chest. Her thoughts were a happy jumble, but the only thing that came from her mouth was, "I'll have coffee waiting."

"We'll catch this guy," Ryan said before getting into his car and backing out onto the street. Not taking his eyes off her, he smiled and gave her a small wave.

Kate waved back as he drove away. When his car rounded the corner and disappeared, so did her feeling of safety. Fear crept along her spine. She gazed up and down her deserted road, then turned to face the woods. A profound sense of loneliness swept over her. It made the fear inside burn. *With eight billion people on the planet, why am I alone so much?*

The shadows in the woods shifted. The wind rustled the leaves. It was a short run to the back of the house and the safety inside, but she pictured a man charging out of the brush. She'd never make it before he grabbed her.

Kate swallowed and shook her head. "Ryan's coming back. He'll be back soon."

Somewhere in the forest, a branch snapped.

Kate started quickly gathering up the tools, one thought now repeating in her mind.

What if the stalker comes back when Ryan's not here?

7

Kate sat on the couch, forwarding the latest round of perverted texts to Ryan. Whoever he was, the creep was a prolific writer. He'd sent her pages of messages, some rambling, others just a few choice words. All of it made her want to take a shower and scrub her mind, but there was no unseeing what she'd read.

A new email from Michelle flashed on top of the screen and she hurriedly opened it.

No worries about the drone! Sending you out a replacement. Sorry for the delay. Can't wait to read your review. I'm sure it will be smashing! (pun intended!) Lol!!!! M.

Kate cheered. Finally, some good news. She'd finish the review and hopefully turn it into even more work. Better yet, she could list it on her résumé.

The front doorbell rang. Kate glanced at the clock. She had no idea when Ryan was going to show up, but this was earlier than expected. She hurried to the door. Staring out the peephole, all she saw was the empty steps.

Okay, this is creepy. I know I heard the doorbell…

She flipped the deadbolt, cracked open the door, and peered out into the darkness.

"Boo!" Donna jumped out of the bushes, waving a bottle wrapped in brown paper.

Kate shrieked and almost pushed her down the steps. "What is wrong with you?"

"You mean, what is wrong with you? You should never open the front door like that."

Kate pictured Scott standing at the front door saying "a stalker would never come to the front door" and wanted to smack herself for listening to him again. She stepped back into the house, dragging Donna with her.

"I looked through the peephole first, and when I didn't see anyone there, I thought I was losing my mind. But you're right." Kate locked the door, turned the deadbolt, and attached the chain. "What are you doing here?"

"I thought you could use some company."

"You have to work tomorrow. You don't need to babysit me, Donna."

"After all the sleepless nights you spent listening to me crying? I owe you."

"No, you don't, but I'm glad you're here."

"I texted you I was coming over."

"You did?"

Donna leaned forward and sniffed Kate's breath.

"Shut up. I haven't been drinking." She gave her a playful push, and Donna shoved her back. Kate checked her phone. Sure enough, there was a text from Donna, but it was marked as read. "I must have accidentally clicked it while I was forwarding the perv slush pile to Ryan."

"Are you getting more?"

"Dozens."

"You need a gun, girl."

"I don't think I'm a good candidate for a gun. I would've just shot a nut hiding in my bushes. Seriously, Donna, this stalker thing is freaking me out, and you're not helping."

With the flair of a magician pulling a rabbit out of his hat, Donna yanked a bottle of wine out of the bag. "Well, I've got the perfect mellow-maker right here."

Kate's smile faded as fast as it had appeared. "We both have to work tomorrow. And the police are coming by. I don't think getting drunk right now is the best idea."

"Don't worry, I only brought one bottle, not a case. I can't stay too long anyway." Donna started toward the kitchen and waved for Kate to follow.

Kate rechecked the lock and jiggled the deadbolt, then headed into the kitchen.

Donna took two wine glasses out of the cabinet and put them on the counter. "One glass will take the edge off. Where do you want to dish—couch, kitchen, or back deck?"

Kate shuddered at the thought of going out into the dark. "Not the deck, that's for sure."

"Okay, yeah, bad idea." Donna took her arm. "Come on, couch potato."

Under the circumstances, Donna was probably the only person who could get Kate to loosen up right now and definitely the only person she shared her fears with.

While Donna sipped her wine, Kate fought the urge to polish hers off in one long slug. She was about to take a sip when she remembered last night. "Actually"—she set the glass down on the table—"I'd better not have any. I've had some side effects from my antianxiety meds. I emailed the doctor, but he hasn't gotten back to me."

"What side effects?"

"I've been saying stuff aloud."

"I talk to myself all the time." Donna took a big sip of her wine. "That doesn't make you crazy."

"But last night I think I was sleepwalking. I haven't done that since Andy was born."

"Did you, like, go out somewhere and have a good time without me?"

"No. And it's not funny. It's… I woke up in my office chair. I'm just off. I'm forgetting to pay bills and… now this."

"You're the poster girl for stress, Kate! I'm surprised you haven't gone kinda nuts, especially now that someone is stalking you. But you didn't just stop taking your meds, did you?"

"No, but I did go back to my lesser dosage." Kate took out her phone. Still no email from the doctor. "And on top of everything, I have a guilty conscience because I lied. I want to tell Ryan the truth, but Scott thought that was a bad idea."

"About the drone? I can't believe I'm going to say this, but I agree with Scott. Don't be stupid. If you tell the cops the drone is yours, they're not going to believe you about anything. Cops are like that. With them, *one little lie* and you're done. Branded a liar. They'll think you made the whole thing up."

Kate rubbed her temples. "All I know is that lie blew up in my face. Don't tell anyone, okay?"

"I'm not the one you should be worried about. I guarantee Scott's going to tell Tammi."

"He may not take his marriage vows seriously, but when it comes to the law, he won't break that trust."

"I wouldn't bet on it. But I'm serious," Donna said, leaning forward. "You need the three Gs."

Donna had a colorful vocabulary, but Kate hadn't heard this one before. "What're the three Gs?"

"A guy, a gun, or a German shepherd. Preferably all three."

"I don't need a guy."

"One already fell right into your lap. But don't sweat it. If Ryan doesn't work out, you can have the dog chase him down and then shoot him."

They both giggled.

The beads in Donna's hair clinked as she let her head roll over her left shoulder, and she stared at Kate. She took a deep breath, her face thoughtful. "I hate to break it to you, but even when they catch your stalker, you still have a major problem on your hands. The drama with Tammi won't stop on its own. She's relentless." Donna stared into her glass and swirled the liquid around. "I haven't told you this story yet. It involves Scott too, so you might find it... interesting."

Kate tucked her feet beneath her legs as Donna began her story.

"Tammi and I never got along, as you know. She was a stuck-up priss even in elementary school. Freshman year of high school, things blew up." Donna settled back on the couch. "I dreamed of becoming an actress back then. I mean, I really, really wanted it, and sometimes I think it's actually because of Tammi that I gave up on my dream. The spring play was *Romeo and Juliet*, starring—"

"Oh, no, not the famous production with Tammi as Juliet and Scott as Romeo? I've seen pictures. He looked like such a dork in those tights."

"I think he padded."

Kate snickered so hard she snorted.

When their laughter died, Donna went on. "Anyway, I was Tammi's understudy. And I was nailing the part. Think of it—a black Juliet! Tammi felt threatened, and…" She wrapped her arms around herself and seemed to get smaller. "One day, Tammi couldn't rehearse—she broke a nail or something—so I had to cover for her. Finally, my chance to walk in the sun. Anyway, Scott suggested he and I should practice beforehand, and he asked me to meet him backstage." She set her empty wine glass down, picked up Kate's, and took a nervous sip. "And then he said he wanted to work on Act One, Scene Five." She rolled her eyes and shuddered.

"What's that?"

"The kissing scene."

"You kissed Scott?" Kate's chuckle faded when she saw Donna's eyes glistening with tears.

"Scott was the first guy I ever kissed. I was, like, a total theater nerd—braces, thick glasses, the works. We rehearsed the scene, and Scott stuck his tongue down my throat. I knew up here"—she tapped the side of her head—"something was off, but he told me that's how they kiss onstage, and I went along with it. Right after, this guy Billy came backstage, and Scott told me Billy was his understudy so I needed to do the scene with him too. After Billy, Scott spun this story about how the flu was going around and the director was nervous, so Billy had an understudy too."

Kate saw where this was going. "That scumbag!"

Donna rubbed her eyes. "They had a bet to see how many guys I'd be stupid enough to make out with. I know it sounds ridiculous, but I didn't even catch on until two more understudies had stuck their tongues down my throat and copped a feel. What can I say? I'm a moron."

"You didn't do anything wrong." Kate grabbed Donna's hand and gave it a firm squeeze, the secret handshake of women everywhere who've been set up, felt up, and put down. "Scott, that little padded—" She let fly a stream of salty swears.

"I had no idea you could swear like that! You would have made a pirate blush." Donna polished off Kate's drink. "Anyway, Tammi found out about it and carved the word WHORE into my locker. Lots of people told me later she'd done it. And that was just the start of the fun. After that, I was on her hit list."

"Wait a second. Are you saying… ?"

"I guarantee Tammi keyed your van."

Kate held up her hand. "Whoa. I have no love for Tammi; the truth is, I actually want a piñata that looks like her for our next girls' night. But don't you think the stalker did that?"

Donna shook her head. "I think Tammi keyed your van, and the stalker is some other psycho following you around. But don't worry. I'm gonna catch El Creepo." She smoothed out her dress and flipped back her hair.

"The police are already on it." Kate waved both her hands in front of Donna, hoping to derail her crazy plan before it left the station.

"Right or wrong, I get a free meal and some drinks for my trouble." Donna checked the time and frowned. "I haven't got a date yet, so don't sweat it. Anyhow, gotta go."

Kate stood, and the room spun. Donna hugged her and Kate wrapped her arms around her friend to steady herself. "I don't like it," Kate said, "but trying to stop you doing something is like trying to stop the sun rising."

Donna gave her a peck on the cheek and headed for the door. "Lock the door and keep your curtains closed!" She checked the peephole and opened the door. "Stay safe, and I'll get you that piñata!"

Kate clicked the lock closed, shut the deadbolt, and reattached the chain. But the actions didn't bring the sense of security she'd hoped for. They reinforced the fact that out there in the darkness, someone was watching her.

It was almost eight and there was still no sign of Ryan. She pictured him smiling at her, buffer in hand, brown eyes sparkling. Had something else come up? Something with work? Something more important? The emptiness inside her grew a little bigger.

Adding to her loneliness, she had missed a call from the kids. She'd already spoken with them twice today, but Ava always called before going to bed. Kate listened to the voicemail:

Ava: "Hi, Mommy!"

Andy: "Hey, Mom."

Ava: "Grammie says we need to go to bed, but I wanted to tell you I love you. Bye, Mommy, sweet dreams, and don't forget your prayers. God bless you!"

Andy: "See ya, Mom. Love you."

Kate clutched her stomach and covered her face with her other hand as a sob racked her body. Another night without her children. And if

Tammi got her way, this would become the norm. *Two weekends a month is not happening.*

She wiped her eyes, blew her nose, and began tidying up the house. Doing the dishes was too low key; she needed to move. But dusting the shelves in the living room only added to the aching loneliness. She hadn't had the heart to change the photos yet. Almost every one of them was a picture of how her family used to be before the divorce shattered it. She touched the picture of Scott throwing Ava in the air, then swallowed when she turned to the picture of Scott and Andy. Andy had a goofy grin; she hadn't seen that grin in a while. Each image was a reminder of what she'd lost, but one cut her to the bone.

Emma.

Her favorite picture. Kate and her little sister at the beach, their arms draped around each other's shoulders. Emma had written *Friends Forever* in the sand.

Before she could turn away, Kate felt the question screaming in her soul. Why? Why? Why? Could she have done something to stop it? Was it her fault?

From the kitchen, a faint click echoed down the hall. Setting down the picture and the duster, she listened until she heard the light tap again. She snuck down the hallway and stopped at the kitchen threshold. The room was empty and dark. After flicking on the light, she waited a few moments, but everything was quiet. She turned to go back, but the distinct click of something tapping against glass made her gasp and spin back around.

Kate stared into the shadows of the room. Someone could be hiding in the corner or behind the kitchen island.

Click. Click.

Each tap dug into her skull as she searched for the source of the sound. Click.

The noise was coming from outside, on the back deck. Kate crouched, ready to flee, but then a bump at the sliding door revealed the source of the noise. The wind had picked up and the patio umbrella was rocking about in the breeze. She went over to the slider, opened it, and stepped outside.

The door slipped shut behind her, followed by a muffled thump.

She pulled at the slider. The locking bar Scott had installed had closed along with the door. Like all Scott's do-it-yourself projects, he'd messed it up, and now she was locked out of the house.

Kate swore.

The front doorbell rang.

Oh, no, not now!

She gave the slider another tug before hurrying around to the front of the house. Ryan Daley and Detective Tills were waiting on the front porch with a duffel bag and a box at their feet.

"Hi." Kate gave a quick wave, the heat rising in her cheeks. "I accidentally locked myself out," she explained as she headed over to the fake rock next to the front steps.

Tills groaned. "Don't tell me you keep a spare house key in such an obvious place."

Kate nodded. "Duly noted." The fake rock was another stupid idea of Scott's that he'd talked Kate into. "Thank you for coming." She moved between the two men and unlocked the door.

"So, you just came from the backyard?" Detective Tills asked.

"The slider door to the deck locked behind me."

"Oh." He scratched his jaw with the back of his thumbnail. "You didn't feel uncomfortable being out back—alone? All things considered."

Kate stared. "Uh. Well, I didn't feel comfortable, but the patio umbrella was bumping against the window. I went to close the umbrella and—"

"You locked yourself out." Tills's phone rang. "Got it. Can you two excuse me for one moment?" he said, taking out his phone.

"Certainly."

Kate and Ryan went inside, and the other detective stayed on the porch.

Ryan shut the door and lowered his voice as he said, "Please excuse my partner. He's a little rough around the edges, but he means well."

"If he's still upset about my spoiling the first stakeout—"

"No, it's not that." Ryan walked away from the door. "Mark's like an old hunting dog. He barks a lot, has a pretty gruff disposition, but he gets the job done, so you tend to overlook the fleas." Ryan comically scratched at his neck like a dog.

Kate laughed. Her feet seemed to have a mind of their own, and she stepped closer to him.

"How are you holding up?"

"Stressed out would be an understatement, but…" *Your handsome face is a welcome distraction.* "I'm doing better."

"Better is good." Ryan smiled.

"What I mean is…" Kate stammered. "You're so… I feel so…"

Tills knocked on the front door and opened it. He focused on Ryan. "Just the sheriff making sure we're handling everything for Ms. Rochester's daughter-in-law." He handed Ryan the duffel bag, then brought in their box of equipment and set it on the floor.

"Former daughter-in-law," Kate said. Something about the gruff detective bothered her. Was Tills a member of Tammi's fan club perhaps? Or Scott's?

Ryan turned to her, cleared his throat, and gave the slightest shake of his head, which Kate took as a sign to change the subject. "Would you mind giving us a tour of the house?" he asked. "We need to see where we should set up."

"Certainly."

Kate took them upstairs first. They spent less than a minute in each room. Ryan would look out the window, he and his partner would exchange a few words, and they would move on.

After the brief tour, Ryan told her, "We'll set up in the dining room. We have two unmarked patrol cars stationed down the street north and south."

"Wow." Kate breathed easier. "I didn't expect all this."

"Neither did I," Tills muttered as he took some equipment out of a thick case. "What we need from you is for you to go along with your normal routine. Leave your shades open in the other rooms and the lights on. Try to forget we're even here."

Kate took one look at Ryan and dismissed the idea of forgetting him. He was already on her mind far too often, and with him inside her house, it would be impossible.

"I made some coffee and sandwiches."

"We're fine, ma'am." Tills opened a large gym bag and took out a tripod and camera. "And please don't bring any food out to the undercover patrol units."

Ryan scratched his neck and winked at Kate.

Kate grinned, nodded, and slipped out of the room. Typically, the detective's surly behavior would have upset her for the rest of the night, but Ryan had a way of chasing her worries away.

She tried doing some simple chores to keep her mind off the realization that she was bait dangled out to attract the predator, but it was useless. Each time she passed a window, she imagined eyes out in the darkness following her every move. She gazed at her hands, which appeared to be locked in a wrestling match, the tops covered with red scratches where her nails had dug into her skin.

I'm such a coward.

Ryan appeared at the open dining room door. He placed both hands against the doorframe and stretched. His broad chest expanded and became massive. He was a powerful man. It was easy to picture herself wrapped in those strong arms, his hot breath against her neck.

His deep voice broke her out of her fantasy. "Is that offer for a coffee still open?"

Kate turned and hurried down the hall. She was halfway to the kitchen before she realized she hadn't responded. "Back in a snap," she called out too loudly.

Smooth, Kate. Real smooth.

She poured two coffees and opened the refrigerator. Next to the tray of prepared sandwiches sat the pastry box Scott had brought by. She set the sandwiches on the tray and grabbed a plate for the pastries. When she opened the box, she made a face. The end of one of the cannoli was speckled green.

"He must have got the day-old, marked-down manager special—"

She tossed the pastries into the trash, trying to ignore the fact she'd eaten one earlier, then lifted the dinner tray, set her shoulders, and headed for the dining room.

Ryan held the door open and grinned. "You're a lifesaver. Thanks."

If I'm a lifesaver, I'd like to give Hartville's finest a little mouth-to-mouth resuscitation. She watched his face to see whether she'd said the words aloud. He was still grinning, so she squeaked, "Hi," as she slipped by him and over to the table.

Tills rose from his chair and barked out, "Can I use your bathroom?"

"Of course. The first door on the right." Kate pointed down the hall.

Tills gave her a curt nod and left the room.

Kate glanced at the window and the drawn shade.

Ryan pointed at what looked like a telescope mounted on a tripod near the window set up to peek out. "Infrared camera."

"Will he come back tonight?" Kate pressed her elbows against her sides.

"I hope so." Ryan's hand alighted briefly on hers. "We'll get this guy."

She tried to smile, but her lips weren't cooperating and they curled down. Worse still, they trembled. "I'm sorry. It's just…"

"You have nothing to be sorry about. It's a horrible feeling, being targeted." Ryan's voice softened. "Everyone's hoping we'll catch him tonight, but the truth of the matter is, this may take time. Is there someplace else you could stay? Visit family?" He pointed to a picture on the wall. It was a photograph of Kate, her parents, and her sister.

"My mother passed, and my father and I… we're not on the best of terms."

"Is that your sister? Any chance of you staying with her?"

Kate shook her head. "Emma died before Andy was born."

"I'm sorry."

Me too.

Ryan squared his shoulders. "We'll catch him, Kate."

Tills walked in the door and frowned.

"Thanks again for the coffee," Ryan said as Kate left the room.

She wiped at her eyes as she hurried back to the kitchen. Her heartbeat slowed as Emma's beautiful face filled her mind. How old would she have been now? Kate bumped into the counter and sent a knife skittering into the sink. She clamped her eyes closed and tried to drive out the memory of them lowering Emma's white coffin into the ground. With a shake of her head, she shoved the faucet handle up, and she cupped her hands beneath the water and laid them on her face to cool her burning cheeks. But the old anger bubbled, hotter than ever. Why? Shame? Guilt? Pain?

Probably all three.

She felt lightheaded and her vision blurred. As she reached for a paper towel, outside, along the dark tree line near her neighbor's house, she was sure she saw rising smoke. Her eyes followed the vapor trail. Crouched beside a pine tree, like a hunter stalking its prey, was the silhouette of a man.

Kate stepped away from the sink. *Remain calm. Back away slowly.* But she froze. Every muscle in her body, including her heart and lungs, seemed to seize up. Her mind was in overdrive, shouting out warnings: *Don't make a sound. Don't make any sudden moves.*

Kate bolted down the hallway and right into Ryan's arms.

"Kate!" Ryan grabbed both of her shoulders and stared straight into her eyes. "What's wrong?"

She opened her mouth to speak, but fear strangled the words in her throat. She waved a trembling hand toward the kitchen window. "Outside. I saw him."

Ryan rushed to the slider as Tills barreled into the kitchen. "Suspect on north side of the house," Ryan called into his radio as he and his partner dashed out onto the back deck.

They snapped on their flashlights and ran toward the trees. Ryan raced through the undergrowth while Tills tried to keep up. Their flashlight beams bounced off the branches until everything was engulfed by the shadows.

Kate watched the blank patch of window anxiously until, after several minutes, Ryan and Detective Tills emerged from the woods, joined by two policemen. Kate's hand hesitated on the slider door. The darkness deepened.

They hadn't caught him. He'd gotten away. The man was still out there. Somewhere.

The four men spoke for a few minutes, then the detectives came over to the deck and the police headed to the front of the house.

Ryan looked disappointed, but she couldn't tell what Tills was thinking. He looked grumpier than usual, if that was possible. He stopped at the stairs to the deck and waved Kate outside.

She slid the slider open and stepped out onto the deck.

"We didn't see or hear anything out there," Tills said, plucking briars out of his pant leg.

"Can you please show us where you saw the man?" Ryan asked.

Kate looked across the dark yard to the trees in front of her neighbor's home. She pointed to the large pine tree. "There. He was crouched next to the pine tree. I saw the smoke from his cigarette."

Tills and Ryan walked over to the spot Kate had indicated and shone their flashlights at the ground. They paced in ever-widening circles until

Tills headed over to a group of white birches ten yards away. He shone his flashlight on the large compost pile beside it and gave it a kick with his shoe. Steam from the rotting vegetable matter rose into the cool night air. He shook his head and said something to Ryan that Kate couldn't hear. They came back, snapped off their flashlights, and craned their necks to look up at her standing on the porch.

Detective Tills pressed his lips into a thin white line. He jerked his thumb back to the compost pile. "Is that what you saw? The steam from the compost looks just like cigarette smoke. And that pile could look like someone crouching—"

"No." Kate pointed at the pine tree. "He was over there."

Tills didn't say anything. He stared at Kate, searching her face.

"I saw him."

"No one's saying you didn't," Ryan said.

"We'd better call it a night." Tills stomped up the steps. "If he was here, there's no way he's coming back now." He grabbed the handle to the slider and pulled.

It didn't budge.

"Shoot." Kate winced. "It's locked."

"Great! Just perfect." Tills yanked on the door again, to no avail. "All our equipment is in there. Don't tell me you left your keys inside?"

"They're in my purse. And you told me not to put the spare key back in the fake rock!"

"Let me try a window," Ryan offered.

Kate shook her head. "They're all locked." She had made sure of that.

Ryan moved over to the first-floor bathroom window. It slid right up.

Tills cleared his throat.

"I—I locked it. I'm certain."

As Ryan disappeared through the window, Detective Tills didn't say anything, but the look on his face said it all. He didn't believe her. Not about locking the window. Not about seeing the man.

Kate turned away from the detective to stare out into the dark woods. The man was somewhere in that forest. He had been scared off tonight—but he wasn't done.

He was going to come back.

Whether the police believed her or not.

Kate made it through another agonizingly boring day at work, managing not to fall asleep. Lack of sleep was making her dead on her feet. If it wasn't for coffee, she didn't know what she'd do. At least Berman and Marshall were out of the office. It was a mixed blessing, however. With no one there, Kate found herself staring at the door all day, wondering if the man following her was doing the same thing from the other side.

The ride home was just as bad. Kate swerved and jumped at shadows until she skidded into her driveway. After she'd hurried into the house, locked the doors, and checked every room and every window, she collapsed on the couch.

Her phone rang. It was another blocked number.

Kate swore. Her phone was slammed with pervy texts and voicemails of heavy breathing or the sound of porno movies playing in the background. She wished she could change her number, but the police were building a case and trying to catch the guy. She forwarded another batch to Ryan, along with screenshots of all the unknown phone numbers.

No sooner had the phone stopped ringing than it started again. But this number wasn't blocked.

Andy's school.

Kate sat up and answered. "Hello, Kate Gardner."

"Kate? It's Dr. Green. Cushing School's therapist."

"Is Andy okay?" Kate was instantly on her feet, reaching for her car keys.

"Andy's fine. I'm calling regarding our appointment."

Kate's eyebrows traveled in different directions. She had an upcoming appointment but couldn't remember when. She knew it wasn't today, because she'd checked her calendar this morning.

"Yes. I replied to your email, and we're scheduled for…" She spoke slowly, stalling for time as she checked the calendar on her phone.

"Our meeting was supposed to be today at five thirty. I rearranged my schedule to stay after school specifically for you."

Kate stared at today's date on the calendar. The appointment for Dr. Green was listed with a star next to it. How had she missed it?

"Dr. Green, I am so very sorry. I can come right now—"

"Unfortunately, I have another parent already waiting. They're here early."

"I apologize. If we could reschedule—"

"I'll need to check my calendar and email you. I have a few concerns regarding Andy that need to be addressed. I've already met with his father and I hoped you'd be as accommodating."

Kate gritted her teeth. Scott was his own boss. In order for her to get time off, she had to go through the employment agency, who contacted Mr. Berman.

"Whatever time works for you, Dr. Green. It's just—"

"I'll email you later. Good day."

The phone clicked.

Kate glared at her calendar. How had she not seen the appointment? She'd checked her schedule this morning. She always did before she got out of bed. She flopped back on the couch and rubbed her eyes. She wasn't getting enough sleep and the days were starting to blend together.

Her phone buzzed with another incoming text. Audrey Rochester's name flashed on the screen.

MY HOUSE. NOW.

Kate broke into a sweat. She texted back. ARE THE KIDS OKAY? WHAT'S WRONG?

THE CHILDREN ARE FINE. WE NEED TO DISCUSS THIS NEW CUSTODY ARRANGEMENT.

Kate pressed her hands against her face, then bit her finger to stifle a scream.

Can this day get any worse?

She grabbed her keys off the counter and trudged to the car. Simply being outside was a nightmare. At every intersection on her way across town, Kate twitched, expecting a runaway bus or falling satellite to put her out of her misery—and half wishing for it. Stopping at a red light, she gazed up at a half-dozen birds perched in a dead oak tree. For a moment, she could have sworn they were vultures, waiting to swoop in and pick the dead remnants of her soul clean. She shivered, but when she looked up again, they were nothing more than common crows.

Kate took her glasses off and rubbed her eyes. She still hadn't heard back from Dr. Sprouse. She'd cut back to her regular dosage of the yellow happy pills, but they weren't even taking the edge off her stress.

The light changed and she sped through the intersection. She wanted to turn around and go home, safe behind locked doors. But she couldn't hide from Queen Audrey. She'd been summoned.

As Kate parked in front of the palatial mansion and slogged to the door, her heart constricted. Maybe Audrey would tell her that from now on, Kate was on her own. Maybe Scott had convinced his mother to stop helping with childcare. It would definitely give a boost to his appeal for full custody. If Audrey backed out of watching Ava, Kate was finished. Without the scheduling flexibility Audrey provided, the already tricky job search would become impossible.

Worse, what if Scott had enlisted Audrey's help with the legal side of things? Audrey retained an army of attorneys, including specialists in divorce law. Why hadn't Audrey used them to help Scott annihilate her in the divorce? Perhaps because it hadn't been necessary. Kate scoffed and shook her head. After all, she had let Scott destroy her with barely a whimper.

Audrey's doorbell rang like the bells of Notre-Dame Cathedral. Audrey whipped open the door and stared down from the top of the steps with all the warmth of a stone gargoyle. She stepped aside and Kate entered, bracing herself for the inevitable verbal flogging to come. Audrey still didn't speak as she directed Kate to the sitting room and, with one glare at the Victorian sofa, commanded her to sit, which she did, like a well-trained family dog.

"Mary is running errands with the children," Audrey said as she poured herself a glass of straight scotch and jammed the gold-trimmed stopper back into the crystal decanter. Her hand trembled as she raised the tumbler to her lips.

Surely the tremors had nothing to do with age and everything to do with the verbal tsunami Audrey was preparing to unleash.

Kate sank deeper into the couch and stared at her own trembling hands. "I want to say, I can't thank you enough for all the help you've given. What with watching the kids—"

Audrey set the glass on the marble-top bar with a loud click. "When will you stop being the helpless little pushover and focus on the real issues at hand?"

"The real issues? I—I don't understand."

"No, you don't." Audrey finished the scotch and held the empty glass in her hand as though she were appraising it. "This is Baccarat crystal, made in France in 1902. My mother gave me the set." Closing her eyes, she held the heavy crystal tumbler high over the bar sink and opened her fingers.

The glass shattered and shards sprayed high into the air.

Kate's jaw dropped as she stared at the glittering broken pieces.

After a second, Audrey continued calmly, "The set is also missing a wine glass. My grandmother broke it against the dining room table when she found out my grandfather had been unfaithful. Grammie held the broken stem to his groin and informed him the next time he strayed would be his last." Audrey turned back to the bar and poured herself another scotch in a fresh tumbler. "You will, in turn, tell Ava that Grammie broke the glass that is missing from her set the day she told you to stop being a doormat."

Kate sat straighter. Audrey never got this upset—nor did she ever drink, for that matter. Scott was more than willing to imbibe, but Audrey, never. The bar served as an obligatory part of the stage set.

As if she'd read Kate's mind, Audrey said, "I don't normally consume alcohol, but I'm allowing myself a new vice. I'll explain momentarily." She turned back to Kate and fixed her with a commanding gaze. "First: this new custody arrangement cannot go ahead. I will not have my grandson become a spineless cuckold, or my darling angel turn into a vapid tramp like her stepmother. But unfortunately I will not be around to assist. The responsibility, therefore, falls on you to ensure my grandchildren escape the tragic future I see unfolding."

Kate stared at this woman she had known for over a decade yet didn't seem to know at all. "'Not around'? What do you mean? Are you moving?"

Audrey gave Kate a hard smile. "I'm dying. Cancer. The doctors believe I have less than a year, and frankly part of me is grateful. The pain is quite unpleasant." She took a sip. "But I'll find a way to soldier on. That is why you are here. Has Scott ever shared my personal history with you?"

"You're dy—" Kate put her hand to her mouth, pictured her children's sweet faces, and swallowed a lump in her throat. "No, no, he didn't."

Audrey strolled over to the wingback chair and sat down. She always controlled the conversation by letting the tension build during her silences. It was awful. But now? This silence proved her amazing self-control and power.

"We are far more alike than you realize, Kate. Scott's father took everything I had when he left. I was a girl of means from an aristocratic family, yet I blindly yielded everything I had to a thief who left me for a shinier plaything. Our similarities end there, my dear. I had been holding out such hope for you. I even tried to help you behind the scenes. I gave Scott an ultimatum I thought would restore your marriage. Return to his family and he would remain in my will. Or go ahead, marry that trollop, and be disinherited."

Audrey had been trying to help her?

Audrey's ring tapped against her glass. "Despite my efforts…"

"He went ahead with it anyway." The wound cut all the deeper.

Audrey looked at Kate as if she were as dumb as a stump. "He's a fool. Scott thinks like his father. He plays at being a self-made man, but you and I both know his success was built on your shoulders and with my purse strings. Right now, the boost you gave him is still keeping him aloft, but in time he'll fall like Icarus. It's not an outcome I relish. He is my son, and I do not want to see him fail. But he will; it is simply a matter of time. He's weak. He had privileges and smart and capable women to support him— and now he has hitched his cart to a blond donkey. I can only hope falling flat on his face will knock some sense into him."

Audrey took a slow sip of scotch, then fixed her stern gaze on Kate once more. "What he did to you was barbaric. If you were a man, you would have been his business partner…" She shook her head. "It's immoral."

Kate's mind whirled. "But it was because of you that I signed the prenup."

"Me? Is that what he told you?" Audrey scoffed. "Not only did you believe him without so much as verifying it with me, you went ahead and signed it. How foolish."

Kate hung her head. "I wish you had told me some of this before."

Audrey let her eyes flutter to the ceiling. "Oh, please. Did you envision the two of us flopping on my settee in sweatpants and commiserating with each other over what louses our first husbands turned out to be? This is my point: *move on*. I had hoped you would show the ovarian fortitude to do it on your own, but it has become exceedingly clear you are lacking in that department. So here is the carrot." She paused and spread her arms wide. "You will be named trustee of everything. And in turn, you will distribute it to Andy and Ava at the appropriate time. But…" A much longer pause ensued, during which Audrey took a slow sip of scotch. "The carrot comes with a stick. If you can't pull yourself together in the next three months, I will give it all away."

"You'd cut off Ava and Andy too?" Kate stammered, bewildered.

Audrey scoffed. "Cut them off? I'd be freeing them—for their own good. Power should be given based on ability, not lineage, especially in my own family. I have no doubt Tammi would find a way to leverage my inheritance to her own ends, no matter to whom I left it. And under her tutelage, I shudder to picture how warped my grandchildren would become. Do you know how that woman said she would honor me?"

Unsure whether to nod, shake her head, or shrug, Kate waited.

Audrey paused. "When they have a child, of either sex, she will name it Audri—with an *i*. Under those circumstances, it would be better for my grandchildren to find their own way in this world." Her eyes flashed. "Speaking of which, I forgot to mention another stipulation. Do not inform the children of my illness. I will not have my last days spent in sadness."

Kate was struggling to take it all in. She rubbed her thumb across the back of her hand, until Audrey stopped her with a look. "What exactly do you want me to do?" she asked.

Her former mother-in-law rose and loomed over her. Kate's breathing hitched.

"I want you to fight, Kate. Life is hard. Did your precious little boat of dreams hit an iceberg? Then swim for a lifeboat! And if there's no room in the lifeboat, push someone aside and make room. If there are no lifeboats, you float on the wreckage, and if there's no wreckage, you drift on the carcass of someone who gave up—but whatever you do, you fight. That is the lesson I expect you to learn, Kate. That is the lesson I want you to teach my grandchildren. Not in a speech, but by example. You are going to go out there and fight for what you want in this life."

Kate found herself pressed back into the sofa. Audrey was right. It was exactly what Kate needed to do, but any promises she could make would ring hollow.

Audrey grimaced and her hand tightened around the tumbler. Kate noticed a fresh-looking bruise on her wrist as she took a tiny sip.

Audrey walked back to the bar and placed her hands on the marble. "You have three months. Now get to work."

Kate didn't want to go back home. Her house no longer felt like her sanctuary, especially without the kids. She needed a place to think, but also somewhere she wasn't alone and vulnerable. There was only one place that fit the bill—the library.

As she passed through the front doors, Darlene, one of the librarians, smiled and gave her a big wave. "Hey, Kate. Your seat's available. Should I put you down for an hour?"

The library's resource room had become her go-to job-searching office. Kate spent a couple of afternoons a week there while Andy was at soccer practice, using the computers to scour job boards and send out résumés.

Kate smiled back. "Not today. Thanks, Darlene." Today she wasn't going to spend hours hunched over a keyboard or reading another self-help book. She wanted to think.

Kate walked straight to the spiral staircase. Her heels clicked on the old metal stairs as she circled down into the basement. Down here, the sound of the jackhammers outside faded to a muffled rattle. The west wing had been under construction since Kate had moved to Hartville. It didn't matter. She loved it here—the cold marble, the high vaulted ceilings, the busts of writers and philosophers. She zipped past the rows of books, steering straight for the ladies' room in the rear corner, and locked the old wooden door with its pebbled glass behind her. Then she collapsed against it.

On the one hand, she'd just gained the most powerful ally she could ever hope for. On the other, Audrey had said Kate was on her own in this fight. If Scott sought full custody now, a sympathetic judge wouldn't have to look far for justification to support his request.

And Audrey was dying. She and Kate had never been close, but the kids adored their grammie. Her loss would crush them.

She turned on the heavy brass faucet and splashed water on her face. She wasn't going to lose it—not here, in the bathroom at the public library. Water still dripping off her chin, she looked at her reflection in the mirror. It stared back at her with a mixture of disbelief, scorn... and age. The fluorescent lighting highlighted every flaw. With the dark shadows around her sleepless eyes and her dry, ashy skin, she looked like an inmate in a gulag.

When did I give up on myself?

The question pierced something inside her, and deep within her chest, a heat spread. Kate gripped the edges of the cold porcelain sink and pulled herself closer to the traitor in the mirror until she was nose-to-nose with the woman she had become—a woman who wasn't anywhere close to what she had once dreamed of being.

She thought back to when she first met Scott. From the beginning, she'd put him on a pedestal. He was Prince Charming come to rescue her. Kate was less than average in every department. Scott was the exact opposite. Rich, handsome, and popular, he was everything she wasn't, and he was offering her a life that seemed straight out of a Hallmark movie. The flawless husband would give her the ideal family and make her something she dreamed of—special. It was perfect. It just went wrong at the end, but it was perfect, right? She hadn't always been a doormat. She was strong. The divorce had broken her. Yes, it was the divorce.

No. She had to face the truth. It wasn't perfect. *You gave up your own goals; you bent to his will. And for what?* Scott wasn't flawless. He was a narcissistic, selfish, pompous ass focused on his own dreams and desires. Kate had made every excuse for his behavior, burying his wrongs, blaming herself, and pretending everything was fine. Yes, she had always been a doormat.

She was the one who had abandoned her ambitions. She was the one who had chosen to sacrifice herself beyond the point of reason for the sake of her husband. Yes, Scott had capsized their marriage—but long before that, Kate had already betrayed herself. She'd based her entire identity on her roles as wife and mother. She'd entrusted her fragile, beautiful heart to a man who treated it like Audrey had that crystal tumbler.

She hung her head, letting the awful realization sink into her tired bones. If she expected another Prince Charming to rescue her, she should head to the psychology books and start self-diagnosing because she was delusional. What happened next was all up to her.

Kate looked up at herself once more. She sagged into the counter. Her determination was already waning. Kate wasn't Audrey; she didn't possess her mother-in-law's mystical powers. She didn't have any power at all.

An image of Ava appeared—tears streaking her face. A makeshift cape lay at her feet. She had been wearing it and running around the yard, thinking it would allow her to fly... but it hadn't.

"I'm not a superhero!" she cried to her brother. "I don't have superpowers."

Andy shook his head. "You don't need superpowers to be a hero. What about Batman? He doesn't have any superpowers. Anyone can be a hero."

Kate stared into the mirror. "Audrey doesn't have superpowers. She made her own. And so can I."

Straightening her shoulders, Kate held her head high. A newfound strength blazed in her chest; her cheeks had some color; her eyes shot sparks. She was done waiting around for someone to solve her problems. Audrey was right. Kate needed to fight. And that fight started now.

Kate was passing the reference desk when Darlene called out to her. Holding a telephone in one hand, the librarian waved Kate over with the other.

"I'm on hold, and the poor woman in the resource room is having a hard time. She's looking for a job. Can you give her a hand?"

Kate didn't hesitate. "Of course I will." She headed to the resource room and stopped in the doorway.

The sight before her was all too familiar: a middle-aged woman clutching a tissue and struggling with the library's computer system as tears ran down her cheeks. Except this time it wasn't Kate sitting there crying.

As Kate walked over, the woman dried her tears.

"Darlene, the librarian, sent me in to see if I could help." She pointed at the chair beside the woman. "I'm a frequent flyer on the job boards. I'm Kate, by the way."

"Susan." The woman nodded politely. Her eyes were red-rimmed and she looked prepared to cry once more. "I can't log in. I know computers, but every time I try, it rejects my credentials!"

"You need to clear the browsing history, exit, and start again," Kate explained as she sat down.

Susan's hand shook as she moved the mouse. She followed Kate's instructions and managed to log in. "I can't thank you enough!" She gave Kate a broad smile, but her lips trembled.

Kate placed a comforting hand on her shoulder.

"My Bill was always the one I'd call with computer questions. He was a help desk manager. For the hospital."

Kate nodded.

"Heart attack," Susan said.

"I'm so sorry."

"Me too." Susan sniffled. "But now I've got to find some kind of work. It's been four months, and he didn't have much insurance…" Susan's voice trailed off and she stared at the screen. Her head slumped forward. She covered her eyes and sobbed. "I have no idea what I'm doing!"

Darlene appeared in the doorway, but Kate motioned that it was okay as she rubbed Susan's back. "Take a deep breath." She pulled her chair closer to Susan's. "Why don't I give you a hand getting started."

Over the next hour, Kate helped Susan begin her job search. But as soon as Kate saw Susan's résumé, she realized that she was helping someone who would be in direct competition for any position that Kate wanted. Their backgrounds were remarkably similar. Still, Kate felt for the poor woman. Susan had three girls in their early teens to feed and keep a roof over.

Their backgrounds may have been the same, but Susan's résumé was very dated. As they worked on reformatting it, Kate opened her own résumé to use it as an example.

Susan's eyes widened and then narrowed. "We're competing against each other."

Kate chuckled. "No, we're not. Every job gets hundreds of applicants. We're competing against them, okay?"

Kate gave Susan a thumbs-up and she returned the gesture. With that, Kate uploaded Susan's newly formatted résumé to the cloud. As Susan went to get a printout of it, Kate performed a search for new jobs. She froze. There was a fresh listing. It was a bit of a stretch skill-wise for Kate, but she had a shot of getting hired for the position. The position was perfect for Susan, however.

Kate sat staring at the screen. *It's a rough world. Every woman for herself, right?*

Susan was walking back over.

Kate moved the mouse. The cursor hovered above the button to close the window.

"Thank you again for helping me." Susan's eyes began to water again as she sat. "I'm sorry for blubbering like a baby. I just felt so alone."

Kate swallowed. She knew loneliness, but Susan's was different. Kate could still pick up the phone and call Scott, even if he was a louse.

"Check out this job. They posted it a minute ago." She took her hand off the mouse. "It's perfect for you."

Susan's smile faded as she read the listing. "It's perfect for you too."

"Tell you what, why don't you go for this one. It's more up your alley."

"Are you sure?"

Kate nodded confidently. "Besides, I already have a job, right?"

Susan hugged her and thanked her half a dozen times as they exchanged contact information.

Darlene waved as Kate exited the library. Although Kate had given away the best prospect for a job that she'd seen in a long time, she'd never felt better. Until she walked out the door and into the darkness. She'd forgotten the parking lot lights on the north side of the building were out due to construction.

And, of course, that was where she'd parked.

Kate muttered as she hurried along, her footsteps sounding overly loud in the deserted parking lot. How could she have been so stupid? Someone was stalking her, and she'd let her guard down. She took out her phone and held her finger over the emergency button but didn't press it.

"I'm on the phone with 911!" she called out. *If loud noises scare away bears, maybe that works for stalkers too!* "Just so you're aware, I have a raging yeast infection and diarrhea!"

The night closed in around her. Her van seemed a mile away, although it couldn't have been more than thirty yards. She was perspiring and breathing heavily by the time she reached the driver's side. She checked the backseat before jumping in and locking the door.

Her hand was shaking so much that as she tried to stick the key into the ignition she dropped it. She snatched it up from the floor, slammed it in, turned the key, and started the engine.

"Get a grip, Kate!" She seized the steering wheel with both hands. She could do this. She had fixed the vandalism on the van. She had helped Susan. Now she needed to fix and help herself. The first step in doing that was to stop being so afraid. And for that she knew exactly where to go.

Big Ed's Army, Navy, and Police Supply was a landmark in Hartville. Partly because of the old WWII tank parked in front and the Korean War fighter plane on the roof but mostly because of Big Ed's TV ads. In college, Kate's teachers would have torn Ed's marketing to shreds, but there was no denying it worked. The ads were as showy as Big Ed, but his message was simple: he sold protection for you and your family.

And that was exactly what she needed.

As she strolled through the front door, lights flashed in her face like paparazzi cameras and a recording of Big Ed boomed over a speaker. "Welcome to Big Ed's. Here, you're a star!"

"Welcome to Big Ed's." A far less enthusiastic clerk waved from behind a gun case. "Looking for anything in particular?"

"Just browsing," Kate said and headed down the closest aisle. She wasn't looking for a gun. She didn't have a problem owning one, but since Scott had one and wasn't as careful as he should be with it, she may have to use that in the custody fight and she didn't want to appear a hypocrite.

She rounded the corner and bumped into the back of a man built like a brick wall. Kate's glasses slid sideways on her face. She would have fallen over if the man hadn't grabbed her arm.

"I'm sorry," she said, straightening her glasses, and looked up—into Ryan's warm chocolate eyes. "Oh, hello."

"Hey. Wow. I didn't think I'd run into you here."

Kate's nose wrinkled. "I kinda did the running into you."

Ryan laughed and let go of her arm. In his other hand he was holding a bright-pink package of pepper spray.

"Red might go better with your blue suit," Kate said. "But pink works."

Ryan's mouth dropped open, then he chuckled. "It's not for me." The color rose in his cheeks as he rubbed the back of his strong neck. "I was actually thinking about you—your case, and I, uh, thought that you might need..." He held the package out toward her. "It's a good choice for personal self-defense." He moved beside her and pointed at the different pieces contained in the package. "The pepper spray is attached to a keychain with an emergency whistle. The whistle emits three distinct sounds at a hundred and twenty decibels each. It has a locking clip, so all you have to do is pull for the alarm to go off. And the pepper spray is police grade."

Kate nodded. She'd heard some of what he said, but she was still back at the part where he said that he was thinking about her. "Me? Did you really come here for me?"

"I needed to pick up a couple things for work too."

She raised a puzzled eyebrow until she realized she must have spoken her thought out loud. Now it was her turn to blush. "It's perfect!" Her voice was far too high and loud. "Great." She winced as she'd lowered the pitch too much. She cleared her throat. "Do you have any recommendations for home security?"

"I'm glad you brought that up. The first thing I'd recommend is to lose that fake hide-a-key rock."

"Already threw it out!" Kate grinned.

"Over here, I saw they had some cameras and security alarms."

"Exactly what I'm looking for." *Unless I can take you home?*

She followed Ryan around the store as he explained the different products and their pros and cons. At first he came off like a teacher giving a presentation, but the more she joked, the more he relaxed. Soon they were both laughing and they even had to go get a cart as they picked out an array of electronics to secure Kate's house. She'd have to put all of this on her credit card, but what choice did she have? She'd heard about people spending thousands on a boat and not buying life preservers. If the alarm would protect her, she was getting it.

After checking out, Ryan insisted on walking her out to her minivan. She didn't even consider saying no.

"I'd get those things installed as soon as possible," he said while loading the packages into her van.

"I'm going to start tonight."

"Good for you." Ryan gave her a smile that made her spine tingle. "Do you want a hand?"

Abso—freaking—lootly! "Are you sure? It's kind of late." Kate wanted to smack her own face to make herself stop talking. "I'd love the help, but if you have to work tomorrow…" *SHUT UP!*

"I'm actually off tomorrow, so it isn't a problem."

"Great! Hop in."

"How about I follow you?"

"You drove here. Of course. I'll see you at my house." She didn't know where to place her hands. She folded them behind her, put them on her hips, and settled on crossing her arms.

"I'll be right behind you." Ryan jogged to a large pickup.

Kate had a hard time not speeding home. She bounced in her seat as she zipped along, Ryan's headlights wrapping her car in a protective glow.

After unloading the van, she started a pot of coffee and they got to work. Kate loved every minute of it. From getting distracted by the warm touch of Ryan's fingers as he helped her hold a camera while they screwed it into place to getting caught staring at his cute behind as he stood on the ladder, she was having the best night she'd had in a long time. They talked about everything and nothing—his growing up in Texas, movies and TV shows, and more as they placed electronic sensors on the windows and doors to alert her if they were opened. But when Ryan said *Tommy Boy* was his all-time favorite movie, her hands trembled and she looked down.

"I take it you don't like comedy?" Ryan asked.

Kate tucked an errant strand of hair back behind her ear. "No... actually, I like it. It's just... my sister loved that movie." She smiled thinly. "That'll leave a mark!" she said in her best Chris Farley impression. "Emma was always saying that. She was a bit of a klutz."

Ryan climbed down from the ladder and stared into her eyes. "I'm not one to give advice, but sometimes it helps to talk about people we've lost."

Kate swallowed. "Sometimes it doesn't." She picked up another window sensor.

"True." Ryan nodded and moved beside her to hold the device as she screwed it in. "But it helped me."

Kate focused on the screwdriver in her hand, determined not to look into his brown eyes. "You?"

"I lost my older brother. He was twenty-two."

"What happened?"

"He was breaking up a fight. Guy stabbed him."

Kate dropped the screwdriver. Ryan caught it before it hit the ground.

"I'm so sorry. What was his name?"

"Caleb. Seeing how protective you are with Andy reminded me of my mom. She became a single mom when I was born. Caleb was six years older than me and she always called him the little man of the house. He took care of us."

Kate turned toward the window so she didn't have to meet his gaze but ended up staring at Ryan's reflection in the glass. Her emotional defenses were cracking, and it hurt. "Does it really help thinking about him?"

Ryan rubbed the back of his neck and chuckled. "I know Caleb's in Heaven, but it's almost like I can hear him sometimes. Like right now, he's telling me I sound like a doofus."

Kate laughed so hard she covered her mouth to stifle a snort.

Ryan handed the screwdriver back to her, and she finished attaching the window sensor. She wanted so much to touch him that she found her hand reaching out toward him. She turned in the opposite direction—and bumped her head on the ladder. Rubbing her forehead, she muttered, "That'll leave a mark."

Ryan laughed as he took her chin in his hand and tilted it up. He looked at her forehead for a moment and then lowered his eyes to meet hers.

Kate's breathing hitched. His fingers were rough, but the delicate way he was cradling her chin made little waves of warmth radiate down her chest. She moved closer to him. Her hands rose to his waist and touched something metal on the side of his belt—his gold detective shield.

Ryan's eyes followed hers. He stiffened and stepped back.

Kate panicked. It was an invisible thing, but a wall slammed down between them. Somehow she knew he was thinking about his job. He was a detective and she was a victim.

Though she reached out to him, Ryan just awkwardly shook her hand and nodded. "Thank you," he said, then marched over to his coat. The wall between them solidified. She saw it in the distance in his eyes and the stiffness in his shoulders. He was back to being a cop. "It's good to see... a citizen taking security steps. I'm glad I could help."

A citizen? He sounded like RoboCop. "I'm the one who should be thanking you."

"I should go." Ryan grabbed his jacket off the couch and headed for the door.

Kate followed him. She was about to protest, but then she saw the first rays of sun lighting up the sky. It was morning already, she had to work, and she hadn't slept at all.

"Thank you again!" she called out as Ryan descended the steps.

He stopped and turned around. He looked like he was going to say something, but then he pressed his lips into a tight smile and nodded formally, like a salute.

Kate waved and watched him back his truck out of the driveway. He didn't take his eyes off her.

While she wanted to shout, *Come back*, she couldn't do that to him. Ryan was a cop and was working her case. They couldn't get involved. He could get in trouble.

Stupid stalker. Not only was he keeping her kids away, but now he was driving away the first man she'd been interested in for a long time.

Her hands clenched at her sides.

Fix it, Kate. You fixed the van. You helped Susan. You secured your home. You can catch this creep following you. And then you can ask Ryan out.

Kate sat at the reception desk, her eyelids feeling as if they weighed twenty pounds apiece. She hadn't slept at all. Last night had been wonderful, but this morning was brutal. The clock on the wall seemed to be stuck. It wasn't possible that it was still only a few minutes past ten.

Marshall Whitman hurried through the front door and headed straight for her desk, his briefcase swinging in his hand and his tan jacket billowing out behind him. His usual salesman smirk had been replaced by a tight-lipped grimace. His eyes darted to Morris Berman's office door, and his shoulders flinched upward as if the door might fly off its hinges and he'd be sucked inside. He gripped the edge of the counter with an intensity that drained the color from his knuckles and whispered, "Did you say anything to Berman?"

"About what?"

"The missing envelope. Did you say *anything*?" His breath reeked of coffee and stale cigarettes.

It took Kate's sleep-deprived brain a few seconds to remember what he was talking about. "I told you I have no idea where it is."

Marshall ground his teeth and pushed off from the counter. He made it to outside Berman's door, then marched back to her desk. He glared down at her. "You admitted to taking it." The cords stood out in his neck.

"It was a joke!" She shifted back a bit in her seat, unnerved by the stressed-out, sweaty man towering over her. "It's like saying, oh, yeah, I know where Jimmy Hoffa's buried—under my house, next to Elvis and JFK."

He muttered something, spun on his heel, and trudged back to Berman's door. But then his whole posture changed. He set his briefcase down and draped his jacket over it. He straightened his shoulders, brushed back his hair, and shook out his hands. A smile lit up his face. Confidently, he rapped three times on the door and stuck his head in. "Hey, boss. You wanted to see me?"

"Five minutes ago," Berman snapped from inside. "Get in here and close the door. We have a problem…"

The door clicked shut, and Kate couldn't hear any more of the conversation. If she hadn't had so many issues of her own, she would have been mildly intrigued about what those two men considered a "problem," but her main concern right now was keeping her eyes open. The pot of coffee she'd drunk before work wasn't keeping her awake, plus she now had to make her third trip to the bathroom.

Not wanting to miss a call, she hurried to the ladies' room and set some kind of record for taking care of business. As she exited the bathroom, Marshall stepped out from behind her desk, holding up a pen and talking rapidly.

"Mine died… I grabbed one of yours, okay? I'll give it back after I meet with the warden," he said, tipping his head toward Berman's office.

Marshall looked pale as if he too hadn't been sleeping well lately, but he didn't leer at her like he usually did. She supposed she should be grateful for that. The bar kept getting lower. She nodded as Marshall walked over to Berman's open door.

She trudged back around the desk and slid into her chair. Her foot bumped her purse, and it tipped onto its side and fell open. When she picked it up, she saw the outside zipper was pulled back.

Her stomach plummeted. She never, ever left her purse unzipped. Marshall! *Needed a pen, yeah right.* She plopped her purse on her lap and burrowed through it like a squirrel hunting for a buried acorn. Her wallet and credit cards were still there.

Kate sank deeper into the office chair. Was it possible she'd left it open? She was so tired her thoughts were getting jumbled. She settled her elbow on the desk and propped her head on her hand like a kickstand. She should clean her desk. Or stand up. The last thing she wanted to do was…

Mr. Berman's meaty hand slammed down on Kate's desk.

She jerked to attention in her chair. "I wasn't sleeping."

"You were snoring." The short man's chest rammed the counter. His face—jowly and toad-like at the best of times—was flushed and splotchy.

Marshall stood beside him, looking just as outraged—and also a little smug. "You know how hard I work to get clients in here," he said to Berman. "What if it had been a client who caught her drooling on her desk and not me? How would that have looked?"

"I—I'm so sorry," Kate stammered. "You see, last night—"

"I do not want to hear about last night." Berman's splotchy face turned crimson. "Leave your personal life at the door."

"Mr. Berman, please let me explain. I must have dozed off. You're right—it's inexcusable." *Please don't fire me, please don't fire me.* "I didn't sleep at all last night because some man has been stalking me and—"

Berman huffed. "Ms. Gardner, I'm not here to discuss what you do on your own time." Marshall smirked behind him, pretending to look at his cuticles. "The point is, as the receptionist, you are the first face people see when they come into this establishment. I've ignored rumors about your unseemly behavior—"

Kate stood up so fast her chair rolled back and hit the wall behind her with a thunk. "How dare you! What rumors?" She leveled her gaze at both men. "Someone is *stalking* me. My van was defaced in this very parking lot! The only reason I didn't come to you—"

Berman cut her off. "You fell asleep on the job. Third violation, end of discussion. Your services are no longer needed here, Ms. Gardner. I'll inform the employment agency. You can work out the details with them."

Knowing that she would be paying into the swear jar for a very long time if she opened her mouth again, Kate pressed her lips together and grabbed her purse. She was marching around the desk when Berman stepped in front of her.

"There is one matter that still needs to be addressed before you leave the premises."

The secure door behind her opened and Bruce, the IT guy, walked out. "Sorry," he muttered as he tried in vain to tuck his shirt into the belt that struggled to hold back his large belly. "It's the weirdest thing. Kate Gardner only has front-door access. I deactivated that, but I couldn't find any computer logins for her. What department is she in?"

"Reception. I'm right here." Kate gave Bruce a slight wave. He was the only person in the entire place who actually treated her like a human being, even if he had forgotten her name. "I've never had computer access."

Understanding dawned on his big, affable face. "Oh, you're Kate Gardner? Sorry about that."

"No worries." Kate shrugged.

"Ms. Gardner," Berman butted in, "before you leave this building, security needs to check your handbag."

Kate cradled the purse to her chest as though she were protecting a baby. Her eyes narrowed as she looked up at Marshall's smug grin. She was wide awake now.

"When I came out of the restroom, my purse was open and he was behind my desk." She pointed at Marshall.

He scoffed. "Oh, come on. I borrowed a pen, that's all."

"My purse was open, and I never leave it open."

Marshall flung his hands at the ceiling theatrically. "And you only say something when your purse is about to be searched?"

"Enough," Berman barked. "Ms. Gardner, your handbag. Please."

Kate's fingers tightened on the leather. She knew she hadn't done anything wrong, but...

"If you don't turn over your handbag to be searched, I'll have no other option but to contact the police." Berman pointed at the phone for emphasis.

Kate handed her purse to Bruce. "It was open when I got back from the restroom," she repeated.

Bruce set the purse on the reception counter. As he removed each item and placed it to one side, Kate's anger, embarrassment, and shame grew. Wallet, lipstick, kids' Band-Aids, antacids, hand wipes, a wadded-up tissue, her prescription bottle of happy pills, crumpled receipts, panty liners, and the usual junk every mother of small children carries around without even realizing it—a toy from a supermarket vending machine, straws still wrapped in paper, two ponytail bands knotted with hair, a water bottle cap.

After it was all stacked in a heap, Bruce shook his head. "That's it."

Kate nodded, her claim validated—she hadn't stolen anything from Mr. Berman or Marshall.

"The fact remains," Berman continued, "you fell asleep on the job. I'm sorry, I have no choice but to terminate your employment. Good day."

Bruce looked apologetic as he held out her empty handbag to her.

Kate stuffed her belongings back one by one. When she reached Ava's rainbow unicorn Band-Aids, her eyes moistened. Fired. Before this job, she had never even gotten a bad review, let alone had to endure the walk of shame. She swept everything else back into her purse, stuffed it under her arm like a football, and walked at the steadiest pace she could manage out the door.

As soon as she got outside, she struggled to hold back the tears. She was already on the edge of financial ruin. She needed this crappy job. Without it, the upcoming custody battle with Scott would shift in his favor.

I can't lose my kids.

She got into the van and drove home as quickly as she could through the blur of tears that were threatening to spill over. After shutting off her new security alarm, she checked the house from top to bottom—her pepper spray with the emergency alarm clutched in her hand.

Kate stopped in the kitchen. She pictured herself telling Andy and Ava. They wouldn't understand, but Ava would try to make it all better with a rainbow unicorn Band-Aid. She would kiss Kate's cheek and ask where she should put the Band-Aid.

Over my broken heart.

Kate had read in a gazillion self-help books that crying was therapeutic. Whether it was true or not, she couldn't hold back the waterfall. Her marriage. Her job. Her privacy. Her sense of safety. Her sister. What else was going to be taken from her? Her kids. Scott would win. He would—

Kate took out her phone and furiously stabbed the keys, texting a message to Donna. Would she even understand? Donna loved her job.

There's nothing worse than losing a job you hate but really need.

She rubbed her hands together and stared at the place where her wedding ring used to sit.

Okay, some things are worse.

She stalked up the stairs to the bedroom and collapsed on the bed. She was exhausted and needed to regroup. Yes, she'd gotten fired, but she could bounce back from this. How? She had no idea yet, but maybe after getting some sleep...

Her phone buzzed with a text. Kate sat up in bed, rubbing her eyes, and grabbed her phone. The text was from Andy.

HELP, MOM!!!!!!! I NEED MY CABIN + REPORT!! CLASS IN 30 MIN!!!

She jumped up from the table and dried her eyes. Andy had spent all last week making a Popsicle-stick replica of Abe Lincoln's boyhood home to accompany a book report. With all the chaos, he must have forgotten to take it with him to Audrey's. Kate swooped down the hall and into Andy's room with a newfound determination. Sitting on his desk were the large cabin and the plastic-bound report. She carefully put the cabin in a large shopping bag along with the report, then texted Andy back.

MOM IS ON THE WAY!

Juggling the report, the cabin, and her purse, she dashed for the garage. This was one job she wouldn't screw up. She backed down the driveway, making sure the garage door closed, before pulling out onto the road. Barreling across town in her restored-to-imperfection van, Kate powered down the window and let the wind blow through her hair. She might be a loser at everything else in life now, but she was still a good mom. That had to count for something.

She peeled into the school parking lot and skidded to a stop in front of the entrance. She ran from the car as fast as she dared and made her way to the principal's office. Andy was waiting in the hallway outside. His face lit up when he saw her and he frantically waved her forward. They made the handoff, and Andy gave her a quick kiss on the cheek, yelled, "You're the best mom ever!" and dashed down the hallway. Before he turned the corner, he gave her a big thumbs-up and a huge grin.

Kate gave the office assistants a cheery smile—which they returned. *Best mom ever—did ya hear that?* She attempted to stroll down the hall back toward the entrance, but as soon as she was out of sight of the office staff, she had to double over, put her hands on her knees, and catch her breath. For a slightly overweight, under-exercised mom, she thought she'd done pretty well at the hundred-yard dash in less than four seconds, but the aftermath was a killer.

Even in victory, she was fighting back the tears. "Good," she wheezed. She'd done something right, and her kids still loved and needed her. Kate stood straight and looked for a tissue in her purse to wipe her eyes and blow her nose. *One step at a time. Time to look for another job. Keep the momentum going.*

"Ms. Gardner?" A wiry man with slicked-back and thin gray hair was marching toward her—Dr. Green, the school psychologist.

She froze.

"Ms. Gardner? Do you have a moment?"

Every warning bell in Kate's system went off. *Did I just speak my thoughts aloud again? Oh, no… Did he hear me?*

"Hi. Sorry again about the missed appointment," Kate said.

"Well, I'm glad you stopped in now. So, are you available to talk?"

"I—"

"It shouldn't take long," Dr. Green said.

She couldn't get a read from his face; it was completely neutral—not worried, but not friendly either. What did he want to discuss, and why now?

"I'd like to give you an update on Andy." He pushed his round glasses higher up his square face. "We can meet in my office."

"Of course."

Kate followed the man in his sneakers and brown suit and tried to remember every word Andy had said about school during the last couple of months. Her heart was racing again as she slid into a comfortable recliner across from Dr. Green's desk. She tried not to picture Andy in the oversized chair and failed. The image made her little boy seem even smaller and more overwhelmed.

Dr. Green took off his glasses and cleaned them, prolonging her agony, and she didn't have any conversational openers rehearsed for this unforeseen situation. Finally, he folded his hands and leaned back in his chair.

"You asked me if everything was all right, Ms. Gardner. That's a good place to start. Is everything all right with you?"

The doctor's simple question made Kate's mouth go dry. She couldn't let the school therapist think that she was at her wits' end, barely hanging on. "Fine. Under the circumstances."

He nodded, interlacing his fingers. "Of course. I had a meeting earlier in the week with Scott and he brought me up to speed on the situation. That's why I wanted to discuss some possible changes to Andy's routine."

Kate's fingers tightened on the arms of the chair like they did when the drill was turned on at the dentist's office. The "discussion" that followed took much longer than a few minutes. Dr. Green didn't just beat around the bush before getting to a point; he had to circle the entire park. He talked at length about the need for changes in Andy's schedule, including weekly check-ins with him as well as with the family therapist, instead of bi-monthly. It was lousy that even more free time was being taken from Andy's cramped schedule, but getting him out of additional therapy was a battle she couldn't win.

Finally, Dr. Green glanced at his watch. "I'm glad we had a chance to go over some details. Thank you for your time."

She'd been waiting for the other shoe to drop, but all he'd done was recommend the additional therapy. She stood up, enormously relieved. Once again, her anxiety had thrown rational thought over the cliff, and she'd wasted half an hour worrying over nothing.

"Of course, and thank you, Doctor." Kate shook his outstretched hand.

"I'm certain all this will work out. The new custody arrangement will be difficult for Andy at first," Dr. Green said, "but with the extra therapy, we can keep a close eye on him and get him through it."

Kate froze. "Excuse me? What new custody arrangement?"

"I'm sorry? That's what we were going over."

"What new custody arrangement?"

"My apologies. I thought... Mr. Gardner contacted the school and indicated... I assumed that you were aware of the changes—"

"There's been a misunderstanding, but I can assure you, I'll work it out." Kate lowered her rising voice as she added, "There have been no changes to the custody of my children, nor will there be."

Kate didn't wait for his reaction; she just headed to the door. Letting her anger and vulnerability show was not the right move and would undoubtedly become the next topic of discussion in poor Andy's weekly therapy sessions. She would do some damage if she stayed in that office another second.

She strode out of Dr. Green's office as calmly as she could, leaving the door open because that was the only way she wouldn't slam it. The bile in her throat made her stomach heave. She made her way to the restroom next to the office, dashed into a stall, and threw up. All the stress was doing a number on her insides. She rested her hands on her knees, hoping the nausea would pass.

Fifteen minutes later, she had nearly made it to the front doors of the school when the bell clanged, making her heart miss a couple of beats. Classroom doors flew open and students flooded the hallway, chattering and laughing, flowing around her, taking no notice of her as they banged their lockers shut and rushed out the front door toward the buses and cars waiting to take them home.

Kate moved with the stream of children, like a dead fish drifting along with the lively kids. When Kate passed by a mother she knew from Boy Scouts, she was glad that her transition lenses hid her puffy eyes as she managed a polite nod. In return, a complex series of contortions crossed the woman's face, ending somewhere near pity, before she turned away.

Outside, cars and buses were honking, and some parents were shouting rudely, "Hey, lady! Is that your van?" In her haste to get to Andy, she had parked in the bus lane and was holding up traffic, which, as she'd been told numerous times, was a big no-no. She walked faster. She didn't want to give someone a valid reason to be upset with her.

A group of young boys standing on the curb beside Kate's van erupted in fits of laughter. She lowered her head, yanked the door open, and slid into the driver's seat. Someone had stuck a flyer underneath her wiper. *Oh, please, I don't think I can take another bake sale.* Grumbling, she reached for her door handle—and froze. The photo on the flyer short-circuited her thought process. She shoved the door open and ripped the paper out.

The honks and jeers of the impatient drivers faded away as she looked at the photographs printed on the flyer. They were all of her. One showed Kate sitting in a chair with a male stripper in a leopard-skin thong thrusting against her face. Another showed her in front of the mirror, naked. A third was a close-up of her bare breasts. Across the top of the flyer, printed in an enormous red font, were the words DIAL-A-SLUT followed by Kate's cell phone number.

Laughter rippled toward her from the students, still pouring out of the doors, getting into cars, and boarding the buses. Dotted on cars in the parking lot were more flyers. Several people had them in their hands or were lifting the windshield wipers to get at them. A group of boys who looked to be about Andy's age weren't even bothering to contain their whoops of laughter as they imitated her poses in the photos. Parents were shaking their heads and giving her sideways glances.

"No, no, no, this can't be happening!" She got out and started yanking the papers off the cars, grateful Andy was going to Audrey's today and not witnessing the spectacle.

The principal, Holly Monahan, strode through the crowd, followed by several teachers. "Gather up every leaflet," Holly ordered. The teachers fanned out across the parking lot, and the students and parents quieted.

The cavalry had arrived, but too late. Several boys stuffed the flyers into their pockets.

Holly wrapped an arm around Kate's shoulders. "Why don't you come with me back into the school?"

Kate bit her lip so hard she tasted blood. She wanted to go. Anywhere but here. She shook her head. "I need to go home." Her voice didn't sound like her own. It was thin and stretched.

"We've contacted the police."

Kate tried to gather a deep breath, but it ended in a choked gasp. "I need to go home," she whispered. "Please."

Holly motioned to the crossing guard, who cleared the way while Kate got back into her van.

She drove home in a daze. She should have her therapy appointment moved up from next week. At this rate, she'd never make it. She parked the van and slunk into the house. The alarm's high-pitched whine hurt her throbbing head. She punched in the code, and the keypad beeped twice and went silent. *Crying is supposed to be therapeutic. Come on, cry.* She slammed her fist repeatedly against the door frame. *Cry! Get it out!* She punched and punched with all her force. She glanced down and saw a bruise, but she felt nothing. Her whole body was numb.

Her phone buzzed with a constant hum as dozens of pervy texts poured in. She turned her phone off. Then swore. She couldn't do that. The kids would need to get a hold of her. And where the heck was Donna? She hadn't responded to Kate's SOS text. She powered the phone back on and stuffed it in her purse.

Kate made her way upstairs, clinging to the railing as she pulled herself up, each step feeling like she was scaling Everest. In her office, she flopped down in her chair and turned on the computer.

A half hour later, with the lights off and the shades drawn, she read the instructions on her computer monitor for the seventh time. She glared at the settings on her phone. Even though the photos were no longer on her phone, what she hadn't realized—until now—was that copies had been automatically uploaded to the family cloud account, and both she and Scott—and therefore Tammi—had access.

Just as she'd thought, that witch was behind the flyers. The world spun around her. How long had it been since she'd eaten? Had she eaten today?

The doorbell rang. Kate's leg whipped up and banged against the desk. Swearing and muttering, she wiped at her tears with the back of her hand and headed for the door.

"Coming!" she yelled.

Her head throbbed. She knew she must look terrible, but she didn't care. Hoping it was Donna, she put her eye to the peephole—and realized what a terrible mistake she had made not running a brush through her hair at the very least.

Ryan Daley stood on her porch.

She unlocked the deadbolt and opened the door. Burning with embarrassment, she stepped aside to let him enter. Ryan had no doubt seen the pictures of her—all of her.

"You must be very upset." He cleared his throat, a look of pity on his face. "I want you to know how sorry I am that this happened."

Kate kept her eyes on the floor. "Can we have this conversation inside? Not that it'll make it any less awkward."

"I can arrange for you to speak with a female officer if you'd feel more comfortable."

"No, thank you. It's better to get it over with."

Ryan followed her into the living room and took out his tablet. "I'm sorry, but I need to ask you some questions. Were those photographs of you, and if so have they been altered in any way?"

Kate cleared her throat. "They're mine, and they're unaltered, but I didn't realize that even if the pictures were deleted from my phone, copies remained on the cloud. I just changed the setting, but it's like locking the barn after the horse is out. And oh my gosh, I'm not judging, but I swear

I don't do strippers—I didn't even have a bachelorette party when I got married. But my friend Donna hired one to surprise me after the divorce, you see, and before I sent him packing, she took a few photos with my phone. And the other ones... I took them after a skin exam. The doctor wanted me to keep a record."

Kate's fingernails dug into her palms. She was supposed to take photos to check if her skin spots changed over time. How could she have known she'd end up as the poster girl for DIAL-A-SLUT?

Ryan nodded but kept his eyes on the floor. "Who else has access to your photos?"

"Scott has access to our cloud account with the photos. That means Tammi does too."

"Tammi Yates? Your ex-husband's fiancée?"

"Yes. We're not on the best of terms."

Ryan paused for a second before continuing with his notes. "The school is pulling their security video, and there were several witnesses who saw someone putting the flyers on cars."

"Was it Tammi? She's my height. Blonde—"

"I'm not at liberty to say, but I'll be reviewing the school's security video. And we'll interview Ms. Yates."

Kate took a quivering breath. The police relaying her suspicions to Tammi would likely cause World War III, but this had to stop. She rocked her head from side to side and dropped her chin to her chest. "My son may have seen those pictures. I can take the whispers, the humiliation, but Andy..." Heat rose to her cheeks and she couldn't go on.

She wanted the bullying and scare tactics to end, wanted her children back, wanted Scott and Tammi to mind their own business, and wanted Hartville to leave her alone. That was all she wanted.

Ryan touched her arm. "Accessing your photos and distributing them in a school zone is a serious crime. Add in the stalking and vandalism, and the perpetrator is looking at lengthy jail time. I know that doesn't make up for what's happened, but we will stop this and you'll be able to go on with your life."

His words gave her some hope. His touch gave her more.

"In the interim, try not to worry too much, okay?"

"The ship has sailed on that one."

Kate followed him to the front door. He paused with his hand on the knob, and she thought he was going to say something more, but instead he shook her hand, said goodbye, and let himself out.

Kate's phone vibrated against her leg, causing her to utter a little cry. She didn't need to look at it; all unknown callers were set to vibrate. She knew what it was. A call to DIAL-A-SLUT.

She locked the door behind Ryan, realizing the action was useless. Even with the new security system, she couldn't keep the monsters outside; they could get to her anywhere. The last time she'd feared monsters, she was eight years old. But now the monsters were real and a whole lot meaner.

Kate archived fifty-eight text messages for the police with a quick flick of the thumb. That was just the harvest from the last couple of hours, but she was getting better at it. Her next job was to push through her embarrassment and explain to Andy what had happened. It was his school and he needed to know.

A text from Scott made her stomach drop. He had found out about the flyers and already told Andy about them. She burned with shame and frustration. Why had Scott talked to Andy without her? Had he explained why she had taken the pictures? Did Andy understand? How could he? He couldn't un-see those pictures.

She sagged down into the couch, remote in hand. But before she could turn on the TV, Audrey's voice echoed in her mind. *"Stop being a doormat... you have three months to get your act together."*

Sitting up straight, she mustered the energy of Queen Audrey. She was done cowering. She was on the offensive now.

She opened her phone, flipped over to her email, and scrolled through the long list of rejection letters from companies she'd applied to. All of them looked like standard computer-generated forms and basically said the same thing: *Dear Loser, Thanks but no thanks. We're telling you we'll keep your application on file, but please be informed we've already shredded it. Yours insincerely, Potential Employer (Not).*

As she was filing them one by one in her rejections folder, Kate's finger froze over an email from MG Uniforms. *Availability for an interview?* She read the subject line twice before opening the email. With a trembling hand, she scrolled down the message. They wanted her to interview for a job—tomorrow morning!

"THANK YOU, GOD!" she shouted at the ceiling but seized up mid-cheer. She poked her potbelly and dashed upstairs. Would she still fit in her interview outfit?

Stupid chocolate. Stupid, stupid pasta! Kate cursed as she rushed to her closet. It had been over a month since she'd had an interview and she'd been blowing her diet all over the place.

Please fit. Please fit. Please—

The jacket was tight, but she could leave it open. Time to tackle the skirt. She sucked in her stomach as far as she could, and the zipper shot up and sealed her in. She couldn't breathe, but she was in the sausage casing of a skirt. Taking shallow breaths, she inched over to the bed and started to sit down. It seemed to be working. With some heels, taking small steps, wearing Spanx of course, and acting very dignified, she could make this work. She sat gingerly on the edge of the bed and held out her hand to her imaginary interviewer, but as they shook on her accepting the new job, threads popped, the zipper gave way, and suddenly she could breathe again. Kate couldn't even cry if she wanted to.

She did want to, but she didn't have the time. She wiggled out of the skirt and dressed quickly. As she rushed to the front door, a wave of nausea swept over her. Her head spun and her vision blurred. She clung to the doorknob for support. Hanging her head, she took deep breaths until the dizziness passed.

She glanced at the clock. If she hurried, she could still make it to TJ Maxx, where she'd bought the skirt, before the store closed. After taking a quick picture of the jacket, she raced outside and to the van.

Saying a silent prayer of thanks that the mark of shame on the van was no longer visible, she raced across town. Kate had always been a believer in prayer, but that had crumbled into the moral wasteland of divorce. She'd begged God to save her marriage, and when that didn't happen, she'd stopped asking for anything. But now she found herself on the edge of the abyss. She needed this job and was desperate for all the help she could get. Feeling like a complete hypocrite, she mumbled, "Please let me get this job," then added, "Sorry. In Jesus's name, amen."

And with that, completely oblivious, she drove straight through a red light. Horns blared, vehicles swerved, fingers were thrust high into the air, and cursing ensued from all directions.

"Sorry!" Kate yelled over her shoulder and pivoted her head, scanning for flashing lights. Grateful for the lack of police, she pulled into the mall parking lot and headed for the store at the end.

The large lot was dotted with cars. She parked in the nearest space and hurried for the door, clutching her pepper spray. The automatic doors swooshed open and a smiling teenager greeted her.

"We close in ten minutes."

Kate made a beeline for the rack where she'd found the suit a few months ago. That time, there had been several identical suits in different sizes, but now only one remained. She snagged it off the rack, but her joy shattered when she realized the skirt was a size smaller than the one she'd busted out of. Dejected, she placed it back on the rack and thumbed her way down to the business skirts. Her hand stopped on a blue skirt that looked very similar to hers. She pulled it off the rod and checked the size. It would fit. Better than that, when she held it up against the picture of the suit jacket, she saw it was a perfect match.

Cradling it to her breast, Kate hurried over to the checkout counter.

The young clerk took the skirt and turned it over, searching in vain for the price. "There's no tag. Is this part of a suit?" she asked.

Kate was done lying. She had to have the skirt, but every time she lied, it bit her in the butt. "It is, but I didn't see the jacket."

"I can't sell it individually."

That's what I get for telling the truth!

"I'll pay the price of the full suit. I have a job interview tomorrow."

The teen shook her head. "I'm not supposed to sell it if I don't have both pieces. It will mess up inventory."

"Okay, I'll go find the jacket." Kate dashed over and scoured the rack for the matching coat—in vain.

The lights blinked off and on, and the intercom crackled. "Attention, TJ Maxx patrons. The store is closing. Please bring your purchases to the checkout line."

Kate's stomach flipped—there wasn't time to find a whole new suit. The store was closing and another one wouldn't be open this late... Her skin prickled and her throat constricted as a panic attack rolled over her.

The clerk walked up along with another woman. The shiny gold name tag on her dress read *Beatrice Kay—Store Manager.*

"I know you're closing," Kate said, gulping air. "And—I understand it's store policy that you can't sell the skirt without the jacket, but I have this job interview tomorrow... The skirt actually fits me! It's a miracle! Mine self-destructed because of pasta and..."

The woman was smiling as she waved her hands to stop Kate's rant. "Don't worry. I understand. Believe me, I've been there." She gestured to the girl standing next to her. "Zoey was simply following procedure."

"I know. Look, I'm willing to pay for the whole suit, but I can't find the matching jacket anywhere."

"Well, how about I take fifty percent off the skirt?"

It took a second for Kate to absorb what she'd heard. "What? Really? That would be great. I can't thank you enough!" She wanted to hug both women.

"Like I said, been there." Beatrice smiled so widely her eyes almost disappeared. "Matter of fact, it was my interview to get this job. I went to the store two towns over to find a plus size. The manager called around to other stores until she found one. Guess who interviewed me the next day?"

Tears beaded Kate's lashes. "That's so awesome. Thank you again." She let go of the rack and walked toward the register.

Several minutes later, Kate strode triumphantly out of the store with her purchase. Now she was ready—almost. She looped the suit over her arm and fumbled for her phone. Typing a quick reply email, she thanked the company for the opportunity to interview and assured them she'd be there tomorrow.

Footsteps behind her made her glance over her shoulder.

Standing on the sidewalk outside the store was a large man. The shadows concealed his features, but he was tall and wearing a dark jacket and a baseball hat. And he was staring directly at her.

Kate spun on her heel and hurried for the car. She didn't turn back around, but from the sound of his boots on the tar, she knew he was following her. There were still a few cars in the parking lot but none close by, only hers. She was exposed and alone. She unzipped her purse and her trembling fingers touched a round cylinder.

Remembering Ryan's instructions—*"all you have to do is yank and the emergency alarm will go off"*—she tightened her fingers around the pepper spray.

"Hey!" the man called out.

"Get away from me!" Kate ordered as she turned to face him. "Leave me alone!"

The man was only a few feet away. He reached out his hand.

Kate ripped the pepper spray out of her purse and pointed it at the man's face. "Back off!" she screamed, but her words were lost in an ear-piercing shriek as the emergency whistle blared to life.

The man jumped backward, his wide eyes blinking rapidly as he covered his ears.

A police cruiser driving by sounded its siren, and its blue and white lights flashed as it swerved into the parking lot.

The man waved a hand in the air, a piece of paper clutched in his fingers. "She dropped this. I just wanted to give it back!" he yelled over the alarm as the officer leaped out of the cruiser.

Kate's stomach knotted. Up close, she saw her would-be assailant was an older man—tall, but his shoulders were quite rounded. His baseball cap was dark orange, not blue with a circle. He didn't seem threatening at all but confused and determined to explain himself.

Kate clicked off the alarm.

"She dropped her receipt. I tried to give it back, that's all." The man took his cap off and ran a quaking hand through his gray hair. "I was just trying to give it back."

Kate cringed. "I'm so sorry. I can explain…"

Even though she apologized repeatedly, the officer insisted on taking down her name and address, as well as those of the good Samaritan, Ed Forbes, who hurried off as soon as he could, shaking his head the entire way back to his car.

The young policeman lowered his notepad and his eyes rounded in concern. "Are you sure you're okay, ma'am?"

"I'm fine," Kate reassured him, placing a trembling hand in her pocket.

As she pulled out of the parking lot, the policeman spoke into his radio and followed her with his eyes. He shot her a look that seemed to say he wasn't convinced that she had it all together. She didn't want to imagine what he might be reporting or what Ryan would think when he heard about it.

The blue light from the computer monitor reflected off Kate's glasses as she read the screen. She was exhausted, but from the moment she'd gotten home, she'd been researching MG Uniforms and the man she'd be meeting with, Dennis Munson. She'd read not only the company's websites but Dennis's social media pages as well. He was a former soldier, and posted mostly about the military, but in one post, he grumbled about work and moving from RO Reports to the cloud.

Desperate for a boost, Kate popped the last of the rum balls in her mouth. She gazed at the palm trees on the cover of the candy box. *No, no, no. Do not go down the rabbit hole of regret. Focus, focus... on the now.* She reached for another rum ball, then tossed the empty box off her desk and into the wastebasket.

She knew RO Reports like the back of her hand. She'd taken a class on it in college and done so well with it that the teacher had gotten her an internship at Wilson Packaging. But she didn't know cloud reporting—at all.

Kate started snapping her fingers, then made a face. It was a habit she'd picked up from Scott and now she felt dirty doing it. She needed to spin her work experience, but she wouldn't lie. How could she turn virtually zero knowledge of a software product into a positive?

The front doorbell rang and her phone buzzed with a text from Donna. IT'S ME. DON'T JUST OPEN DOOR. LOOK 1ST! :)

Kate chuckled and hurried downstairs and peered out the peephole.

Donna was dressed to the nines in a tight green dress, dangly gold earrings and cherry-red lipstick.

"Wow! You look gorgeous!" Kate said, opening the door.

"Thank you. You have a package." Donna pointed at the large white cardboard box on the porch.

Kate's eyes went wide. "But I didn't order anything."

Donna scooted around behind Kate and swore. "I don't see a delivery label. Did the stalker put it there?!"

"Calm down." Kate stepped onto the porch and examined the package from a distance.

"Call Detective Dreamy! Don't touch it!"

Kate picked it up and turned the package around. On the side that had been facing the house were the address label and a note: *X-192 Drone. Replacement for Kate Gardner.*

"It's another drone from Michelle!" Kate grinned. "At least I haven't been terminated from my side gig."

"Sweet! Aren't you glad you didn't panic and spray it with the hose like I was about to?"

Kate laughed, carried the package inside, and locked the door.

Donna's head tilted to the side and she pursed her lips. "I got me a date tonight."

"Louis?"

Donna shook her head. "We decided to go our separate ways. It was cordial. He's moved back to Augusta."

"He's already gone?"

"He saw an opportunity and went for it. I can't blame him for that."

"Who's the date with then?"

An impish smile dawned across Donna's red lips.

"No, you didn't." Kate walked into the living room and set the box down beside the end of the couch. "Please don't tell me you're going through with this plan to catch the creep. It's dangerous."

"No, it's not. I'm meeting him at Flagstaff Tavern. I'm buds with the bouncer. Relax, I got this. It's you I'm worried about. You look rough. Have you been sleeping?"

Kate shook her head, but when she remembered the job interview, a rush of adrenaline kicked in. She grabbed Donna's hand. "I got a job interview! Tomorrow with MG Uniforms!"

Donna gave her a hug, her beads dangling against Kate's cheek. "Berman didn't deserve you. You're going to nail this interview, Kate. Is it a marketing job?"

"It's in sales, but they do have an in-house marketing department. I figure I could work my way into marketing after I prove myself."

Donna gave her a high-five. "See! Things are turning around. You'll get this job, I'll catch your creep, and then you'll bed SuperCop."

Kate blushed. "None of that has happened yet, and I don't like you trying to catch this guy on your own. SuperCop is already working on it."

"So am I! One guy already texted me four times today. I bet he would have been at my house this morning if he wasn't working."

"That's what I'm talking about, Donna. That's so not cool."

"It is very cool! It means my plan is gonna work. I've got this superpower where I attract weirdos the way honey attracts Tigger."

"Winnie the Pooh is the honey luvah."

"Whatevah. Either way, my efforts will be rewarded with a steak and a really nice glass or three of wine." Donna checked the time and frowned. "I've gotta bounce." She hugged Kate and made a beeline for the door.

"I don't like it," Kate said, following, "but there's no stopping you when you've got your mind set on something. Don't go anywhere but to the Flagstaff, okay?"

"Yes, Mom. I'm a big girl. I'll be fine." Donna gave her a peck on the cheek.

"I'm serious, Donna. And promise me that you'll call me when you get home."

Donna struck a pose like she was swearing on a Bible, her left arm bent at the elbow and her right hand held high. "I promise I'll call you and give you all the salacious details as soon as I get home."

In spite of the churning in her stomach, Kate smiled. "You'd better."

"I just swore I would. You want a blood oath? Do you have a knife?"

"Shut up and be safe."

Donna checked the peephole and opened the door. "Don't worry." She patted her purse. "I have Harry!"

Kate flipped the lock, set the deadbolt, and reattached the chain then grimaced. She took a deep breath, bracing herself for another night of terrifying solitude.

"Kate!" someone screamed.

Kate stared straight ahead, but all she saw was blackness. Her fingers touched her face. Her eyes were open, yet she couldn't see. Not even shapes or shadows. Nothing.

Stumbling forward, she felt her way along, her hand touching rough wood.

The ground beneath her feet was spongy. Damp. Uneven.

Her feet were bare. Why?

An odd sense of peace washed over her. Kate stood still, yearning to lose herself in the comforting silence. For a moment, the thought of stretching out her arms and falling backward as if to land in a fluffy snowdrift was almost overwhelming.

A breeze blew softly across her face. Her hair tickled her cheek.

"Kate!"

It was Emma! Calling her from far away.

"You're in trouble. You need help."

Kate's eyes fluttered and opened. She was staring up toward her bedroom ceiling. But the problem was, she wasn't in her bedroom.

She wasn't even inside her house.

Her legs buckled and she sank to her knees, pressing her hands into the grass. Kate stared at the back of her house. The rear slider was wide open. The moon was high overhead and stars twinkled above.

She willed herself to rise. She was standing beside the elm tree. Standing now in the exact same place where Ryan had found the cigarette butts. The spot where her stalker had stood watching her bedroom.

Move! Move! Kate's mind screamed, but her body wouldn't listen. The hairs on the back of her neck rose. She wanted to turn around, see if someone was standing directly behind her, but she was paralyzed.

Run!

Kate's feet finally obeyed. She took four halting steps forward before breaking into a mad dash for the house.

She flew up the stairs and into her kitchen, yanking the slider closed behind her.

Napkins blew off the kitchen table and onto the floor. Her bare feet were freezing and muddy, leaving small tracks on the tile.

She turned and glared out at the blackness. It was happening again.

No! She couldn't deal with that. Not again.

She turned and bolted upstairs. Grasping the phone off her nightstand, she searched for any message from Dr. Sprouse.

Nothing.

She flipped to her sent folder, ready to forward her previous message and demand that he get back to her, but there was no previous message to Dr. Sprouse. None in her sent folder or her drafts. But that was impossible. She'd sent him an email, hadn't she?

Maybe she hadn't. Maybe she'd never even written it. No. She remembered writing it after the last episode of sleepwalking.

What if she hadn't? What if that had just been part of the nightmare too?

Kate retyped her earlier email from memory, adding this latest incident, and pressed send.

I'm taking control. I'm fighting back. I won't take any more of that medicine until I hear back from the doctor. I'm getting help.

Kate sobbed at a sudden realization.

I'm losing my mind.

11

Kate woke up like a kid on Christmas morning as the first rays of dawn filtered through the window and hope rose along with the sun.

Today will be different. Today will be awesome.

The prospect of a job! The nightmare of stalkers, vandalized vans, and those hideous flyers would soon be over. It had to be Tammi behind everything. Kate had been too blind to see it.

"Donna was—"

Kate sat bolt upright and grabbed her phone. She swore loudly. Because of all the pervy messages, she'd silenced her phone. There was no phone call from Donna and no text either. Kate hit speed dial. It went straight to Donna's voicemail.

"You *promised* you'd call me," Kate said, trying to keep her rising panic in check. "Call me back as soon as you get this."

Kate texted Donna the same message and slid out of bed. She took her time showering and getting ready, making sure she had a good breakfast, but the nervous feeling in her stomach was growing. The suit looked great, and as she applied subtle makeup to highlight her cheekbones and eyes, she ran over her notes on the company, her résumé—with the years of working for Scott for free described as "marketing consulting"—and rehearsed her pitch.

Donna still wasn't picking up, so Kate left another message, then picked up her folder, threw open the front door, and marched out to the porch. As she locked the house, tires squealed around the corner of her street and then Tammi's new, enormous black Escalade skidded to a stop, half in the driveway, half on the lawn.

Tammi charged out, her hands balled into fists. She was scowling so deeply that, despite all the Botox, wrinkles marred her perfect face.

"How dare you!" she shrieked, leaving the SUV's door open as she stomped over to Kate. "You called the police on me?" She stopped only inches away, her shoulders pulled back and her chest thrust forward.

A surprising sense of calm spread through Kate as she stared into the wild eyes of her nemesis. "I didn't call the police. It was their idea to speak with you. Did you confess?"

Tammi looked like she was choking on peanut butter. Her mouth opened and closed repeatedly, and her eyes bulged out. "You—how can you—I had nothing to do with any of that! I want nothing to do with you! I want you to crawl back to whatever backwater swamp you came from. Get out of Hartville and GET OUT OF OUR LIVES!" She screamed the last words, the veins in her neck and forehead protruding.

Kate stepped back, and as calmly as she could said, "Tammi, I have an appointment. Whatever you have to say to me will have to wait. But you did have access to my family photo account. You're the one who created those flyers."

Tammi leveled a trembling finger at Kate. "You're crazy! Scott told me all about your past breakdown. He said you're a psycho. He said your sister went nuts too! I guess it runs in your family."

"You're a liar! Scott never said that." Kate started towards her car, but stumbled as the bands of anxiety tightened around her chest.

Tammi lunged in front of her and snarled, "I didn't have anything to do with those flyers. Do you think I would run all over a school parking lot putting those things up?" She thrust her hand into her tight back pocket and pulled out her phone. "Everybody knows you're a slut." She unlocked it with a long red fingernail and held the screen up in Kate's face. "Like I told you at the coffee shop, I thought you were advertising your services."

On the screen was an ad for an escort service—"Secret Fling"—and the woman in the ad was Kate!

Kate's eyes widened. The ad had been posted last week. The pervy texts, the flyers, and the word SLUT etched into her car must have all been a result of this ad.

Why would her stalker do that?

And since the photos used in the ad were the same ones used in the flyers, Tammi wouldn't have needed access to Kate's account to get them. Anyone who'd seen the ad on the Internet had access.

Kate could hardly speak. She was equal parts angry and horrified, and more than anything, she wanted to call Ryan right now. Worse, Tammi was smiling. Kate could see the glee in her eyes.

"How do I know you didn't make that ad too?" Kate finally croaked out.

"Because you made the ad, you psycho! I figured you needed the money."

"Only you, Scott, and I had access to those photos…" Kate swallowed. Donna had access to the family photos too. Kate had given Donna the login when she made the Speedy Date profile. Had Donna given access to someone else? Kate's head was reeling. Maybe Tammi wasn't responsible? Her indignation at being accused seemed genuine.

"I can't talk about this now. I have to go." Kate tried to get around her.

"We're not done." Tammi shoved her phone back into her pocket and blocked Kate's way. "Scott and I tried to fight it, but you can't help who you love. You can't seem to help it either. I see how you look at him, how you use every opportunity with the kids to text or call, and now you've invented a stalker. You have to get it through your crazy head, you're just someone he used to love. Past tense. I'm his now. I'm his future." Tammi shoved the enormous engagement ring in Kate's face to prove her point.

"I thought the same thing when Scott put a ring on my finger."

"Here's another promise for you, Katie. If you continue to falsely accuse me or try to slander my good name in this town, I will make your life a living hell."

Tammi turned on her heel and stormed back to her car. She jammed the car into reverse and created even more ruts in the grass as she backed across the lawn and into the street.

Kate watched her go. Then she snatched her phone out of her purse and texted Donna.

CALL ME ASAP! 911!! NEED 2 TALK NOW!!!

Her next text was to Ryan.

TAMMI JUST SHOWED ME AN ESCORT AD W/ MY PICS + CELL #. SHE DENIES POSTING IT. AM ATTACHING LINK 2 "SECRET FLING." THANK U.

Kate marched to her van, trying to get her emotions in check. Her world was falling apart, but there was no way she'd be late for this interview.

At 10:35, Kate sat in the little waiting room outside the sales manager's office, going over her notes again. She had done as much research about MG Uniforms as she could in one evening scouring the Web. The company had been in business for seventy-five years, starting as a textile factory and manufacturer of durable gear for farmers, then changing with the times to become a wholesale distributor of uniforms for fast-food restaurants. It had been glacially slow in upgrading its software, and that was good news for Kate. She had already formulated a plan to spin the negative of her outdated software knowledge into a positive. The office was only fifteen minutes from her house, which meant more time with the children—

"Ms. Gardner? Mr. Munson will see you now."

"Thank you, Stephanie." Kate had read in some employment guide to make a point of thanking the secretary, but today she did it out of empathy. She'd sat behind a desk exactly like that and been shocked by how invisible she'd felt.

Kate knew from her prep work that Dennis Munson was one of the firm's principals and had managed the sales department for years. His office was so cluttered, Kate had to walk past a stack of boxes to see him behind his desk. The balding older man pointed to a chair across from his desk as he adjusted his glasses, never taking his eyes off his computer screen. He frowned and held up a hand while pecking at the keyboard with the other one.

"One second. I need to respond to this." He typed with two fingers while Kate straightened her new skirt and tried not to look anxious.

After brief introductions, he asked Kate to go over her résumé. She launched into her well-rehearsed speech, careful to highlight her college background and awards.

Dennis frowned. "We're moving to a new Web-based portal and cloud reporting suite. I didn't hear you mention any experience with that."

Kate was prepared. "I worked for Wilson Packaging for three years during college, and they used the same RO Reports software that you're upgrading from. I know RO Reports backward and forward. I doubt any candidate walking through that door knows it like I do, and your expert has retired."

"You've done your research." He crossed his arms, clearly impressed. "But I need someone who knows the cloud. With this new system, we're looking for someone with a technical background to spearhead the rest of the staff."

Kate lifted her chin. "Respectfully, sir, I know where you're coming from, and I can lead your team in this transition. IT will handle the technical part of the upgrade. What you want is a bridge between the old system and the new one, somebody with a background in sales and marketing. I'm perfect to act in that role." She crossed her fingers. "The way I see it, my inexperience can be turned into an asset."

She could tell by the way Dennis leaned forward that he was interested. She mirrored his movements, following another suggestion from the interview guide.

"Your upgrade is still two months out. I'm going into the new system like one of your employees. So, as I learn, I will document what I go through. I will make sure the new system covers the same functions as the old one and that everybody understands how the changes work."

Dennis pressed his hands together, his fingertips forming a pyramid that he tapped against his chin. He was thinking about it, and from the slight bob of his head, she could tell that so far, he agreed with her assessment.

Kate glanced over his shoulder at the Army Strong plaque on the wall and the faded photograph of a group of soldiers. "I can be your first boots on the ground, doing recon." She almost added "sir," but decided that would be over the top.

He folded his hands behind his head and rocked back in his chair, nodding. "You make some good points, Kate."

She clamped her mouth closed. Another interviewing article mentioned that many job candidates actually talk themselves out of a job by overselling themselves—and right now she was looking good, so it was time to shut up.

Dennis took over, talking about the company and the direction it was headed. He spoke of five- and ten-year plans, but Kate was having a hard time focusing because he was talking to her in a way that made her feel like she was already an employee. She couldn't help projecting into the future, picturing coming in here every day, having her own office with a door, wearing professional attire, like the moms on TV—modern chasers of the American dream, struggling but perky.

Dennis was open and revealed a good head for business. She relaxed into the interview and responded quickly when he asked her questions, sometimes with a little humor. His enthusiasm was infectious, and when he mentioned the salary they were offering, based on her experience, she nodded coolly and said it was acceptable. It was much more than she'd hoped for.

With a broad smile he added, "Of course, that's just to start."

After a few more minutes, Dennis thumped one hand down on his desk and stood up. As he pumped her arm, his grin widened. "We still need to speak with some other candidates, but I do have to tell you, Kate, it's been a pleasure."

Kate was so happy she felt like she was floating two inches off the floor. It felt like accepting and signing the papers were only formalities. "The pleasure's mine."

"I'd like to wrap this up by next week, so we'll be in touch." She was almost out the door when he cocked his head to the side. "Gardner... You wouldn't happen to be related to Scott Gardner by any chance?"

She suddenly felt very hot and her Spanx bit into her flesh. "No, we're not related." Technically, it wasn't a lie, and she didn't want to admit that Scott was her ex.

"Just wondering. My niece just got engaged to a man named Scott Gardner. Small world."

Kate forced a smile. If Dennis spoke to Tammi, there was no way he'd hire Kate, and if he found out afterward...

His desk phone buzzed and the receptionist's voice came over the speaker. "Mr. Munson, sorry to interrupt. You have a call on line one. Your niece."

"We'll be in touch," Dennis said in a cheerful voice as he picked up the phone. "Well, speak of the devil, I was just talking about you, honey… Yes, that's right… You don't say." His smile faded and so did Kate's. "She's standing in my office right now."

Kate watched her dream job implode in a puff of smoke. She gave him a small nod, but he wasn't even looking at her now.

When she hurried past the reception desk, Stephanie smirked, and Kate realized she was a member of Tammi's coven. It was no coincidence that Tammi had called when she did. Like a real witch, she had her crows spying for her, and Stephanie had let Tammi know Kate was there.

Kate rushed out to the van, hopped inside, and started driving with her purse still slung over her shoulder. Her dream job hadn't died, it had been murdered. By the same woman who'd stolen her husband, created a humiliating ad, defaced her van, shamed her in front of the whole town, and plotted to take her children. The news that anyone had access to those pictures didn't change anything. Tammi was behind it all; Kate was certain of it. Her knuckles turned white as she gripped the steering wheel. Tammi was making good on her threat. She wouldn't stop until she'd destroyed everything that Kate had ever loved or possessed or hoped to achieve.

"I am officially in Hell."

Kate pulled over at the side of the road. Her head slumped forward until her forehead was resting against the steering wheel. She wanted to scream. So she did. It wasn't the mournful cry of the defeated, though. It was a battle cry that would have made Ava proud.

Kate may have lost that job, but there were other ones out there. And she knew someone else who was perfect for the one at MG Uniforms. Kate texted Susan. ANY WORD ON JOB U APPLIED 4?

I DIDN'T GET IT.

I'VE GOT ANOTHER LEAD 4 U.

Kate typed a long email and attached all her notes about MG Uniforms. She outlined exactly what Dennis Munson was looking for and ended the email with a warning to Susan not to mention that she knew Kate.

After hitting send, she made a note to herself to apply for the job that Susan hadn't gotten, before switching over to her messages and scrolling down the list of pornographic texts. Still nothing from Donna since she had gone on her date. Kate hit speed dial. Her friend had a lot of bad habits, but dropping off the face of the earth wasn't one of them. And regardless of the possibility, Kate was sure Donna had nothing to do with the fake escort ad. But she had to hear it from Donna herself.

"You are freaking me out now," Kate said when Donna's voicemail picked up. "I'm going to crash your work day and make sure you're okay."

Kate sped across town to the offices of Firewall Life Insurance. When she arrived at the building, she drove through the parking lot but didn't see

Donna's car. Kate pinched the bridge of her nose as her concern threatened to turn into full-blown panic. She parked in a visitor spot.

A girl who looked young enough to still be in high school sat at the front desk, twirling her hair. Kate recognized the look of sheer boredom.

"Hi, I'd like to speak with Donna Trucci, please."

"I haven't seen her today. Do you want to leave a message?"

"You haven't seen her all day?"

"Nope. But I'm not the regular receptionist. Can you hold on a second and I'll go check?"

"I'd appreciate that."

Kate paced in the foyer as the girl disappeared into a side office. Printed on the nameplate outside was *Gary Lewis, Manager*. A minute later, a bear of a man ambled out.

"Are you a friend of Donna Trucci's?" Gary wiped his hands together.

"Yes, and I haven't been able to reach her by phone, so I came here to speak to her."

"Donna's off today. Everything okay?"

Kate's back stiffened. "I don't know. I've been trying to get in touch with her and I'm getting worried. If she does contact you, please have her call me as soon as possible." She grabbed a pad of paper and a pen off the receptionist's desk and wrote down her name and number.

Gary exchanged a concerned look with the receptionist. "I will. I hope she's okay."

Kate nodded, but she was already heading for the door. "Thank you for your time."

The ride to Donna's apartment took less than ten minutes, but it felt like forever. Donna's car wasn't there either, and no one answered the door.

Kate got back into her car and headed for the last place she knew to look: the Gas-and-Go. Lori, Donna's friend and neighbor, was working the register.

"Have you seen Donna?" both women asked at the same time.

"I guess that's a no." Lori leaned against the checkout counter. "I was hoping she was staying with you because of your… situation."

Kate cringed. "Donna didn't stay with me. When's the last time you spoke with her?"

"Yesterday. With all the drama Donna went through with the divorce, I keep a close eye on her. I'm a little worried."

"Me too. Did she say anything about where she might be going?"

"Well, I don't want to sound paranoid, but there was a new guy who'd been texting her and they were supposed to hook up last night. I stayed up to ask her how the date went, but she didn't come home."

"Did she say who the guy was?"

"I don't think she mentioned his name."

"Can you check your messages? Maybe she texted it to you?"

"Good thinking."

After a couple of minutes of scrolling through her text messages, Lori shook her head. "Sorry. I don't see a name."

"Well, if she reaches out to you, please tell her to call me."

"I will. You too!"

Kate nodded and headed for the door. She drove across town to the Flagstaff Tavern, hoping someone there had seen Donna. She fired off another text and sped up. She frequently checked her rearview mirror and even took a few fast turns to see if she was being followed. Right now, if she did see her stalker, she'd run him over.

The tavern was empty except for the bartender. At night the little bar was too loud and too rough and tumble for Kate's taste, but Donna liked it, so Kate had been with her a few times. She recognized the bartender but didn't know his name.

"Hi."

"Sorry, we're closed." The bartender stopped slicing lemons. "We open at four."

"I'm trying to find a friend of mine, Donna Trucci. I'm worried about her."

"Donna?" He smiled. "She was in last night."

"Were you working then? Did you see her?"

"You can't miss Donna. That girl lights up a room like fireworks."

"Did you see who she was with?"

The bartender set his hand down flat on the bar. He pressed his lips together like he was debating whether to say what was on his mind. "I'm not judging, but Donna could do much better. She's not only out of that guy's league, it's like she's playing a different sport."

Kate took out her phone and opened the Speedy Dates email she had forwarded to Ryan. She pulled up the pictures of the five men she had talked with. "Which one of these guys was it?"

The bartender took his time looking at the photos. He scrolled through them twice before shaking his head. "None of them. The guy had a face that looked like someone'd hit it with a shovel. Flat."

"Do you know his name? Is he a regular?"

The bartender shook his head. "Never seen him before."

Kate glanced around the ceiling of the bar, searching for any cameras. "Do you have a security system?"

"Yeah." He chuckled. "I keep a twelve-gauge under the bar. No cameras if that's what you were asking."

She swallowed. "Was the guy she met short?" She prayed the bartender would nod, but he didn't.

"Big guy."

Kate's legs shook along with her hands as she took a bar napkin and wrote down her name and phone number. "If you hear from her or remember anything else about the guy, will you please call me?"

The bartender took the napkin, his bushy eyebrows knitting together. "I sure will. Please keep me posted. Donna is a doll. I hope she's all right."

"Me too."

The bartender swore. "I knew I should have said something to her. I got bad juju from that guy. He was really pouring on the good ol' boy routine."

Kate thanked him for his time and headed outside. A second later, the door banged open behind her and the bartender called out, "Hey! I remembered something. The guy was wearing a baseball cap. A blue one."

Kate was reading over the information she'd put on the missing person report one last time when Detective Mark Tills strolled into the police waiting room.

"Hello, Detective. Is Detective Daley in?" Kate asked hopefully.

"He's in court this week testifying on a case. But I'm glad you came in." He folded his hands in front of himself. "I had a couple of questions regarding your case."

"Certainly, but that's not why I'm here." She pointed to the form she was filling out. "My friend is missing."

"I'm sorry to hear that." He stepped closer and peered down at the form. "Missing persons are in my domain too. What's going on?"

"Her name is Donna Trucci. No one has heard from her or has been able to reach her since last night."

"Normally, we don't even start looking for a missing adult for seventy-two hours."

"This isn't a normal situation. Donna thought she could find out who my stalker is."

The detective crossed his arms, the wrinkles in his face deepening. "Please continue."

"She was convinced he's one of the men I met at the speed dating event. Last night, she was supposed to meet one of them at a bar, and I haven't heard from her since."

"That's why civilians should leave police work..." Tills clicked his tongue. "We've already interviewed all the men you spoke with on Speedy Dates. They've all been ruled out as suspects."

"Donna went to the Flagstaff Tavern and she met this guy. He—"

"Maybe they hit it off?"

"Donna's not the one-night-stand type."

"She could have just gone away for a couple of days. Does she have any family she might be staying with?"

"Only some distant cousins; she doesn't keep in contact with them. And I've checked with another friend of hers, Lori Delmonico—they're pretty close, and they're neighbors. Lori can't reach Donna either, and she didn't come home last night."

"Was Donna's car at her apartment?"

"No."

The detective's skeptical look faded a little. "Do you know the make and year?"

"A purple VW Bug. It's at least ten years old. Her license plate number starts with P-A-X, but I don't remember the rest."

"We can pull that from the Registry of Motor Vehicles. Did she mention any plans to go away?"

"No." Kate crossed her arms over her churning stomach as the real possibility that something ominous had happened to Donna began to sink in. "But see… she came up with this plan to catch my stalker."

Tills's eyes fluttered as if he were struggling not to roll them. "You said that Donna was supposed to meet with one of your previous dates but didn't. How do you know that?"

"I showed the pictures of the men from Speedy Dates to the bartender—"

"You did what?" The detective's voice rose.

"I… I didn't know which guy Donna had the date with, so I showed the bartender the profile pictures I had. But he said it wasn't any of them. He said it was a guy with a face that looked like it'd been hit with a shovel. A big guy. He was also wearing a blue baseball cap. The man on the drone videos was wearing a blue hat too."

"I'm glad you brought up that drone, Ms. Gardner. That was one of the questions I wanted to ask you. How come you never noticed it?"

"Excuse me?" Kate swallowed as she realized her stupid lie had resurfaced like a nasty rash.

"That drone was flying right over your head. You didn't see it?"

"Of course I did." Blood rushed to her throbbing temples as she scrambled to cover one lie with another. "I thought it belonged to some kids. Two of Andy's friends own them. I also saw a few at the soccer game. They're everywhere now." It sounded plausible to her.

Tills scratched his jawline with his thumb.

Kate changed the subject. "What about the perverted text messages I've been getting? Have you traced any of them?"

"We have. So far, all the men we interviewed said they only contacted you because of the escort ad. IT is still working on finding out where the ad was created."

"What about the flyers? The school has security cameras."

"It does, and we've reviewed the video from the day the flyers appeared. Unfortunately, the woman putting the flyers on the cars was wearing a long coat and a wide-brimmed hat, so her face was obscured."

Kate's head flinched back. Rising heat made her stomach flutter. "It was a woman? Not the stalker? Are you certain?"

Tills nodded. "Several witnesses reported the same thing, and video doesn't lie or get confused. It was a woman, about the same build as you."

"It *wasn't* me."

"No one said it was you. All I said was, she was your build."

"I was speaking with the school counselor when the flyers were put on the cars. I can't be in two places at the same time."

The detective's brows drew together and his face pinched. He took out his phone and flicked it with his thumb. "Your meeting with the counselor was over at three o'clock?"

Kate thought for a moment. "I believe so. I remember leaving the school when the bell rang."

"School gets out at three thirty. That's when the video shows you leaving. Did you go speak with anyone else after your meeting with the counselor?"

"The meeting with Dr. Green ran over, and then I went to the ladies' room. My stomach was very upset, if you must know." A sheen of sweat dampened her brow. "Wait. Are you investigating *me*? You're not thinking that I somehow snuck out of the school and put the flyers of myself on those cars, are you?"

"You are on video carrying a large shopping bag into the school. You don't have the bag when you exit."

"My son's school project was in that bag, not a coat and an oversized hat!"

"Please lower your voice, Ms. Gardner."

"My ex-husband's fiancée, Tammi Yates, had access to the pictures used in the flyers. She's my height."

"I'm aware. I spoke with Ms. Yates yesterday."

"And she of course denied it?"

"Vehemently. Tammi even offered to take a polygraph." Tills looked down at the missing person report. "Ms. Gardner, I do need to ask you…" He looked up and his expression softened. "Are you under psychiatric care?"

Kate inhaled slowly. She could only imagine the things Tammi had told the police about her. "I started seeing a therapist because I was going through a difficult divorce, yes."

"I was under the impression the divorce was finalized months ago."

"It was. I…" Kate closed her eyes and counted backward from five. "Is seeing a counselor against the law?"

"Of course not, but what I'm asking, Ms. Gardner, is…" He cleared his throat. "Believe me, I know how hard divorce can be. I've been through three of them myself. But could all this be your way of looking for help? If it is, you're not alone. There are resources—"

"Hold on." Kate held up a hand. "Are you suggesting I made this all up? Why would I do such a thing?"

"Are you on any medication for your mental health?"

"For anxiety. Someone is stalking me, Detective—I'd call that a cause for anxiety! I can't believe this. What about my van?"

"Let's try to calm down and look at the facts." Tills crossed his arms. "Your van was defaced, but it was parked in an area of the parking lot where none of the cameras saw who defaced it. And even though the lot was crowded, we haven't been able to track down a single witness. We got a police detail to watch your house, but the only person who saw anything suspicious was you. Last night a police officer on patrol reported that you accused a man of harassing you outside TJ Maxx. That man turned out to be a retired minister."

Kate's legs shook. The best proof she had that someone was actually stalking her was the videos from the drone, but her lie had screwed that all up. If she confessed to Detective Tills about the drone, he'd never believe that she didn't know the man following her.

"All I'm asking, Ms. Gardner, is whether or not everything you're telling us is true. If I was a cynic, I might look at the situation like this: You're feeling depressed and alone, so you gin up this idea of a stalker to get some attention. When that doesn't work out, you move on to your 'missing' friend." He made air quotes.

Kate shook her head and closed her eyes for a second. *I was wrong. Tammi is a great actress. She convinced Tills I'm a psycho—a needy, lonely kook. Does he actually think I'm so desperate that I fabricated the whole story?*

"Would you please clarify your last statement, Ms. Gardner." Tills looked at Kate with eyes rounded in concern.

She had uttered her thoughts aloud, again. Kate pictured Audrey's crystal glass smashing into a million little pieces in the sink. Something so beautiful shattered in an instant. Her life was like that glass. But she was done breaking. She stepped forward.

"You want to think I'm some crazy woman looking for sympathy and that I'm making this all up? You don't know me at all. I'm a good mother and I would *never* do anything that would scare my children as these stalking incidents have. While your opinion of me disgusts me, I will not have it impact my friend. Donna has nothing to do with any of this. She's missing and could be in trouble. I don't care what you think of me, Detective, just do your job and find her."

Tills took a step back and straightened his tie. "I'm going to look into your friend's disappearance. But you need to hear me loud and clear on this. If I find out that Donna's disappearance was staged, or that any of this stalker business was made up so you can get attention, I'll make sure the DA charges you with filing false police reports, and that's a felony."

"Find Donna, and then you can do whatever you want to me." Kate walked around Tills and shoved the door open. "Find my friend."

As her heels clicked down the cement steps, her fears about Donna rose. Detective Tills thought she was crazy, that was obvious, but what about Ryan? Her gut clenched.

Even if she told him the truth now, would he believe her?

13

Kate drove without paying any attention until halfway home, when she skidded to a stop at a red light. She seized the steering wheel in her hands, her arms thrust out straight, pushing herself back against the driver's seat. As she did so, a wave of panic swept over her. She could feel the darkness beckoning to her. It would be so easy, so easy to just lean into it, let it take her. Though passing out would only last a brief moment, it would be a reprieve.

Her marriage. The kids. Donna. Audrey. Her job. Her dignity. All in flames.

She had tried to run from the fire, but each door she opened provided more oxygen and brought her into a room blazing hotter than the last.

Just as she felt the final wave of dizziness, the moment before the black, her phone buzzed in her lap, bringing her to the light—another text from Lori.

ANYTHING FROM DONNA?

FILED MISSING PERSON REPORT. THEY'LL FIND HER.

"Find her?" Kate muttered. "They're probably not even looking."

The light changed, and Kate jammed the gas pedal to the floor. The minivan wined and chugged through the intersection. Once again, Kate realized that Tammi was the cause of her misery. From Tills's questions, Kate was sure Tammi had told him about Kate seeing a therapist. Had she also mentioned Kate's postpartum depression? Her panic attacks? All true, but out of context they sounded pretty bad. Tammi must have made it sound like no one should be surprised if one day Kate ran through town naked and screaming and killed everyone with an ax.

But I never confided any of my medical history to Tammi…

Kate's hurt shifted to righteous indignation. Scott must have betrayed Kate's confidence, along with their marriage vows. She pictured Scott and Tammi lying in bed together—Scott, his hands folded behind his head on the pillow, painting his verbal pictures, snide and sarcastic, picking apart all of Kate's weaknesses, insecurities, painful and embarrassing moments while Tammi laughed.

The tires of the minivan squealed as Kate turned onto her street. A jet-black Audi was parked in her driveway. She didn't know anyone who drove one except Marshall. Why would he be at her house? She parked next to the Audi and quietly closed the van door. From the custom pinstripe on the side, she was certain it was Marshall's car, but he wasn't inside. He wasn't standing on her porch either.

Then she heard it—noise from the back of the house.

Kate crept down the driveway, staying on the grass. What was he doing out back? The skin along her arm prickled with goosebumps, but all of her frustration and anger stiffened her spine. She noticed one of Scott's forgotten golf club's lying next to the sandbox. Ava had found the club in the garage. She liked to pretend she was Deborah driving the Canaanites out of the Promised Land with it. As quietly as she could, Kate picked up the discarded club with its slightly bent, rusted shaft and felt the weight of it in her hand.

This should do.

She tightened her grip, crept forward, and paused at the corner of the house.

Footsteps on wood. Someone was walking on the back deck.

Kate leaned around the corner.

Marshall stood on the deck, his hands cupped to his face and pressed against the glass of the slider, peering into her kitchen.

"You son of—" Kate's growl cut off her own words as she charged up to the base of the steps, raising the golf club over her head.

"Whoa, whoa! Kate, it's me, Marshall!"

"I know who you are. What I don't know is why you're trying to break into my house!"

"What? I'm not breaking in." His eyes darted to the steps and he took a step forward.

Kate climbed the steps to cut off any chance of his escape. "Then why are you at my back door?"

"I went to the front. I thought I heard you inside and I thought maybe you had headphones on or something. I need to talk to you. Please?" Marshall's voice rose high. His eyes were bloodshot and his hands were shaking.

She lowered the club slightly.

Marshall managed to put on a crooked salesman smile. "I need to ask you something. Please. Just between you and me. It's kind of awkward. Can you let me off the porch?"

"No offense, Marshall, but no. This is creepy. I didn't even know you knew where I lived."

"Fair enough. Look, I need to get that envelope."

Kate was tempted to hit Marshall with the golf club, and if he mentioned that stupid envelope again, she would, but he was clearly flustered and she was curious as to why.

"First," she said, "admit that you went into my purse."

"What? You're out of your mind."

Kate raised the club higher.

"All right, fine. Yes. I peeked. Because I—I need what's in that envelope. It's a USB stick."

"I told you, I never took your stupid envelope. Now get off my porch or I'm screaming for the police."

Marshall held his hands up. "Please. Can you think if you saw anyone else take it?"

Kate lowered the club as the answer to the mystery hit her right between the eyes. "Look, Marshall, I don't know what you're trying to put over on the company, but if anyone took the envelope, it had to be Mr. Berman."

Marshall went pale. "What makes you say that?"

"Mr. Berman may be many things, but stupid isn't one of them. If you're trying to pull a fast one—" Marshall opened his mouth, and Kate held up her hand and cut him off. "I don't want to hear what you did. It's your mess. But believe me, if you copied the client list or took a bid on the side…"

Marshall flinched. He took a step back. "It was only a few clients. Some ex-employees started up a business and asked if I'd join them. I thought I'd reach out to a couple of clients I knew weren't happy with TRX and make them an offer. They were on their way out the door anyway. What's the harm in that?"

"It's illegal. It's also a fireable offense." Kate scowled.

"But Berman doesn't know. If he did... why did he have Bruce search your purse?"

"Maybe he's gathering more proof against you and didn't want to tip his hand right then. He was going to fire me for falling asleep anyway. If you ask me, Berman has your envelope, and it's only a matter of time before he talks to you about it. Possibly with a lawyer and the police present."

Marshall pressed his hands to his eyes. A sob racked his body. Without another word, he shuffled down the steps and took off.

Kate set the golf club down on the back porch. Even though Marshall deserved whatever was coming to him, his misery didn't bring her any vindication. In fact, it was just sad that everyone seemed to be grabbing what wasn't theirs and trying to justify or cover up their indiscretions.

She waited until she heard Marshall start his car before she headed around to the front of what used to be her haven. Kate bounded up the front steps, opened the door, and locked it behind her, making sure the deadbolt clicked into place. She punched in the code to shut off the alarm. The keypad beeped once. She raised an eyebrow. Normally, it beeped twice. Had she done something wrong? She entered the code a second time and pressed the unlock button. Again, the alarm only beeped once.

"I'll have to check the stupid manual," Kate muttered.

The house was completely still and silent. No sounds of Andy screaming in excitement as he beat a level of his latest game, no sounds of Ava running around and talking in whatever accent matched her current character. No sounds at all. Nothing. Even the noise of the two kids fighting would be welcome. She grasped her chest, feeling a stab of pain, then checked her phone. Four more perverted texts, but nothing from Donna.

There was a text from Dr. Sprouse, however. He agreed she should cut back to her earlier dosage and wanted her to come and see him as soon as possible.

That would have to wait until she found Donna.

Kate kicked off her shoes and unfastened her bra as she headed through the living room. She pulled her bra out of her sleeve and tossed it on the couch as she mulled over her next move. If she didn't hear from Donna soon, she was going to start driving around and searching for her car.

With her new plan set, Kate headed up the stairs to change. She carefully hung her interview suit back up in its place. She picked out black jeans, a charcoal-grey shirt, and boots. The outfit matched her mood, and as she stared at herself in the mirror, she realized she looked a little tough. And that was exactly what she needed to be.

The doorbell rang. *Donna? Please be Donna!* She raced down the stairs.

"Where have you been?" she snapped as she whipped open the door.

Ryan stood there, his hair rumpled, his tie crooked, wearing no jacket against the chilly fall air. "Kate." He cleared his throat, his warm breath making fog, and his eyes searched hers. The stale smell of smoke from his shirt made her nose twitch.

"You smoke?" The words tumbled from her mouth.

"I quit years ago, but… I picked up a pack this morning." He ran his hand down his face and his jaw clenched.

She could almost feel the frustration emanating from him. "Are you okay? What's wrong?"

Ryan lowered his voice as he said, "I've been removed from the investigation. I wanted to tell you in person."

"What? Why?"

"Detective Tills and the sheriff believe that my feelings for you are impacting my impartiality."

Kate opened and closed her mouth twice before she found her voice. "But that's not true. Is it?"

Ryan stepped closer. The corners of his lips curved upward. "Actually, they're right."

Kate's pounding heart slowed to a deep, steady rhythm. His admission simultaneously sent her over the moon and caused a peace to wash over her. She opened the door wider and stepped aside.

Ryan stood his ground. "I need to caution you that while I'm not on this case, I'm still an officer of the law."

She gave a one-shouldered shrug. "At this point, I'll take my chances. I really need to talk to you." She led him into the living room.

"I heard about your friend. I put out an APB on her car before I was taken off the case."

Kate grabbed his hand. The fact that he believed her and was helping to find Donna made it hard not to leap into his arms. "Donna promised she'd call me. She always keeps her promises. I'm so worried…" Her lip trembled.

Ryan pulled her close. He held onto her and she let go of her pain and cried. Tears rolled down her face as he rubbed her back, silently reassuring her that everything was going to be okay.

Kate dried her eyes and stepped back. "Sorry about that."

"Don't be." Ryan brushed another tear away from her reddened cheek. "You've been through a lot."

"I have to tell you something." She swallowed. "You've heard that expression 'The truth shall set you free,' right?"

He nodded warily.

"The drone—"

"Is yours."

"What? How did you know?"

"The lab enhanced the video footage. Not enough to identify the stalker, but in one of the shots, you looked up. When you did, the drone moved. That, and I interviewed your friend Donna."

"Donna wouldn't have told you."

Ryan smiled lopsidedly. "No, but she went way over the top trying to make it clear to me that the drone was in no way, shape, or form yours. The line 'The lady doth protest too much, methinks' came to mind."

Kate sighed. Although her friend wanted to be an actress, keeping secrets wasn't one of her strengths. "Does Detective Tills know?"

"Methinks he suspects," Ryan said with a crooked smile. "But I'm the one who reviewed the videos. And I haven't told him—yet. I wanted to talk to you first. Why did you lie?"

"Because I'm a coward." She motioned to the couch and Ryan sat down. She sat on the opposite end, even though she wanted to cling to him right now. "It all started at Andy's soccer game. I was reviewing the drone for a freelance writing job. A friend of mine is an editor for a tech magazine and she gave me the gig as a favor. Anyway, I put the drone in follow mode and forgot it was even there. It ran out of juice and hit me in the head. I was lying on the ground with my dress up around my waist and my self-respect around my ankles. I was beyond embarrassed, so I lied when everyone asked whose drone it was. And that lie grew…" She was tempted to point out that Scott, acting as her lawyer, had advised her to lie, but she wouldn't do that to him. It was her lie and she'd own it.

Ryan nodded but remained silent.

"I'm sorry. I thought you wouldn't believe me about everything else if you knew I'd lied once."

"The police get a bad rap about that," he said. "We're human. We understand. I understand."

Kate reached for his hand but stopped herself. "Do you believe me?"

"I do. Even if the drone is yours, someone is following you." He stood up, running both his hands through his thick hair.

The invisible barrier between them was palpable. He was trying to help her, but he could only do so much without risking his job. She had to cross her arms so she wouldn't reach out for him. Something about him drew her to him, and from his posture, she thought the feeling was mutual. Ryan's whole body was leaning toward her, his arms slightly raised, as if at any moment he'd spring forward and wrap her in another comforting embrace. She wanted to lean into him but didn't trust anything anymore, least of all herself. They stared at each other, together yet opposed, pulling and pushing with their eyes.

"I can't believe I'm going to say this," Ryan said, "but for right now, don't say anything about the drone to Detective Tills."

"Why not?"

"Because he doesn't believe you. About anything." Ryan started pacing. "I told you he's like an old hunting dog, but the problem is, he caught the scent of that lie about the drone and now he won't let it go. He sees all the evidence through tinted glasses. And that puts you in real danger, because someone really is after you."

"What about Donna? Is Detective Tills looking for her?"

"I think Donna could be in danger too. We need to find her."

Kate's fingernails bit into the palms of her hands. "Well, let's get busy. I'll go grab my purse."

Ryan nodded. "I'll drive."

She practically flew up the stairs. The freedom that came with confession had liberated her, and hearing that Ryan had feelings for her had given wings to her determination to find Donna. She hurried through her office and then into the bedroom. Her purse was on the floor next to the dresser. She bent to grab it, but when she straightened up, the room spun. The blood rushing to head made her lose focus. She felt for the edge of the bed and slumped down. Pressing her palms to her eyes, she rocked slowly as a wave of nausea washed over her.

I have to see Dr. Sprouse. This is ridiculous.

Ryan was waiting for her downstairs, but she couldn't risk standing without throwing up. She sat there slowly rocking until the feeling passed.

A loud thump sounded from downstairs.

"Ryan?" Kate called out.

Silence.

She lurched to the top of the staircase and peered down. Had he gone out to his truck?

The front door was closed. She made her way down the stairs.

"Ryan?"

The sound had come from the back of the house. Had he seen something outside? Had he gone out the back door to go check?

As she walked down the hallway toward the kitchen, a putrid smell hit her. Puzzled, she continued forward, wondering if she'd left something on the counter that had spoiled. But her kitchen didn't smell like rotten food, it smelled like the corner of a subway station. The reek of body odor mixed with stale cigarettes made her gag, and fear pinned her feet to the floor.

Ryan was lying on the kitchen tiles face down. His eyes were closed and blood streamed from his scalp and down his cheek. He groaned softly.

Ryan! Kate willed her legs to move toward him, but her feet stayed firmly planted. Someone had toppled her white knight. Ryan was large, strong, and had a gun, yet he now lay unconscious on the floor. She had to run. She needed to go get help.

A shadow in the far corner of the room next to the window shifted. She screamed. A tall man wearing a blue baseball hat, light-brown jacket, jeans, and work gloves stepped forward. The odor emanating from his unwashed clothes made her eyes burn. His scruffy beard did little to hide the scabs on his face. Kate had seen enough meth heads on TV to spot one in real life.

The man ran his tongue over rotting teeth. He squinted like he was having trouble focusing on her, then smiled.

"Kate? I'm ready to help you now." He had a deep, rich voice that should have belonged to a radio announcer. It didn't fit him at all and added to the surrealism of the moment.

Run, Kate. Run. Why couldn't she move? She was going to die.

"Please, leave me alone. Just go." Her voice was a thin whisper, but she was surprised any sound came out at all.

The man's smile widened. "You won't worry about a thing after I help you." He stepped forward, the rusted golf club clasped in his hand.

The bathroom was only a few feet behind her. She took a step back. "I don't need your help."

His eyes skittered around and back to her. "It's okay. I understand. Life is hard. So hard. It's better this way." He took another step toward her.

She glanced at the flimsy bathroom door. No, she wouldn't be safe there. She needed to get out of the house.

Kate held up her hand as if she were warding off a dog. She did her best to summon the withering look her mother-in-law used like a Jedi power. "Stay where you are! Drop that golf club!"

The man stopped and opened his fingers, and the club clattered on the tile.

A spark of hope flashed in her chest.

The man reached into his jacket pocket. "Close your eyes." The glint of metal in his hand made Kate's knees shake. "I'll make it real fast." He raised a long hunting knife. "You won't feel anything."

Kate grabbed a family portrait in a heavy frame from the wall and flung it at his head. As he ducked, she darted for the living room, screaming as she ran. She only made it a few feet before he caught her by the hair. She cried out in pain. He yanked her back toward him and right off her feet.

Please, God. No.

Kate's hands closed around his thick wrist as she dangled, her feet swinging inches above the floor. It felt like he was scalping her. Her scream mixed with the shattering of wood and glass as he slammed her into the coffee table.

She landed on her side, and he fell on top of her, squeezing the wind from her lungs. This was it. This was how she would die.

Nothing happened. She looked at his hands. Empty. No knife. She breathed. No knife.

Like a panicked bird, his eyes darted around the room. He squinted toward the TV. The knife lay out of reach of his long arms.

She screamed again and struggled to get up.

He rolled her onto her back and grabbed her throat with both hands, leaning forward, using his weight to try to crush her windpipe. The leather from his work gloves creaked as he tightened his fingers.

Audrey's voice echoed inside Kate's pounding head. *I want you to fight, Kate.*

And like an erupting volcano, all the years of bottled-up pain spewed forth. A fire raged in her. She thrust her knee upward into the man's groin. His eyes bulged out, and she jammed both thumbs into her new targets. The man howled in pain, releasing her throat to cover his face.

Shrieking, Kate kicked and scratched her way out from underneath him. As he tried to scramble to his feet, she searched the floor for something, anything to use as a weapon. Her fingers touched a coaster, a television remote control, then closed around a heavy hardcover book. She seized it with both hands and used it like a sledgehammer, bashing him repeatedly over his head until the binding cracked.

He collapsed to the floor. He was still alive, but he wasn't moving.

Kate was breathing heavily and blood trickled down the side of her face as she stared down triumphantly at her tormentor. The man who'd been hunting her lay defeated at her feet. She'd vanquished her enemy, just like Joan of Arc, but instead of a sword she had used—a crooked smile crossed her face when she saw the title—*The Power Is in Your Hands.*

It was the best advice she'd ever gotten from a self-help book.

Kate woke up in a hospital bed and reached for the nurse call button. Everything after the attack was a blur. Calling 911. Trying to wake Ryan. The police arriving, along with an ambulance. The paramedics placing Ryan on a stretcher. The EMTs had wanted to take her in a separate ambulance, but she'd insisted on riding to the hospital with Ryan. They were whisked to Mercy General with sirens blaring. Then she was scanned and x-rayed, cleaned up, and put to bed.

The door opened and a nurse hurried in. "Are you all right?" she asked as she glanced at the machine beside Kate's bed.

"Rya—" Kate's throat burned as she tried to talk. Remembering the beast who'd tried to crush her windpipe, she was surprised she could speak at all. "Ryan Daley. Is he okay?"

"He's in ICU."

"Is he awake? Can I speak with him?"

The nurse's face was pinched. "Let me check with the doctor. How are you feeling?"

Kate's hand went to her sore throat. Other than that and the tender left side of her rib cage where she'd hit the table, she felt all right. "I'd really like to know about Ryan."

The nurse nodded. "I'll see what I can do."

Kate lay quietly, listening to the periodic beeps of the monitor beside her. The thin hospital blanket provided little warmth and no comfort. In the distance, doctors and nurses were going about their business. Her room had a strong smell of disinfectant. Who had been in the bed before her? What had they been suffering from?

More questions swirled in her head. Who was the man who attacked both her and Ryan? How had he gotten inside her house? Why did he want to kill her?

The nurse tapped on her door and poked her head in. "You have a visitor," she announced before retreating.

Detectives Tills entered the room. His mask of neutrality was firmly in place. He appeared stoic and all business as he marched over to the bed and took out his phone.

"Ms. Gardner, this is an official visit." Tills's voice was a monotone and, although softer than usual, still loud enough to make Kate's head hurt. "I'm aware this isn't a good time, but would you be able to answer a few questions?"

Kate nodded, wincing as she tried to pull herself higher up in the bed.

Detective Tills pressed a button on his phone and stated the date, his name and title, and then Kate's full name. "Ms. Gardner, you are aware that this conversation is being recorded?"

"I am. Is Ryan okay?"

He didn't look at her while he spoke. "He has a fractured skull. The good news is it's a linear fracture and there isn't any swelling of his brain. He's in stable condition. The doctors should know more soon, but they're hopeful." The detective met her gaze. "Why was he at your home yesterday?"

Kate blinked rapidly. Yesterday? How long had she been sleeping?

"Take your time." He handed Kate a glass of water, which she eagerly drank even though it hurt to swallow.

Ryan said he was taken off the case. Will he get in trouble at work for being at my house?

Through the fog of painkillers, Kate tried to come up with something. She was done lying, but she wasn't going to shove Ryan under the bus. "I forwarded him more texts. He wanted to explain to me that I should be sending all information to you from now on."

Tills nodded, his expression unchanged. "Would you please explain the events surrounding the attack? Start from the moment you arrived."

Slowly, and with significant discomfort, both physical and mental, Kate relayed everything that had happened after she got home till the time the ambulance arrived. He asked only a few clarifying questions.

Trying to quench the burning in her throat, she downed another glass of water. "Donna?" Her voice cracked. "Did you ask him about Donna?"

"We haven't interviewed the suspect yet."

"Why not?"

"He's not capable of providing a statement at this time," Tills said, then paused. "His name is Derek Benson. Do you know him?"

Kate shook her head. "Did you ask at the—" She coughed. She took another sip of water, but it wasn't extinguishing the flames in her throat any longer. "At the bar?"

"We're checking on that. We showed the suspect's picture to the bartender at the Flagstaff, but he wasn't able to say if the suspect was the same man he saw leaving with Donna. You really did a number on Derek," the detective said. "He's got two black eyes and a broken nose. His mother would have a hard time recognizing him."

Kate opened her mouth to ask when they'd be able to interview him, but her words were cut off by a coughing fit. She sipped more water and settled back on the bed.

"One last question, Ms. Gardner. Your new security system was shut off—including all the cameras. Why?"

"I shut the alarm off when I came in, like I usually do, but I thought the cameras would stay on…"

"But are you certain the alarm was on when you first came in?"

Kate grimaced. "I turned it on when I left. I'm sure of that. But when I came in and entered the code, it only beeped once. I think it should've beeped twice. That's what it had been doing."

Tills stared down at her, the lines in his face deepening.

"The alarm system was recently installed," Kate explained. "Maybe I messed it up?"

He cleared his throat. "Thank you for your time, Ms. Gardner. I'll let you get some rest now." He turned and headed for the door.

As soon as the door clicked shut, Kate clamped her eyes closed and prayed for Ryan. He was hurt because of her. Tills had said the doctors were hopeful, but what did that mean? She touched her bruised throat. Even the grumpy detective had to know her story was true now. The proof was written all over her body. She took another sip of water and her thoughts turned to Donna. Where was she?

Kate looked around the room for her phone and finally checked the drawer of her nightstand. There it was, along with a Bible and a pack of tissues. There weren't any messages from Donna. She gritted her teeth and glared at the harsh ceiling light. Something horrible had happened. Kate was certain of it. Donna would not disappear like this.

Someone tapped on the door and it slid open.

"Hey, Kit." Scott hurried over to the bed, a large Styrofoam cup in his hand. His eyes were red and his lips were mashed together in a thin line.

Despite her own pain, Kate's nurturing instinct kicked in. Scott was a crier. "It looks way worse than it is."

He moved to the side of the bed, setting the cup on the table. His hand hovered over her body like he was unsure where to touch.

Kate took his hand. "Thank you for coming."

He picked the cup up. "Vanilla milkshake? I thought something cold might help."

Kate's hand froze as soon as she touched the drink. *How did he know about my throat?*

"I came as soon as I got the call," Scott continued. "You were being treated, so they wouldn't let me see you then. The doctor told me you'd been strangled. He doesn't think there'll be any long-term damage, though."

Groggy from medication, Kate still realized why he must have been notified. "You're still listed as my emergency contact."

Scott squeezed her hand. "I'll always be here for you."

Her eyes narrowed. "Yeah, here today, concerned, and gone tomorrow with full custody." She didn't think she'd spoken her thought aloud, but she must have because Scott shook his head.

"I don't want to fight. Not now. With everything that you've gone through…" He stroked the back of her hand.

He looked sincere. Whether or not it would last, she didn't know, but a truce to all the bickering sounded great to her.

"I was hoping you'd bring the kids."

"I thought I should wait to bring them in, and no offense, but I think I made the right call."

Kate chuckled, and it hurt her ribs. "Have you told them?"

"Yeah. I told them their mommy caught the bad guy." He smiled.

Kate was taken aback. He looked proud of her. Really proud, not some false or halfway placating.

I did. I caught the bad guy.

"The cops arrested him," Scott continued, "but that's all they would tell me. Do you know the guy?"

She opened her mouth and cringed. Scott handed her the milkshake. Despite the cold, it still hurt to swallow.

A knock on the door made Kate glance up. She expected the doctor, but instead, Detective Tills walked in. His usual gruff manner was gone, and that scared Kate to the core.

"Ms. Gardner. Mr. Gardner."

Scott shook the detective's hand.

"I apologize for interrupting your visit, but I need to speak with Kate."

"Of course." Scott gave Kate's arm a gentle squeeze. "I'll stop by with another milkshake tomorrow."

Kate waved as Scott left the room. She was grateful for the gesture but glad he'd left. Detective Tills's unexpected return and change in demeanor made her uneasy.

"There's been a development," the detective said. "They've located Donna Trucci's car, parked behind Poets' Cafe." He paused. "I'm afraid there were signs of a struggle inside the vehicle. They recovered a phone, earrings, and one shoe at the scene. A woman's shoe, size seven. Do you happen to know what size shoe your friend Donna wears?"

Kate's lips moved, but no sound came out. She cleared her throat, trying to loosen the grip of fear on her tongue. She and Donna often traded shoes; they wore the same size.

"Seven."

The machine monitoring her vital signs sounded its alarm.

The first rays of the sun peeking through the windows announced the end of Kate's sleepless night. In spite of the medication, she'd stared at the ceiling all night long, two questions repeating over and over in her mind: Where was Donna? Why hadn't the police been able to get that information out of Derek?

She checked her phone, now clogged with filthy texts, but of course there wasn't one from Donna—they'd found her phone in her abandoned car.

Lori had texted Kate, but she still hadn't heard anything either.

During an early-morning visit from her doctor, Kate was surprised when he announced that she could go home. Delighted she could leave the hospital, even if her ribs ached like she'd been kicked by a horse and her throat was black-and-blue, she dressed quickly.

The nurses hadn't been able to give her an update on Ryan, and she was determined to find out how he was. She finished signing the last of the discharge papers and followed the signs to ICU. The unit was shaped like an octagon with the nurses' station in the middle. Next to one of the patient's rooms, a uniformed policeman sat in a chair.

Kate walked over and the officer stood up. "Good morning. I'm Kate Gardner. I'd like to see Detective Daley."

The cop shook his head. "Detective Daley isn't allowed any visitors at this time."

"Excuse me?" A nurse strode over. "Can I help you?"

Kate held up her arm with the hospital band still around her wrist, hoping it would come off like some form of ID. "I was admitted with Ryan. The same man attacked us."

The nurse's expression softened, but the police officer stepped in front of the door.

"Detective Daley isn't allowed any visitors at this time."

"He's sedated," the nurse explained. "He needs to get some rest, and it looks like you do too. How about you come back later, okay?"

Kate stood there staring at the closed door. Because of HIPPA, there was no way she could get an update on Ryan's condition because she wasn't a relative. But Kate was done rolling over. "I just want to know if he's okay. If you could give me a minute to speak with him—"

The policeman held his hand out but didn't touch her. "I'm going to ask you to step away now, ma'am."

Everyone in the ICU turned to stare.

Kate inhaled slowly and was about to demand to speak with a doctor when she noticed a plaque on the wall thanking all the donors for the new ICU. Audrey Rochester was listed first.

"You're right." Kate smiled at the nurse. "I do need to get some rest. When Ryan's awake, please tell him that I'm praying for him."

The nurse took a step back and gave a slow smile. "I certainly will."

Kate headed back through the maze of corridors, following the signs for the main entrance. She was almost to the exit when her phone rang. Noticing the call was from Detective Tills made the blood rush to her head.

"Did you find Donna? Is she okay?"

"We still haven't located your friend, but I need to ask you some follow-up questions. Would it be okay if I stopped by the hospital?"

"Actually, I was just discharged. I was about to call a cab."

"I can have a car pick you up and bring you by the station. They'll drop you off at home when we're done."

Kate would rather pour salt in her eyes than answer more questions at the police station, but if it would help find Donna, she'd do it.

Five minutes later, a patrol car picked her up and drove her across town to the police station. The officer parked out front. Kate made her way carefully up the cement steps as Detective Tills held the front door open.

"Thank you for coming. How are you feeling?"

She tried not to make a face. Her raw throat burned, her side was bruised and tender to the touch, and she reeked of the hospital. All she wanted to do was take a shower, but she shoved those feelings aside. "I want to help find my friend. Did Derek say anything about Donna?"

"We can discuss that inside."

Detective Tills led her down a long hallway. He swiped an access pass and continued along another corridor before holding open a door.

Kate paused in the doorway. She'd seen enough police shows to recognize an interview room, and this one came complete with a two-way mirror.

"The conference rooms are booked," Tills said, possibly picking up on her rising anxiety. "Sorry about the formalities. It's the nature of the job now. I need to dot all the i's, cross the t's, you know…" He sat on one side of the table and motioned to the chair opposite him.

Kate sat. "I understand," she said, fighting the growing realization that she didn't understand at all.

"Would you like some water?" He offered one of the two water glasses on the table to her, then pressed a button on a metal box. "My name is Detective Mark Tills, and I'm speaking with Katherine Gardner." He proceeded to read a formal interview opening from a card, filling in the date, time, and other details as he went. Then he laid the card on the table, reached over, and picked up a fresh notepad from the small pile next to the wall.

"Did you interview Derek? Did he say anything about Donna?"

"Derek denied ever seeing Donna. We ran some previous mugshots of him by the witnesses from the bar. They all said the guy Donna left with wasn't Derek."

Kate slumped in the chair.

Tills reached over and removed a piece of paper from a folder. He turned his head and spoke to the recorder. "Now showing Ms. Gardner the photo array."

Kate stared down at the photos of eight men on the page. She immediately touched the one of the man who'd attacked her. "That's him. Number four."

"Ms. Gardner identified suspect number four."

"You found him at my house. Why do I have to identify him? Is he denying that he attacked me?"

"No, he isn't." The detective put the paper back into the folder, leaned back in his chair, and crossed his arms. "He confessed. But, Ms. Gardner, I need to ask you again, have you ever met Derek Benson before?"

"No. I've never seen him before the attack."

"Never spoken with him?"

"No. I'm positive, I've never seen him, I've never talked to him. He was the guy following me, right?"

"He confessed to that too."

"If he confessed, why are you asking me all these questions?"

"We're trying to determine *why* he was following you."

"How am I supposed to know that? Ask him."

"We did."

Kate waited.

So did the detective.

An uncomfortable silence settled on the room.

Kate didn't know if it was the painkillers or lack of sleep, but her head was spinning.

The silence continued.

Then Kate sat forward, placing both her hands flat against the table. "What did he say?"

Tills reached over and picked up a different notepad, this one covered with a hastily scrawled script. He removed a pair of reading glasses from his pocket, put them on, and read silently. After a few moments, he removed the glasses and set them down. He fixed Kate with his gaze like he was studying her.

"Derek said you asked him to do it."

Kate coughed as her sore throat clenched. "What? That's crazy!"

"Actually"—Tills leaned back in his chair and crossed his arms—"he said you wanted him to kill you and make it look like a stalker did it."

Kate sputtered again. She took another sip, but her hand was shaking so much, drops hit her chin and landed on the table. "He's on drugs, insane, or both."

"Have you ever been in or in the immediate vicinity of the Love Hut?"

"The adult store? No."

Tills jotted down her answer on the fresh notepad.

"Why would I ask him to murder me?"

"Derek said you wanted to commit suicide but couldn't do it yourself. He said you offered to pay him a thousand dollars to make it look like a random attack."

Despite the pain in her throat, Kate laughed. "Your entire theory is beyond absurd."

Tills tapped the notepad with his pen. He scanned his notes, then flipped to another page and read from it. "'She wanted me to do it at her house when the kids weren't there.'" He paused for a minute, his eyes scanning the report. "He insists you gave him two hundred dollars and promised him another eight once he… completed his task."

Kate leaned forward triumphantly. "How was I supposed to pay him after I was dead?"

"I wondered the same thing. Derek said the other eight hundred would be in your purse. He said there's a hole in the lining."

The hairs on the back of her neck stood on end. The story was bizarre, yet Derek's description of her purse was at least partially accurate. The lining was ripped. It made her want to check her purse right now.

The detective leveled his gaze at Kate. "It's a helluva story."

"You can't believe him," Kate said as loudly as her bruised throat would allow. "The only truth that has come out of his mouth is that he stalked me and tried to kill me."

Tills tipped his head to one side. "There's something that's niggling away up here." He tapped his temple with his index finger. "Normally, suspects lies aren't as detailed. They like to keep them vague. So all these details are making me think." His eyes flicked down to her purse on the floor. "Would you mind if I took a look?"

"Of course not." Kate handed the purse over. "It does have a rip in the lining, but I'd be lucky if there was twenty dollars in there."

Her interrogator appeared to relax a bit. "Thank you for understanding. I need to rule it out."

Kate pulled her shoulders back and nodded.

He opened her purse and shoved his fingers through the hole in the lining. The stitches snapping as they broke sounded like gunshots in the little room. He pressed his lips into a thin line.

Kate felt as though the floor had dropped beneath her when he lifted out eight folded hundred-dollar bills. "Those are not mine."

"They're in your purse."

"Believe me, I'm as surprised as you are."

"Still, the money was right where Derek said it was going to be."

"Maybe he planted it there. He was stalking me."

Tills nodded as though he were considering what she said, but Kate felt as if she were watching a play and he was an actor waiting for his cue. He even stroked his chin.

"I can see that," he said, "but in order for me to believe that, I would have to believe that Derek—who, as you may have guessed, has a serious meth addiction—took eight hundred dollars and, instead of making a mad dash to his dealer, placed that money in your purse so I could find it." The detective's face twisted in theatrical confusion. "I'm not following that logic."

Kate spoke firmly but still had trouble modulating her raspy voice. "I don't know his motive, and I didn't know the money was in my purse."

"No clue?"

"None."

"Is it a new purse?"

"Yes. Well, it's from Goodwill so it's used, but it's new to me. I've had it for a few weeks."

Tills scratched the base of his jaw. "Kate, I want to believe you, but there again, you also said you didn't know the money was there. My wife, she's always going into her purse. It can't fit everything she needs, she says. So she's always organizing it. Zipping, opening, buttoning... Sometimes she dumps everything out and puts it all back in, and by the end of the day, boom! Everything is back on the kitchen table and she's trying to find a spot for it again."

Kate wanted to ask him if that was wife number four but bit her tongue. "So you're saying because I'm a woman, I should know everything that's in my purse? Including underneath the lining?"

He held up his hand as though it were a gun and bent his thumb. "Bingo."

"How many bullets are in your gun?" Kate asked.

Tills stiffened. "Fifteen rounds."

"Well, my ex-husband owns a gun, and he couldn't tell you how many bullets it holds. He didn't even know that a bullet stayed in the chamber until he accidentally shot it into the ceiling one time. So, just because I'm a woman, don't assume that I should know someone stuck eight folded bills underneath the lining."

"Fair enough," he said. "Ex-husband has a gun." He wrote it down, then chuckled. "What did you do after he shot the ceiling?"

"I wouldn't let him keep it loaded anymore."

Tills chuckled again, then turned thoughtful. "Listen, Kate. Look at it from my side. Derek tells me where you put the money, and there it is. Do you have any other explanation for how it ended up in your purse? Has anyone else been in your purse?"

Kate's eyes widened. "Yes. Marshall Whitman. I'm certain of it. He confessed."

He wrote the name down. "How do you know Marshall?"

"I worked with him." She told the detective everything that had happened, from when she'd come into work and Marshall had accused her of taking the envelope, to leaving her purse at her desk and then discovering Marshall there, to getting fired and finding Marshall on her back porch.

Tills took sporadic notes. When Kate was done speaking, he tapped the pen against the pad of paper. "Okay, if I'm understanding you correctly, you now think that Marshall put the money in your purse. And Marshall and Derek are connected... how?"

Kate shook her head. "Connected? No. I don't... You asked me if anyone else had been in my purse and Marshall had."

"So Marshall just happened to put eight hundred dollars in your purse, and Derek, who doesn't know Marshall, knew it was there?"

"That doesn't make any sense." Kate rubbed her now-throbbing temples.

"I agree." Tills sighed, then looked at Kate with what seemed like genuine concern. "Kate, is it possible that Derek's telling the truth here? Maybe with the divorce and these other things I'm hearing about, this is your way of crying for help? Your ex-husband told me about your sister."

At the mention of Emma, Kate winced. "I would never commit suicide." The thought of her abandoning Ava and Andy raised her ire in a way that being fired or stalked or threatened couldn't touch. "I have two children and would never leave them alone in this world. Never."

Tills frowned.

"Detective, professionally, how many cases have you seen where someone hires a homeless man to kill them?"

He shrugged. "This would be a first."

"I don't know anyone who, instead of choosing something reportedly painless like pills or carbon monoxide poisoning, would opt to be hacked to death with a rusty knife in their own kitchen. Do you?"

"Maybe you thought you could call it off?"

Kate pointed to the bruising on her neck. "I did a poor job of that then."

Tills crossed his arms. "Okay. Let's pretend I believe y—"

"But you don't believe me."

"Try to see how this looks from my point of view. If you never spoke to Derek, how does he know so much about you? How did he know how to shut off your security system?"

"I don't know. But I'm not lying."

"Do you know what would go a long way to convincing me that you're telling the truth? A polygraph. Would you be willing to take one, and then we can know if you knew Derek or not?"

"I would be happy to." Kate sat forward. "I've never met the man before." Her hope soared. Why hadn't the detective mentioned it earlier? A lie detector was perfect. They'd have to believe her then.

"Wonderful. It'll take about half an hour to set up. Easy questions. Had you ever met Derek? Did you know about the money in the purse? Had you ever seen that drone before? That kind of thing."

At the mention of the drone, Kate's heart thumped against the wall of her chest. She was grateful she was sitting down because she would have surely swooned.

Grandma Barnes, you were so right.

"See, I have a real issue about that drone," he continued. "Derek is a homeless addict. I can't believe that he owns a high-tech drone, which he used to track his victim. You see my problem?"

Kate groaned inwardly. The stupid drone. But if she confessed the drone was hers now, the police wouldn't believe another word out of her mouth, polygraph or no polygraph. Ryan himself had told her not to mention it to Tills.

"Half an hour?" Kate stood. "I'm afraid I can't wait that long."

"Relax. I'll see what I can do to speed things up."

"Well, the fact is, all this excitement has left me quite nauseous."

"Do you need a trash can? Should I call an EMT?"

"No. I'm… I think I need to go home and lie down."

"There's a private lounge near the captain's office. You can lie down there."

"No…" Kate put her hand on her stomach and shook her head. "I need to go home. I was just discharged from the hospital, for goodness' sake."

Tills's expression hardened. "So for the record, you're now refusing to take a polygraph?"

"Until I feel better." Kate's stomach flipped as she hurried to the door. And just like that, she'd gone from superhero to prime suspect in her own attempted murder.

Two hours after the police unceremoniously dropped her off, Kate paced her living room like an angry hornet in a glass jar. She glared at her phone. Where was Donna? Derek was behind bars, but her friend was still missing. Why couldn't the police get him to talk?

Kate resumed pacing. She had asked Audrey if she could find out anything about Ryan's condition but hadn't heard back from her. Kate's arms felt heavy and a chill shuddered through her, making her whole body tremble. She recognized the feeling. Like the first gentle snowflakes before a blizzard, it signaled a panic attack coming on. Soon, her hands would be tingling and then grow numb, her heart would race, and the bands would tighten around her chest so she couldn't breathe.

She had stopped taking the little yellow pills, but in any case, they'd be useless against the typhoon coming on. There was another way. She stalked into the kitchen and ripped open the liquor cabinet, which had remained almost untouched since the married era, when she and Scott had entertained a lot. She grabbed a bottle of Scott's prized scotch and a glass. She poured half a glass and took a long sip. The liquor burned her sore throat and a coughing fit tore it to shreds.

How does Audrey drink this straight?

She clearly wasn't a grande dame yet, but she wouldn't give up. She had beaten one problem; she'd pound this new dilemma into submission too. *I'm done being a doormat.* Kate looked at the brown liquid as if it were cough syrup, then forced the rest down in one gulp. With her throat on fire, she gritted her teeth and pitched the tumbler into the wall as hard as she could, trying to channel her mother-in-law's grit. She expected the cheap glass to break like the good crystal had, in a dramatic, sparkling shower. Instead, it punched a hole through the drywall and got trapped somewhere inside the wall between the kitchen and the living room.

Kate stared at the crater and swore.

Someday, Ava will be renovating this kitchen, find the glass in the wall, and say, "This is the glass Mom threw when she was pretending to be a badass."

Kate laughed. What would Audrey think of this pathetic attempt? But, as usual, thinking of Audrey automatically made Kate stand up straighter and try to gather what few wits she had. She had told Ryan about the drone, and he believed her. If she confessed to Tills that the drone was hers, then took the polygraph, would he see she hadn't been lying about knowing Derek? Or would confessing seal her fate?

Kate hadn't eaten anything all day, but how could she? She sat in her darkened living room scrolling through the latest harassing text messages, which had slowed to a trickle.

A new text came in from Scott. From the tone it was evident that whatever sympathy she'd earned from him because of the attack was now gone.

COMING OVER TO DISCUSS CUSTODY.

A car pulled in the driveway. "That was a lot of notice," she muttered.

Through the window, she watched as Scott got out of his car, reached into the backseat, and grabbed his suit jacket. He must have come from court because he was wearing his favorite power outfit—gray Armani suit, white shirt, red tie, Italian shoes.

As Scott marched up the driveway, her neighbor, Neil Taylor, ambled over. The two men spoke briefly, Scott mostly nodding while Neil waved his arms around like one of those inflatable tube-men outside an auto dealership. Kate waited by the door until Scott headed toward the house. She opened the front door before he took the liberty of doing it himself. It was her house, after all.

She pressed her thumbnail into her finger, digging it in hard. "Please come in." She stepped to the side.

Scott's nose wrinkled. "Is that scotch? Have you been drinking?"

Kate wanted to say, *Yes, yours*, but ignored his question and asked, "What did Neil want?"

"He wanted to make sure you weren't mad at him. He said you blew him off last week. He saw you near his rental property and tried to wave you down, but you kept walking."

"What? I don't remember seeing him."

"That's what I figured must've happened. But I wouldn't go strolling around the Love Hut. You're asking for trouble in that part of town."

"The Love Hut?" Kate's mouth went dry.

"If you want to shop there, that's your business. All I meant is, be careful."

"Neil must be confused. It wasn't me."

"Forget I mentioned it." Scott magnanimously held his hand out toward the couch. "Do you have a minute?"

Kate didn't budge.

He sighed. "I heard about what happened with your job. It's another reason why it's clearly best for the kids to live with me full time."

"No. I'm contesting. Get out."

"Honey—"

Kate chuckled dryly. "If you think I'm in any mood to be charmed by your nice-guy act, you're out of your mind. I'm not your honey. I'm not your Kit. And I'm no longer your dutiful little wife either. I lived up to our marriage vows, which we made before our friends, family, and God Himself. You're the one who shattered them when you took up with the homewrecker. So from this day forward, I'm going to fight you every step of the way. You are *not* taking my children."

Scott was clearly taken aback. "I don't know what's gotten into you, but you need to face facts, Kate. You've never liked living in Hartville. Why not move someplace you'll be happy and can start over?" He had the gall to bat his blue eyes as though he were delivering a hard truth that was said out of love, with her best interests in mind.

"Is that an option? I'd be happy to take the kids and move far from here."

"You know the kids want to live with me."

"That's a lie. Ava's not old enough to know better, but Andy can't stand it over there. Tammi treats them like dolls. She just wants to dress them up and take them down for parties and events, then it's back up on the shelf where she can't see or hear them."

"That's not true."

"I've kept my mouth shut for too long. Andy says you're working around the clock and he's stuck in his room. When Tammi goes out, it's to go shopping, and she only takes Ava. He's alone all the time."

Scott moved a little closer to her. "I'm worried about you, Kate. I know you're under a lot of stress, but your behavior… It reminds me of that other time."

"What are you talking about?"

"When you had your breakdown. After Emma. You're acting the same way."

"Don't go there, Scott."

"You had blackouts then too. Is that what's going on?"

Kate swallowed. "I didn't have blackouts."

"Blackouts, sleepwalking, I don't care what you call it! You ended up at the park across the street from our house!" Scott's voice rose high and his eyes rounded with concern.

Kate crossed her arms, the horror of the memory of waking up in the backyard fresh again. "The doctor thought it was a side effect of the medicine I was taking." She had no intention of discussing her therapy or her yellow happy pills, which she was no longer taking anyway. He'd just use the information as ammunition in a custody battle.

"Can you make an appointment to see your doctor? You need help, Kit."

She stared into those blue eyes and a wave of self-doubt washed over her. She was stressed. Exhausted. She was having the same symptoms again. Maybe she was losing her mind.

Scott held his hands high like he was surrendering. "I want to help. Please."

As he raised his arms, his suit jacket opened wide. In his shirt pocket, underneath the white fabric, a red button glowed.

White-hot rage rushed up from Kate's stomach. Her cheeks burned and her hands balled into fists. "You're recording me!"

Scott paled and lowered his arms.

"You… lousy… scumbag." Kate marched forward.

Scott hastily retreated toward the front door, reaching into his pocket and taking out his phone as he went. "I just did it in case you forget the conversation, with your blackouts and all. I'm trying to help—"

"You recorded it to use it in court against me! You're despicable! Get out of my house."

"Fine, I'm through arguing with you. I'm taking custody. It's a done deal. Enjoy your every other weekend with the kids."

"No. We don't have a deal, and I'm nowhere near done."

Scott's laugh had a hard edge. He struck his power pose—left foot forward, torso slightly twisted, and chin raised, just as he had practiced endlessly in front of the mirror to use in court. He believed that this pose, combined with his handsome face and silky voice, could convince anyone to bend to his will.

"You're living in a fantasy world. You have little money and no job, and there's a long line of people who will testify you're an unfit mother—mentally unbalanced. Oh, and by the way, now that the kids will be living with me, I'm no longer required to pay the mortgage on this house. So why don't you do yourself a favor and sell it before you face the humiliation of losing it. That way you can save whatever shred of dignity you have left and find an apartment out of town."

Kate stepped forward until she was nose to nose with him. When she straightened up, she was slightly taller. "I moved to Hartville for you and your career. I have a life here now. It's not the life I chose, but I'm going to make it work. This is my house. I'm not asking you to leave, I'm telling you. Get out!"

"Are you threatening me?"

Her fingers were tingling, ready to slap the sneer on his face into the next county. "Considering I just beat the snot out of the psycho who's been following me—and I really liked how it made me feel, you can decide. Now leave."

Scott stomped to the door, and Kate followed him.

"Go ahead and fight custody," Scott said. "But remember this: when you step into the courtroom, you'll be in *my* house. It'll be over like that." He snapped his fingers in her face.

"I've been screwed by you before. And it was always over"—she snapped her fingers—"like that."

Scott turned crimson and slammed the door behind him.

As soon as he left, so did all Kate's bravado. She slumped against the door and slid to the floor. She tried to will herself to stand up again, but she only rose a couple of inches before sagging back down.

He'll wipe the courtroom floor with me. He'll take the kids.

She opened her eyes and stared at the pictures of Ava and Andy all around her. The two of them looked so happy. And they were happy when they were here. She didn't have the money Scott had, but she and her kids were inseparable. They were a family. Ever since they'd moved, it had been brutal on the kids—she wouldn't pretend otherwise—but it had brought them together. Kate needed her kids and they needed her. In that shared pain, the three of them had forged a bond and *"a cord of three strands is not easily broken."*

There was no way she was going to let anyone tear them apart.

She pressed her palms against the wood and shoved herself up to her knees. Tears rolled off the end of her nose and landed on the doormat.

Unfit mother, my eye.

Kate grabbed the door handle and pulled herself up to her feet.

She had work to do.

Kate marched upstairs and turned on the computer. Her hands were trembling so much it was difficult to use the mouse as she opened her photos folder. She searched through the photos until she found one of Donna looking straight at the camera. Her friend's smiling face brought fresh tears to Kate's bloodshot eyes. Drops dinged off the keyboard as she typed the word MISSING.

An email from Susan flashed on her screen and Kate opened it. Susan had gotten the job at MG Uniforms. She thanked Kate repeatedly, promising she'd do her best to repay the favor.

Kate rubbed her eyes with the palms of her hands and got back to work on the flyer. Once she finished it, she'd get a hundred printed and canvass the town with them.

The chatter of a police radio outside alerted Kate to Detective Tills's arrival before he even knocked. She rushed down the stairs and opened the door.

Any sign of compassion the detective had shown for her earlier was gone. He wasn't even trying to appear neutral now—he looked downright angry. And a grim-faced female uniformed police officer whom Kate hadn't seen before stood behind him.

"Is this about Ryan? Is he okay?"

"Detective Daley was moved out of the ICU. That's all I'm at liberty to say. Ms. Gardner, this is Officer Jackson. We need to speak with you. May we come in?"

Tills's tone left no doubt that the only choice he was offering was where the conversation would take place.

"Yes, of course."

Kate led them into the living room; the shattered coffee table, now reduced to a pile of wood and glass, lay in the center of the room.

The detective motioned to the slipper chair while he sat on the couch and Jackson remained standing. "At this time, you're not under arrest, but I do need to advise you of your rights. You have the right to remain silent…"

He continued to speak, but Kate couldn't hear a thing he said. Somewhere between "you're not under arrest" and "remain silent," her brain had exploded. At least that was what it felt like.

"Why are you reading me my rights if I'm not under arrest?"

"I'm letting you know you are under investigation for a crime or crimes." He stressed the *s*. "And you have certain rights. Do you understand those rights?"

"Yes, but… no. Am I under arrest?"

"Not at this time, but I need to ask you several questions. Let me begin by letting you know we apprehended the person who vandalized your van and created those flyers."

Kate sat up like he'd tossed a hand grenade into her lap.

Tills reached down, opened his briefcase, and took out a manila folder. He handed Kate a mugshot of a teary-eyed, middle-aged woman. "Do you recognize her?"

Kate shook her head.

"Her name is Patty Bleacher."

"I don't know her. I swear. Why would she target me?"

"She was upset about your correspondence with her husband, Marty." From the folder, he now produced a photo of a middle-aged man printed off a website.

"I've never seen him before," Kate said.

"But you corresponded with him via email."

"No, I did not."

"That wasn't actually a question." Tills took another piece of paper from the file. On it were two copies of Kate's signature. "Are these your signatures?"

"Yes."

"You admit these are your signatures?"

Kate picked up the paper and looked closely. "They look like it. Where are they from?"

"One is from the missing person report you filed regarding Donna Trucci." Tills put a hand on his knee. "Let me back up here. Patty Bleacher came into the station yesterday evening and confessed to both vandalizing your car and distributing the flyers at the school. She said her husband responded to your escort ad and that you were emailing each other back and forth. She found out about it and asked you to leave her husband alone. When you refused, she became very upset."

"I never sent her or her husband any emails. And I told you that I had nothing to do with that fake escort ad."

"Technology can be tracked. The guys in our IT department took a look at Patty's emails, and they traced the sender back to the library. Do you want to guess where that second signature that you said was yours came from?"

"I use the library computers, but… I didn't email anyone besides prospective employers."

"Really?" He removed another page from the folder and handed it to Kate.

It was a printout of an email with the naked pictures of Kate and a list of sexual services that she offered. Circled at the top were the date and time—which matched the date and time from her library sign-in—Kate's email address, Marty Bleacher's email address, and the subject line: "Come and get it, big boy!"

Kate blinked as she stared at the date. She had been at the library that day, but she didn't know exactly when. And she certainly hadn't emailed the Bleachers!

Without a word, Tills handed her another page. Her hands were shaking violently as she took it.

It was a copy of the email from Patty Bleacher to Kate, a desperate plea from an anguished wife begging Kate to leave her husband alone.

He handed Kate a third page, Kate's supposed reply to Patty. The cruel and disturbing email accused Patty of not satisfying Marty's needs and closed with an invitation for Patty to come along on their next date so Kate could teach her how to please a man.

"I never sent these." Kate tried to hand the printouts back to the detective, but he didn't take them. "Someone is pretending to be me. They created a fake email account."

"Look at the email again."

Kate stared at the printout. The email address was the one she'd been using for years. "Someone must have hacked my account."

"Or you're lying." Tills pointed at the papers in Kate's hand. "Why don't you take another look at Marty Bleacher. You just swore, before Officer Jackson and me, that you've never seen that man before."

Kate shuffled back to the photograph of Marty and her shock was like a gut punch. She had seen him before. He'd stopped by her house the night Scott was over, after the soccer game. He was the man driving the white Ford who said he was looking for a different address.

"You invited Marty over, but your ex-husband stopped by unexpectedly. Both Marty and Scott confirmed it."

"I didn't recognize him from the photo. You have to believe that."

"No, I don't. I think you created the escort ad and emailed Marty. I think you started all of this. You've been lying to us since the beginning of this investigation."

She started to stand, but the detective motioned for her to stay put.

"Believe me, you're gonna want to be sitting for this next part." Tills pulled a large, blown-up photograph from the folder and held it up. It was a grainy picture from a security camera mounted up high. It showed Derek Benson pushing a shopping cart loaded with bags, talking to—

Kate's eyes widened. "That's impossible."

Detective Tills tapped the picture. "That's Derek." He pointed to the woman in the green dress. "And that's you. The hair, the build, the eyeglasses." He gave a low whistle. "Witnesses saw you wearing the same dress at one of your son's soccer games. I've got photos of that too. The security camera behind the Love Hut took this picture a week before Derek attacked you. Derek was telling the truth. That's why he didn't set off your security system—you gave him the code. Want to tell me again you've never been near the Love Hut, or you'd never seen Derek or spoken to him?"

Kate stared at her shaking hands. Was she losing her mind? But no, even if she were having blackouts, she wouldn't visit the Love Hut or email vile messages to a man like Marty, or any man for that matter. Would she? Could she?

"Detective?" Officer Jackson had moved next to the end of the couch and was pointing down. "You'll want to see this."

Tills cast Kate a sideways glance as he ambled over to where Jackson was pointing, bits of broken glass crunching as he went. He leaned down and his eyes widened. "Photograph it. It's evidence."

Kate stood up and looked. Partially hidden behind the couch was the white box for the replacement drone, the packing labeling revealing exactly what was inside—*X-192 Drone. Replacement for Kate Gardner.*

"I need to talk to a lawyer."

"That would be a good idea." Tills nodded and Officer Jackson stepped behind Kate and grabbed her arm.

Cold metal encircled Kate's wrist and the handcuff clicked closed.

The detective stepped nose to nose with her as the other cuff snapped shut. Fury burned in his eyes. "I almost forgot. I lifted your prints off the water glass I gave you when we spoke at the station this morning. The lab came back with the results for the fingerprints on the golf club that was used to bash my partner in the back of the head. Want to guess whose prints were on it?"

Kate shook her head. "Derek wore gloves."

"Save it. Katherine Gardner, you're under arrest."

16

The next hour was a whirlwind. Kate was placed in a police cruiser and driven across town to the police station. There she was hurried into the underbelly of the stationhouse, searched, made to change into an orange jumpsuit in front of a female cop, fingerprinted, and told to stand for her mugshot. She was then allowed to make her one phone call, which she used to call Audrey.

Despite her former mother-in-law's army of attorneys, Kate had to spend the night in jail. And much to her surprise, she had one of the best night's sleep she'd had in a very long time. Maybe it was the fact that she felt safe in her solitary cell, or perhaps it was knowing she wouldn't be sleepwalking anywhere, but she woke up late and very well-rested.

After Audrey posted her bail, Kate waited several more hours to be released and for a cab to drop her off at home. She had never even had a speeding ticket before and now she was facing several serious charges. Audrey's lawyers had told her that the police were holding off on charging her with attacking Ryan until they could get an official statement from him. She desperately wanted to go to him. Picturing him lying alone in the hospital brought fresh tears to her eyes. But part of the condition of her bail was that she was to have no contact with Ryan. She had expected that they'd make her wear an ankle monitor, even though she wasn't thinking of setting foot outside the house ever again. But she was free to come and go as she pleased, provided she stayed in the state.

Free? Her life was over. Hartville's newspaper published every mugshot along with the person's name and the charges against them. First a slut and now a crazed criminal. Her poor kids. Would they be ostracized too?

Standing in the middle of the living room, Kate hung her head. This place, this town had sucked her happiness away and left her a dead husk.

Without any purpose, she headed toward the kitchen, wiping the tears off her face. Through the blur, she saw the pictures lining the hallway—Scott, her, and the kids. That was all gone now. Her future too. Gone.

This wasn't a home anymore. It was a tomb.

Shadows spilled across the kitchen as the last rays of the sunset danced outside. Kate passed the refrigerator and paused. Pinned to the front was a drawing Andy had made in Sunday school. A huge yellow-crayon sun was rising above a brown cross. The word HOPE, written in green, stretched across a blue sky.

More tears fell.

She moved the magnet and lifted the paper off the fridge. Her tears landed on the waxy crayon drawing and ran down until they bled into the page at the foot of the cross.

HOPE.

Kate put the paper back on the refrigerator and lifted her chin. She couldn't give up. Not now.

She closed her eyes and poured her heart out in prayer.

Kate jumped at the sound of the front door opening. *Scott? How dare he just walk into my house!* She swore, muttered a quick apology for her hypocrisy, and hurried down the hallway, but then stopped short.

Audrey was strolling through the front door as casually as if she were arriving at a party. She paused in the foyer and studied the pictures on the wall. As always, Audrey owned the silence.

Finally, she leveled her gaze at Kate. "Where do I even begin?"

Kate shrugged as she tried to remember the thank-you speech she'd been going over in her head. "Please let me start by—"

Audrey held up a hand as she walked past Kate toward the kitchen. "Do tell me you have something stronger than a wine cooler."

Kate followed her into the kitchen. "I'm not sure what's left in the liquor cabinet, but I know there's some scotch."

"I checked with the hospital regarding your Detective Daley an hour ago. He suffered a skull fracture and will be out of commission for a while, but is expected to make a full recovery."

Kate pictured Ryan unconscious on the floor. She wanted to dash to the hospital to see him, but they'd think she was there to finish the job. "Thank you for asking." She opened the cabinet and held out the bottle of scotch.

"May I have a glass, or must I drink from the bottle?"

Kate grabbed a tumbler.

"The doctor spoke with Ryan briefly. He doesn't remember the attack. He did ask about you. Seeing the desperate look on your face, I must remind you of the conditions of your bail: you can have no contact with him until this situation is resolved."

Kate wanted to scream. Every fiber of her being wanted to rush to Ryan's side, but it couldn't be. Not right now. She poured the drink and turned back to her former mother-in-law.

Audrey peered at the hole in the wall. "Your handiwork?"

Kate blushed as she passed Audrey the glass. "I made a toast, and… I was trying to emulate you."

Audrey gave a slight nod. "It appears you failed spectacularly in that regard as well. Sit."

Kate studied Audrey as she took the seat opposite her. If the woman hadn't told her she was dying, Kate would never have been able to tell. Audrey looked better than she had seen her in years.

"You look great." The words escaped Kate's mouth without permission from her brain.

"Great? Your vocabulary is wanting. Radiant? Elegant? Gorgeous would suffice. This Christmas, I'll purchase a thesaurus for you." Audrey set the glass on the table and closed her eyes. She inhaled through her nose as if she were meditating. But when she opened her eyes again, she was anything but serene.

Kate sat up straighter. "I'm sorry. I know you wanted me to lift myself up by my own bootstraps and be more assertive."

"Yes, I wanted you to fight back and prove yourself to me. But did you not understand that I was in your corner? You should have come to me for help long before you did."

"I was going to, but after the flyers, I thought that since I'd brought scandal to your name…"

Audrey laughed loudly. "My dear girl, I was born in scandal, and I thrive in adversity. You said it yourself: I look 'great.'" She glanced once again at the hole in the wall. "Start at the beginning—and tell me everything."

Kate felt a sudden flood of gratitude toward this woman. She told Audrey about the drone, the vandalism, the flyers, the stalker, Ryan, Donna—every detail. By the time she was done, Audrey had long ago finished her drink. Kate waited for whatever wisdom her new mentor was ready to impart.

Audrey drummed her manicured nails on the table. "You've really stepped in it."

"I'm knee-deep."

"A good bit deeper than that, I would say." Audrey sat staring at Kate for what felt like a full minute before speaking again. "I need to know what happened with your sister, Emma."

Kate swallowed. There was no need to ask her why she wanted to know. Audrey would have heard some of the story. It was only reasonable for her to wonder if Kate was at her breaking point too.

"I grew up in a small town like this," Kate started. "I couldn't wait to get out and see the real world, so the minute I could go to college, I left. Emma was four years younger than me. She was always so happy, but her senior year, she changed." She rubbed her thumb against the back of her other hand. "I'd do anything to turn back the clock and get Emma the help she needed. My sister—" She broke off.

"Take a breath," Audrey said. "I'll wait." She got up and poured herself another drink, which gave Kate some time to pull the painful memories together.

"The high school football coach had been molesting her. Emma went to the police and told them. But in that town most people did their praying in the bleachers on a Friday night; for them, the coach was a saint and could do no wrong. People blamed Emma. Even our father."

Kate closed her eyes, but it didn't drive the nightmare away. She remembered it all like it had happened moments ago.

"At first, my father accused Emma of making the whole thing up to get attention. Then it got worse. He said if it had happened, Emma must have done something to lead the coach on."

She pictured their father rambling drunkenly, beer sloshing out of the can. *"What were you wearing? Did you flirt with him?"*

"One night, they had a huge blow-out fight at dinner. Emma didn't cry. She didn't yell back. She just said she needed to get some air and take a drive. And that's what she did. She drove a hundred miles an hour straight into a gigantic elm tree. My father hasn't spoken to me since. He said if I hadn't been so selfish and had just gotten an abortion and come home, Emma would be alive."

Audrey sat as still as a statue, but there was emotion in her eyes. It was a look Kate had seen on the faces of people who had suffered but come through the other side. Maybe that was what she and Audrey had in common—pain.

Audrey finally spoke. "The man's a fool. Most are. Had you taken that route, you would not have Andy." She took a long sip of her drink and continued. "It does one no good to look back. You must press on. Do you understand?"

Kate nodded and remained silent.

"From this point on, take a page from the Mafia playbook and don't say a word to anyone about anything. I'll arrange a sit-down between you and one of my lawyers tomorrow. I'll need you to speak to a private detective too. There is a man in Darrington whose reputation is spectacular, Jack Stratton—he's a former police officer. I'll arrange that too." She pointed at the bottle of scotch. "And pour that swill down the drain right now. Don't get any more. You need to keep your wits about you."

As Kate got up to do as she was told, Audrey seized her arm and pulled her down till their faces were so close together, Audrey's breath warmed her cheek.

"Assure me that you had nothing to do with any of this."

Kate tried to pull her arm away, but Audrey's grip was quite firm. "No. Absolutely not. The only thing I did was lie about that stupid drone. I should have admitted it when it happened, but I was too embarrassed."

A faint smile crossed Audrey's face. "Your reasoning is so pitiful, I believe you." She rose slowly. "I have to go home and mind the children. I was hoping you could visit with them soon, but in light of these new developments, that will have to wait a few more days."

At the mention of her kids, Kate was desperate to go with her. "Could you bring them by?"

Audrey shook her head, her expression softening. "No, but you'll be able to see them soon."

She picked up her purse and strode to the front door with Kate following. Audrey paused in the foyer. "The sheriff is investigating why Ryan Daley was here when he had been removed from the case. Do not reach out to your detective. It will not only violate your bail but will also further jeopardize his career."

Kate let Audrey out. As she watched her mother-in-law drive off, she pictured Ryan atop the ladder as she stared up at him. She had asked him that night, *"When did you decide to be a cop?"*

He'd smiled down at her, shrugged, and said, *"I don't know if it was ever a conscious thing. It's all I've ever wanted to be."*

Kate couldn't ruin that for him. As much as she wanted to speak to him, tell him how sorry she was that he'd been hurt protecting her, she couldn't.

She closed and locked the door. Once again she was in prison, even if this time the bars were invisible.

Long shadows spread across the floor as Kate stood in the living room, staring down at the wreckage from the fight with her stalker. The broken table lay in the middle of the floor and pieces of debris radiated out like there'd been a bomb blast. Fighting back her tears, Kate headed for the closet and grabbed the vacuum and a trash can.

The physical act of clearing the destruction was just what she needed. With each broken bit that she threw away, she felt a little better. After she finished vacuuming, the silence was palpable. But she was done giving in to the quiet. She was done with wrapping her arms around her knees and sitting on the couch alone in the dark. Kate marched to the front window and shoved it open, letting the cold air cool her fiery cheeks.

Donna's little purple VW chugged down the road and stopped in Kate's driveway.

Kate let out a squeal and ran to the front door.

"Oh my gosh! Where have you been? I was so worried about you!" Kate almost knocked Donna off the front steps as she embraced her.

"I am so sorry." Donna looked close to tears. "I spoke with Lori and she told me everything. I'm so, so, so sorry. I don't know what happened. I left a message telling you I was fine and where I was."

"I never got a message from you."

"I called. I had to use Dan's phone because I left mine in my car. I didn't get any of your messages or texts until I got back into town."

Kate pinched the bridge of her nose with her thumb and forefinger. "I was getting a hundred pervy calls and texts a day. I was forwarding them to Ryan, then archiving them in batches. If you called me from an unknown number…"

Donna hugged her again.

"I thought you'd been abducted, or worse…"

Donna gave a sheepish, apologetic grin that showed all her teeth. "Not exactly."

"Oh, no. Don't tell me you just took off for a spa weekend or something!" Kate's anger rose. "Your car was abandoned and there were signs of a struggle. And now I'll be charged with filing a false missing person report."

"Probably. I'm so sorry. I totally backed you up and explained that you didn't know," Donna said. "I stopped by the police station on the way here. That Detective Tills guy is a real jerk. Anyway, I tried, but the police didn't believe me even though I told them the truth."

Kate's hands went to her hips. "And what, exactly, is the truth?"

Donna gestured toward the living room. "I think you should sit down—and not pick up any sharp or heavy objects. Maybe you should sit on your hands. Oh, and promise not to scream."

"I can't promise that."

They went into the living room and sat down. Kate pushed her hands under her thighs.

Donna began. "Okay. So, on Thursday night, I think it was then, I was supposed to meet one of the guys from Speedy Dates at the Flagstaff, but the guy stood me up! You saw how I was dressed, right? The guys at the bar were on me like white on rice. Seriously, I was chasing them off with a stick. I was going to leave when I heard this guy say, 'Donna? Is that you?'"

"Tell me you didn't."

"I turned around, and Dan Felder was standing there. My first love. I know it sounds sappy, but… okay, I'm gonna say it. It was love at first sight all over again."

"You've got to be kidding me!" Kate leaped to her feet.

Donna thrust her hands up with the palms out. "Let me explain. We hit it off again, like, boom! Fireworks. It was like out of a movie or something."

"Just tell me what happened."

"Okay. So, Dan's got this little fishing cabin and—"

"Let me see if I've got this right," Kate broke in. "I went through hell because you ran off with an old boyfriend?"

Donna pressed her hands together. "My soul mate."

Kate couldn't help it; she had to scream. She sat down, and when she was done screaming, she yelled. "Do you realize the police think we set this up together so I could get attention? They think I'm crazy! They think I hired a homeless man to kill me and lied about you being missing! What about the signs of a struggle in your car? That had me scared to death! The door handle was ripped off!"

Donna blushed. "Oh, that. So, Dan and I were in the car talking and fooling around a little… It's a Bug, and he's a big guy, and he put his foot up, and the door handle snapped off. That's when we decided to ride out to his cabin." She got up and paced the room.

"The bartender said he was wearing a blue baseball hat."

"Dan just moved back from LA. He's a Dodgers fan. Sorry."

Kate hung her head.

"Hey, it's your turn to bring me up to speed. Word is, you caught the guy and beat the crap out of him!"

"Yeah, I caught him." Kate cocked her head to the side and shook it. "But it doesn't matter. He came up with this crazy story that I hired him to kill me because I didn't have the guts to kill myself, and the police believe him."

She filled Donna in on everything, all the way to today's surprising meeting with Audrey, and Donna was appropriately shocked, upset, and contrite. By the time Kate was finished, she had a headache.

"Come into the kitchen. I need some aspirin."

"Is your neck hurting? It looks awful—purple, a little greenish, yellow too."

"It's not as bad as it looks, but my head feels like it's about to explode," Kate replied as she headed to the kitchen.

Donna followed. "What are you going to do now?"

"I can't prove anything, so I'm going to listen to my mother-in-law and do nothing until I talk to her lawyer."

"Your former mother-in-law."

"Audrey's helping me. I'd be lost without her."

Donna scoffed. "Did you forget the fact that Scott is Audrey's darling little baby boy?" As they entered the kitchen, she pointed at the hole. "Hey, what happened to your wall?"

Kate stared at the gaping crater that was now a giant reminder that she still had a lot to learn. "Long story. Anyway, it turns out Scott is like his dear old dad. The way that Scott treated me is the same way Scott's father treated Audrey. I think she's trying to break the cycle for Andy and Ava."

"I still don't trust Audrey. And I don't have to, because I'm going to look after you too. You and I already know who's behind all this—Tammi."

"Tammi didn't carve up my van or put the flyers out at school. The woman who did walked into the police station and confessed!" Kate reminded her. "Who knows, she could be a nice lady with a creep for a husband. We've both been there, right? She was trying to keep me from luring her husband away from her."

"But still, what she did was pretty psycho."

"What would you do if you were in Patty Bleacher's shoes? Her husband actually came here to hook up with me. Not *me* me—with slutty me."

Donna patted her purse on the kitchen table. "I'd let Harry set my husband straight. How did the wife find out what her husband was up to?"

"She found his email exchange with the fabricated escort, so she replied, asking me to leave her husband alone. The police traced the fake emails back to the library, which is also where the Secret Flings ad originated. And because someone signed my name in the computer room at the same time, they think I'm behind all of it."

"It has to be someone with access to your family photos. I'm telling you, it's Tammi!"

"You had the login too."

Donna looked like a bug had flown into her ear. "What? You don't think I—"

"No. But did you give anyone else access?"

"Of course not." Donna's eyes narrowed, but her smile returned. "You must still be mad about me taking off." She drummed her fingers on the kitchen table. "I bet Tammi logged in as you at the library. She probably showed up right after you left. One of the librarians could have tipped her off. Becky is a librarian and she's friends with Tammi."

"I think all that sex has messed with your brain."

Donna tapped the side of her head. "You ever think it made me smarter? It releases all those endorphins and stuff. And if that's the case, after the weekend Dan and I had, I must be a genius. Either way, you don't have to be a rocket scientist to know it's Tammi."

Kate popped two aspirin into her mouth and washed them down with a glass of water. "You think Tammi created the Secret Flings ad and emailed this lady's husband?"

"Duh! She stole your husband and now she wants your children. With you gone, she gets promoted from mommy number two to *numero uno*. That is some serious motive." Donna rocked back and forth in the chair, nodding sagely. "She totally set you up. I know it."

Kate folded her arms across her chest. "Tammi's my top suspect too, but believing something and proving it are two separate things."

Donna sat fiddling with her braids. "I'm so sorry. I saw my moment and went for it. I had no idea it would cause the complete destruction of Planet Kate. I swear I called and left a message. I called yesterday too."

Kate stared down at her phone. "I had to stop taking my antianxiety medicine. I was talking to myself aloud and I started sleepwalking again. But there's no way I accidentally deleted two voice messages…" The pieces dropped into place. "If Scott told Tammi my PIN code, she has access to my phone. And if she has access… Oh my gosh. I knew I'd paid my bills, and my phone calendar didn't show my appointment with Dr. Green. I always put my appointments in the calendar. Tammi could have changed those too."

"Tammi's gaslighting you!"

"There's a big part of me that wants you to be right. I want this whole thing over, but the more I run the bogus evidence the police have against me through my mind, the more I want to take my kids and run to Canada."

"I thought you were gonna say, the more you wanna run over Detective Tills."

They looked at each other and burst out laughing.

"I have missed you, D." Kate crossed her arms. "Okay. Tell me your Tammi-done-it theory."

Donna leaned forward. "Snappy title. First off, Tammi knows Derek Benson."

"How? They shoot up together?" Kate joked.

"No, silly, junior high, high school... All Tammi needed to do was dress like you and—"

"Wait! Are you serious?" Suddenly, Donna's wild theory seemed plausible. Until Kate realized there was one massive obstacle. "No, no. It's impossible. There's no way that even a drug addict is going to confuse Tammi with me."

"The guy is on meth. He'd confuse you and me."

Kate shook her head. "I saw the security camera photograph myself. It was grainy, but the woman talking to Derek couldn't have been Tammi. She lacked the bionic boobs."

"Tammi is a Hollywood actress wannabe. I can't stand her, but she can morph herself into any role. I saw it myself junior year when she played the lead in *The Taming of the Shrew*."

"I bet she was fantastic in that role! But was playing a shrew much of a stretch?" Kate said, fighting back another fit of laughter. She was so overtired, she was getting punchy.

"I'm serious, Kate! Tammi played YOU!" Donna was almost shrieking. "How freaky is that?"

"What are you talking about, played me?"

"That's the name of the lead character—KATE." Donna clapped. "She taped her boobs down and wore a wig. That's all it would take to fake out a guy like Derek, right? Give the police the right build, hair, a dress that a field full of people saw you in—plus surveillance footage and eyewitness testimony from both Derek and your neighbor... They don't have a pile of evidence against you; Tammi gave them a freakin' mountain."

Kate's knees went weak. "That's so crazy it actually makes sense." Her mouth dropped open. "That surveillance photo of me talking to Derek. When Detective Tills showed me the picture, he pointed out my eyeglasses."

"But… you do wear eyeglasses." Donna's nose crinkled.

"Yes, but my glasses turn dark outside in the sun. If that was me in the photo, it would look like I was wearing *sunglasses*." Kate sat back in the chair as relief washed over her. For a moment, she had almost begun to believe that she was losing her mind and even suspected herself!

"Oh, oh, oh!" Donna pumped her arm as if Kate had scored a touchdown. "That's how you can prove it was Tammi! Or at least you can prove it wasn't you in that photo."

"That argument isn't going to hold water with the police. They'll just say that I have a second pair of glasses somewhere."

"But if we can find the Kate costume at Tammi's house…" Donna grinned. "Boom!"

"Except whatever we find at Tammi's house won't be admissible in court." Kate rubbed her temples. "I've seen that on a dozen police shows."

"Oh, I didn't think about that."

Kate was stumped.

Donna lifted up Kate's phone. "But if we get video, it will give you credibility where it counts the most—the court of public opinion. That's your only way to fight this."

Kate felt a plan falling into place, and it didn't sound crazy—to her. Except… "No. Audrey said to lie low. I'll wait until I talk to that private detective she wants me to meet with."

"You need to do this yourself. No one's going to help you in the world but you."

Kate laughed.

"You find this funny?"

"You ever hear the story about the guy caught in the flash flood? A boat comes by to rescue him and the guy says, 'I'm good. God will save me.' The water gets higher and another boat comes, but the guy says, 'Naw, I'm fine. God will save me.' Finally, the water rises up to the guy's chin. A helicopter shows up, but the guy says, 'Don't worry about me. God will save me.' A few minutes later, he drowns. He gets to Heaven and says to God, 'Hey, what's the deal? I thought you were going to save me?' Then God says to him, 'What do you want? I sent you two boats and a helicopter!' You're helping me, Donna. So's Audrey. And so was Ryan." Kate turned the palms of her hands up and shrugged. "If we show up at

Tammi's uninvited, it's going to confirm that I'm the mentally disturbed psycho that she's making me out to be."

Kate's phone buzzed in Donna's hands.

Donna glanced at the number and her eyes went wide. "Speak of the she-devil! It's Tammi!"

Kate's mind raced. "Should I answer it? Do you have your phone?"

Donna's eyebrows arched as she took it out of her pocket. "Why?"

"Record this!"

Kate answered the call from Tammi and placed it on speakerphone. Donna's fingers shook, but she managed to turn on the recorder for her phone.

"Hello?" Kate said.

"Kate?" Tammi sobbed. "I'm so sorry."

"What are you so sorry about, Tammi?"

"I need to… I need… It got out of control." She was crying and slurring her words so much it was difficult to understand what she was saying. "I need to talk to you. Are you home?" Tammi sniffled loudly into the phone.

Kate shook her head. If Tammi was drunk, she didn't want her driving. "Where are you?"

"Home. I'm so sorry. Please!"

There was something about the pain in her voice that pierced Kate. It was raw. Desperate. "I'll be right over."

"Thank you."

The call disconnected and Donna thrust both her hands out. "Why didn't you have her come here?!"

"She sounded tanked. She can't drive."

"So what are you going to do? Just walk into the lion's den?"

Kate stared down at Donna's phone and pressed the red stop button. She rewound and made sure the whole conversation had been recorded. It had.

"Is that enough to go to the police with?" Donna asked. "She did say 'it got out of control.'"

Kate shook her head. "Scott could always spin that in court. We need more." She grabbed her jacket off the back of a kitchen chair, turned her own phone on to record, and placed it in the inside pocket of her jacket. "Donna, say something. Talk."

"Talk about what? How crazy you are?"

Kate reached into her pocket to check the recording. She rewound and hit play. "'Talk about what? How crazy you are?'"

"Tammi wants to confess. If I record it on my phone, it may be enough to get me out of the mess I'm in."

Donna straightened up. "Is that legal?"

"We live in a one-party consent state. That means if I know the conversation is being recorded, it's legal."

Donna lit up. "I'll drive."

Donna parked her Bug in Tammi's driveway. "Are you sure you don't want me to come in with you?"

Kate nodded. "Tammi might panic if we both walk up to the front door. I'm going to hear what she has to say." She checked that her phone was recording and placed it in the inside pocket of her jacket. "This will give me the proof I need."

"I don't trust her, Kate." Donna drummed her fingers on the steering wheel. "I've got a bad feeling about this."

Kate didn't want to admit that she did too. "You heard her. She's sorry. I really think she wants to confess."

"That's a hard no. She hates you."

"I know, but... she did say it got out of control. Maybe her harassment grew like my stupid lie. Maybe she just wanted Derek to scare me. What if she really is sorry?"

"Tammi? The day Tammi feels bad about anything is the day Lucifer starts lacing up his ice skates."

"I'm just going to talk with her."

"Scream and I'll come running."

As soon as Kate closed the car door, she began second-guessing her decision. Each step up the walkway seemed harder, like she was sinking into mud. She kept glancing over her shoulder toward the safety of the car and her loyal friend. By the time she reached the front door, sweat was trickling down her back.

She rang the bell and waited a minute. There was no answer, so she knocked on the door, and it swung silently open. The lights inside were on. From down the hallway, the twang of country music played.

"Tammi? It's Kate."

The only answer was the faint sound of a steel guitar playing over the speakers.

Feeling like she was jumping into unknown waters, Kate took a deep breath and stepped across the threshold. She called out once more but heard no answer.

As she made her way down the hallway, she stared at the photos. They were almost identical to those hanging in Kate's house—pictures of Ava, Andy, and Scott laughing and smiling. But instead of Kate standing next to them, it was Tammi.

The music grew louder as Kate approached the first doorway. The room was a study. Scott's law books, certificates, and trinkets lined the walls the same way they had in her home once. Even the desk was the same.

But it was all so different now.

Kate stopped cold.

The gun in Tammi's hand was pointed directly at Kate's chest.

But Kate wasn't afraid.

Not of the gun.

Not of Tammi.

Tammi was slumped over the blood-splattered desk, the gun clenched in her still fingers.

Kate rushed over to her, but from the wound in the side of Tammi's head and the blood, she knew there was no way the woman was alive.

Kate yanked out her phone and dialed 911. In a monotone, she gave the details to the operator, who instructed Kate not to touch anything. When the operator asked Kate to check if Tammi was still breathing, Kate had to look again. She leaned closer. Tammi's eyes were open and unblinking. No breath escaped her painted red lips, which lay above a blood-splattered notepad.

That's when Kate noticed the letter.

Kate,

I'm so sorry. I've always hated you. I hated you even before I knew you because you married Scott. I wanted the life you had to be mine. I let that hate consume me. After the affair, I thought you would leave town—but you didn't. I created the Secret Flings ad to embarrass you so you'd move away. I thought emailing the men who responded would be funny. It wasn't. It got out of control. I never imagined the trouble it would cause and I can't undo any of it. I've ruined my life by ruining yours.

I showed Ava a picture of me when I was little. She asked, "Were you nice then?" At first, I was so mad. Then I looked in the mirror. Ava was right. I was nice then. I changed. I sold out. I don't like the new me.

I'm sorry.

The note wasn't signed. Something dripped onto the page and Kate looked up, puzzled, until she felt the tears running down her face. The 911 operator was telling her something, but to Kate it sounded like the woman was in a different room—her voice was muffled and far-off.

Kate stared at the pictures on the desk. Before, she had only noticed the one of Tammi with her arm coiled around Scott. But now she saw one of Tammi when she was a little girl. Her smiling parents knelt beside their daughter, who proudly held a blue ribbon high.

Their child was dead. And for what? Kate had never liked Tammi. If she were to be as honest as Tammi had been in her letter, she'd admit that she'd hated Tammi too. But seeing her now, Kate wished she had tried a little harder to be nicer.

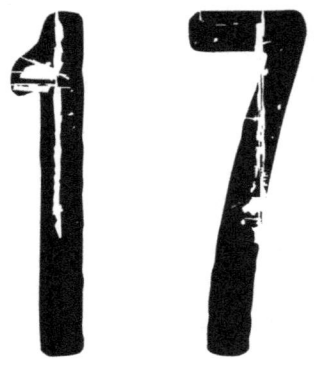

17

It had been three weeks since the funeral. The investigation into Tammi's suicide was still ongoing. But while the cops couldn't find Tammi's phone to check for incriminating evidence, the phone company's records indicated she had called Scott from the Love Hut at the time Derek was there. Kate's lawyers were confident that the charges against her would be dropped, but she wouldn't feel joy at regaining her freedom in such a grisly way. What Tammi had done to her was despicable, but the death sentence Tammi had imposed on herself didn't fit the crime. Yes, Tammi would have had to live with the consequences of her actions, but people, including Kate, would have forgiven her—given time. Suicide had killed any chance of that.

Through the window, Kate watched Andy playing Frisbee and running around with a group of kids next door at his friend Tommy's house. Andy's loud laugh drifted on the wind and made her smile. She prayed again that the kids would bounce back.

Ava ran into the kitchen. "Is Daddy here yet?"

"Not yet."

"Is he bringing my dress-up suitcase?"

"Of course he is." At least Kate sure hoped he was. Ava had left her suitcase at Scott's and she was going out of her mind without it.

The front doorbell rang and the little girl raced to the door. When Kate got to the door, Scott was looking like a kid standing before the principal: head down, eyes lowered, shoulders slumped. Though things were awkward between them, Kate couldn't help but feel bad for him.

"Hi, Daddy!" Ava hugged him, then her suitcase. "Thank you!" She grabbed her prized possession and began dragging it up the stairs to her room.

"Can we talk?" Scott asked Kate.

They walked inside and she sat down on the loveseat, wondering what to say. But when she looked up and saw Scott's weary expression, it hit her again that he had lost someone he loved.

"I'm so sorry about Tammi."

Scott ran his hand through his hair and sank down next to her. "I can't… I can't believe all that Tammi put you through." He looked at her earnestly, intently, and she immediately recognized the signs of tears coming. Andy would get the same look before he started crying, and their resemblance tugged at her heart.

"I want… no, I need you to know that I had no idea about any of the things she did," Scott began. "Tammi must have gone insane—I don't know. There weren't any signs."

He was trying hard to distance himself from Tammi's behavior, and Kate wasn't going to kick him when he was down. Not the time to bring up his role in it all. "Are you okay?"

Scott leaned against her shoulder and cried and talked and cried some more. He apologized for the affair. He took full responsibility—which shocked her. Then he ran down a list of his shortcomings as a husband and father and apologized again and owned them all.

She held onto him, rubbing his back and nodding her head at the appropriate time. "You did some things right too," Kate said.

Scott rolled his swollen eyes and shook his head.

Then it was Kate's turn to remind him of the good things he had done. She was surprised how short the list seemed now and she had to prop up some of the points, but Scott had provided for them, and when he was around, he was a good father.

Soon they were both talking, and the conversation turned to the early days of their marriage. Days when they had nothing but each other and were happy. After a while, the tears had slowed to a stop. Kate handed him the last tissue in the box.

"I'd better get some more—or a towel," she joked.

Scott laughed. It began slow, then built until he was laughing as if she'd told the funniest joke in the world. "That's what I miss about you most,

Kit. Your sense of humor, no matter the situation." He put his hand on her knee and gave it a gentle squeeze.

Kate gazed at her ex-husband. His boyish grin reminded her of the first time she'd met him, in the college's study lounge. He'd laughed at a joke she made then too. That was the moment she'd started having feelings for him. And right now, he looked the same as the Scott she had fallen in love with.

She closed her eyes and she was right back in that lounge, with the musty couch smell and the constant chatter of students. Maybe this was her chance for a do-over? Maybe this time around, she could do things differently and not make the same mistakes?

She opened her eyes.

Scott's grin widened into a roguish smirk and he squeezed her knee again, his hand moving a little higher up her thigh.

Kate said what she wished she'd said fifteen years ago. "Take your hand off my knee or I'll rip it off your wrist."

Scott let go, his eyes wide.

"You just buried your fiancée, and while I feel horrible about that, she tried to have me killed. And I haven't forgotten that during the lowest point of my life, you tried to take away my children and my home. From now on, our relationship is this: If it concerns the kids, you may speak to me. If it doesn't, don't. Is that clear?"

Scott's mouth opened and closed; he seemed entirely at a loss for words. His cheeks flushed and he stared daggers, but Kate didn't care. She had taken the wheel of her own life. She was finally over him. And if he tried to get in her way, she'd drive over him.

His eyes darkened. "Now you listen to me. Do you want to know why I came over?" He paused and the only sound breaking the quiet was the faint tap as he snapped his fingers. "I wanted to talk about us—you and me. I was willing to discuss a reconciliation. I understand you're upset, but you need to calm down and think very carefully about what you're saying, Kit."

Kate sat up straighter. There was no need to think anything through. "It's over between us. And the next time you call me 'Kit,' you lose a testicle."

Their stare-down contest—which Kate felt she was on the verge of winning—was broken when they both looked up at the sound of shoes clomping down the stairway.

"I have a big surprise!" Ava announced as she hid behind the corner of the hallway.

"Mommy and Daddy are having a grown-up conversation," Scott said, gritting his teeth.

"Please, Daddy? I want to give you two a concert. Mommy can record it and send it to Grammie. Please?"

Scott rose and looked down at Kate. "Think about what I said. I'm getting a drink." He stomped into the kitchen.

Kate bit her lip. The last thing she wanted was to continue the fight with Scott, but if he kept it up, she'd throw him out of the house.

"Please, Mommy?" Ava begged from her hiding spot.

"I'd love to hear your concert." Kate forced a smile.

"Are you ready for your surprise concert? Grammie is going to love this!"

"Okay. One second." Kate took out her phone and switched on the video. "Go ahead."

Ava clomped around the corner. She was wearing a pair of women's shoes that were way too big for her. She had a tan handbag slung over one shoulder, and most of her face was hidden behind eyeglasses and a wig.

"Look what I found in my dress-up box, Mommy." She flipped the brunette strands aside, pushed the glasses further up her little nose, and struck a pose. "I look just like you!"

Kate stared at the green dress, then at the wig, which almost engulfed Ava's face but matched Kate's color and style. The glasses were very much like her own too. The little girl's feet were pushed all the way down into the toes of the shoes. How could she even walk in them? They looked like Kate's shoes, but they were far too big for Kate—or Tammi.

"This is for you." Ava clomped over and handed Kate a folded piece of paper with Kate's name printed across the front.

She recognized Tammi's handwriting.

I swear they're not mine. If anything happens to me, bring them to the police. Tammi.

Kate felt as though she had gazed upon Medusa and turned to stone. She couldn't move. She couldn't breathe. She couldn't even blink. The note slipped from her fingers and drifted to the floor. The truth hit her like a dump truck. Tammi hadn't dressed up like her and hired a homeless man to kill her—Scott had.

Kate swiped up on her phone screen. Her finger moved toward the emergency call button.

Footsteps stopped at the back of the couch. Scott leaned forward, his hand landing on the back of her neck, his chest pressing against her shoulder. He wrapped his other hand around hers, still clutching her phone.

"You do look like Mommy, Ava." He pulled Kate back, his grip on her neck tightening. He leaned so close to Kate, his lips brushed her ear. "Drop the phone and send Ava outside to play with Andy, or I swear to God I'll kill you both right now."

Ava clomped over to her karaoke machine and flicked the microphone on. "I'm gonna give you a concert."

"Ava… I think Andy wants to play with you next door. He's at Tommy's," Kate said.

Ava frowned. "But I want to sing for you."

Scott squeezed harder.

Kate set the phone down on the couch next to her. "Yes, later. Right now, I want you to play outside. I'll take you for an ice cream sundae in a bit."

Ava clapped her hands together. "With chocolate and sprinkles and lots and lots of whipped cream?"

"Yes, sweetheart. But you have to go now."

Ava was off like a rocket, kicking off the shoes and dropping the pocketbook, glasses, and wig right where she was. Then the little quick-change artist slipped off the dress, grabbed her flip-flops, and slammed the front door behind her.

Kate reached for the bronze lamp on the end table, but Scott squeezed her neck and she dropped her hand back into her lap.

"Don't do this," she begged. "Please. You won't get anything out of it." Kate tipped her head back attempting to make eye contact.

Scott's pupils were coal-black, the ring of blue around them burning with contempt. "I don't have anything, Kate. My mother cut me off. I'm broke."

"I'll talk with Audrey. Explain it to—"

"Oh, you two are buddies now, are you?" He shook Kate and her phone slid off the couch and landed with a bang on the floor. "All my life, that control freak has looked down her nose at me. She thinks I'm pampered, says I always have my hand out. All I wanted was what's rightfully mine, but she was going to give it to you!" He was panting now and sweat beaded on his brow.

Kate swallowed. "I'd only be the executor. She was giving it to the children—"

"That's still not me. But now you've ruined everything. I was going to take you back and my mother would have forgiven me."

Bile burned in Kate's throat at the thought. "You still can. I love you—"

"Do you think I'm stupid? You and Tammi are the same—pathetic, lovesick pawns who in the end betrayed me. Just like my mother did."

"Is that why you killed Tammi?" The question tumbled from Kate's mouth as Scott forced her head lower.

"She figured it out. Oh, she's the one who created the escort ad. I came up with the idea, of course. I gave her all your passwords and told her to use the computer at the library. I showed her how to forge your signature too. We laughed about it. But Tammi had no idea about Derek. I knew she'd freak out if I took it that far. Tammi wanted you to leave town. I wanted you gone, for good. With you dead, my mom would have had to give the money to me, and as a bonus I'd have had one less shrew making demands of me." Scott's fingers dug into the muscles in Kate's neck. "Tammi found my dress and wig. She must have hidden them in Ava's suitcase. I looked everywhere for them, but I never thought to look in a kid's stupid dress-up box."

"But the phone call? The suicide note?"

Scott laughed. "It wasn't a suicide note. Not at first. Tammi wrote you an apology letter, but I took the second page where she denied having anything to do with hiring Derek." Scott squeezed Kate's neck as he spoke. "She was going to tell you and go to the police. I couldn't let that happen. So I shot her in the head and called you."

Kate looked back at the man she'd once loved and realized she didn't know him at all.

Scott closed his eyes for a moment. "Kate?" he sobbed and slurred. "I need to talk to you." His impersonation of Tammi, drunk and crying, was perfect.

"That was you?"

"I didn't want to be the one who found the body. That Detective Tills is pretty good. Stupid, but he can spot a lie. If I found Tammi, I'd have to cry and wail and carry on. That's a tough sell. But if you found the body?" Scott laughed. "No acting involved. You also helped sell Tammi's suicide. Both you and Donna swore she was drunk and ready to kill herself. Thanks for the assist." He pushed her against the sofa.

Kate braced herself as best she could and one hand slipped between the cushions. Her fingers wrapped around something plastic and a little squishy. "You dressed up like me and hired Derek to kill me!"

"I had to get back in my mother's good graces. I thought it was a win-win. If Derek killed you, I would get what was mine. If he got caught, Audrey would think you'd hired him. She'd believe you were crazy and cut you off. I played it perfectly too. It was easy to slip the money into your purse, and I know all your passwords, all your security codes."

"You gave Derek the security code to the house!"

Scott chuckled. "You always use 0703—Andy's birthday. You use it for your phone too. All I had to do was cancel some bills, delete some appointments, emails, and a voicemail or two, and you started thinking you were going mad, didn't you?"

Kate gritted her teeth as he leaned down close, his cheek now next to hers.

"Remember that medicine they gave you after Emma killed herself? The stuff that made you really lose it? I never threw it out."

Kate's eyes widened. *The green flecks in the cannolis.* "You were drugging me!"

Scott scoffed. "All I had to do was bring by a couple of pastries, a little bruschetta, or a vanilla shake, and you'd chow it down with gusto. You never did have any willpower." He snickered. "And since Derek kept chickening out, I thought I should have a backup plan."

Kate wanted to throw up. All this time, he'd been planning to kill her with a big smile on his face.

"When that drone hit you in the head, I was going to blame your mental health issues on that. And get some good money from the lawsuit.

But going to the cops was my biggest mistake. How could I have known that Derek would have ended up on video?"

"That's why you told me to lie."

"You went right along with it. I had to scramble, but it worked. Everything was falling into place, until Tammi screwed it all up. But everything's back on track now."

"There's no way you can kill me and get away with it."

"Sure there is. Take this." Scott reached over the couch and pressed a phone into Kate's hand. "Now put it down on the couch."

Kate set the phone down.

"That's Tammi's phone." Pride rang in Scott's voice. "The police searched for it, but I've had the phone with me. It's part of my backup plan. I took it along when I met with Derek. I made sure I called my own phone, which I left back in my office, so it would place Tammi at the Love Hut. But now, when the police find Tammi's phone with your fingerprints and the missing dress and wig in your house, they'll believe me when I say that it was you all along. You did it because you still love me. They'll believe me when I tell them that you confessed to killing Tammi."

Kate shook her head. "They'll never believe you."

"Of course they will. They know you lied about the drone. I'll tell them you lied about everything else too. Now, you and I are going to walk out to the van and go for a ride to Houghton's Pond."

"No!"

Scott grabbed her by the shoulders and shook Kate so hard her teeth clacked together and sliced her lip. "If you don't, I'm going to call out to the kids and tell them I'm taking us all for ice cream and pizza. They'll jump into the minivan before I finish my sentence, you know they will. Mommy will be *napping* in the passenger seat, so they'll be extra quiet while putting on their seatbelts. We'll drive toward the Pizza Palace, and as we near Houghton's Pond, I'll put the gas pedal to the floor at the bend in the road with no guardrail. The kids will be strapped in like astronauts in their booster seats. The van will go into the water. I'll slip out my open window and swim to shore, after valiantly trying to save my family, of course. Poor Scott, he didn't stand a chance of getting his family out. What a tragic loss. His ex-wife went crazy and yanked the wheel, trying to kill the whole family." Scott paused and let his threat sink in.

Blood ran down Kate's chin. Her mouth was so dry she couldn't breathe.

"You can either get in the van on your own and spare the kids, or I'll kill all three of you."

Kate swallowed down the vomit that rose in her mouth. He would do it. He would murder them all.

Scott squeezed her neck harder and pressed her head toward the floor.

Kate felt the object in her hand. It had a flip-top cap. She chanced a quick glance. It was Ava's tube of Xtra Sour Lemon Goo candy. Her hopes of stabbing Scott with it faded. It would be like trying to stab someone with a tube of toothpaste.

Her phone was on the floor next to her feet. The red light blinked off and on. There was no way she could reach it to call 911.

Then again...

Kate forced herself to sit up straighter, pressing against the hand Scott was using to push her down into the couch. "You forgot one thing."

He leaned down and smirked. "What have I forgotten?"

"You can't fight your way out of a wet paper bag."

"So?" He sneered.

"I can."

Kate held the sour candy tube in front of Scott's face and squeezed. A stream of neon hit him in the eyes.

Scott shrieked and released his grip on Kate's neck.

Kate grabbed the bronze lamp off the end table and brought it around like Babe Ruth swinging for the bleachers. The first blow hit Scott's forearm, and he howled in pain. She maintained her grip as if her life depended on it—because it did—and brought the heavy lamp down on the top of his head. He collapsed into a heap on the floor.

She rushed around behind the couch and stood over him, ready to swing again, but Scott wasn't trying to get up. His chest rose and fell, but other than that, he was motionless.

Keeping hold of the lamp, she hurried over to her phone. Kate had set it to record Ava's concert. She prayed that when she'd coaxed her daughter to go outside, the phone had carried on recording—and it had. It had recorded everything Scott had said.

Before she did anything else, Kate uploaded Scott's confession to the cloud and forwarded a copy to Ryan. Only then did she dial 911.

Kate was in the middle of talking to the operator when, through the living room window, she spotted Ava and Andy racing toward the house. She dashed over to the front door to cut them off.

Leaning outside, careful to block their view, she said, "There's been a little change of plans."

"We're not getting ice cream?" Ava asked, the back of her hand going to her forehead dramatically.

"Come on, Mom!" Andy chimed in. "You promised."

"It's even better. Auntie Donna is going to come over and take you for pizza and ice cream!"

Andy and Ava broke into the happy pizza dance.

"Now, both of you run back next door to Tommy's and wait inside. Inside, or no deal."

"Okay." They both ran across the yard.

"Stay inside until Auntie Donna comes, even if you see police lights!" Kate shouted after them.

They both stopped. Andy eyed her suspiciously. "Are you and Dad fighting again?"

Kate glanced back at Scott, unconscious on the floor.

"Actually," she said, "we're getting along better than ever."

Kate stood in Audrey's spacious kitchen, filling another pitcher of ice water and staring out through the window into the backyard. Andy's birthday party was in full swing. Donna and Dan—her soul mate—had the kids lined up for the piñata and Ava and Andy were waiting in line with their friends. The sounds of their laughter brought a smile to Kate's face. She prayed again for the kids' resilience, and the signs of recovery were good. They were affectionate and talkative—even Andy! Everybody was sleeping well and eating better—and most importantly, they were together, and nothing could come between them.

Kate had invited some parents and her friends too. Grace, the barista from Screamin' Beans, had twin girls Ava's age, and Darlene, the librarian, had brought her son. Susan was there too, along with her daughters. Kate made a mental note to ask if they were interested in babysitting.

One person was still missing, however.

"Please do not tell me that children squealing will become a regular occurrence now that you've moved in," Audrey said as she strolled into the room.

"Playing with friends is an important part of the children's social development," Kate said, shutting off the water and setting the full pitcher on the counter. She was glad to see Audrey out of bed.

How Kate had convinced Audrey to start chemotherapy, she still had no idea. But Audrey had agreed, on one condition: that Kate sell her house and move in with her. The children were thrilled, and so was Kate. The home was enormous, and Audrey had turned everything except her bedroom and her study into a shared space. With one wave of her hand, Audrey had solved all of Kate's financial difficulties. But Kate was determined to forge her own way in this life and had decided to start her own company—Lighthouse Marketing.

Kate wiped a tear away with her index finger. "I still can't thank you enough—"

Audrey silenced her with a glance as she walked over to stand beside her. She peered out the window. "I suppose the children do need to learn to lead somewhere."

"Learning to play is important too."

Audrey smiled. "Excellent idea. We'll let the other children believe it's a game. Andy and Ava will understand they are preparing for the real world."

Kate hid her smile by taking a sip of water.

It was Ava's turn at the piñata and she grasped the stick like a sword. With a loud battle cry, she swung fast and hard, splitting the piñata in two. Candy poured down and the children swept it up with outstretched hands.

"Oh." Audrey's face broke into a grin. "I like this game." She lifted a crystal tumbler down from a cabinet and reached for the decanter filled with scotch.

Kate poured Audrey a glass of ice water and set it down in front of her.

Audrey's withering stare would have frozen Kate in place before—but she just smiled at her former mother-in-law and now mentor and friend.

"I'm proud of you. Chemotherapy is tough stuff."

Audrey grimaced. "I do need to purchase that thesaurus for you. Tough stuff is a gross under-evaluation of the torturous process of chemotherapy on one's body and mind." She took a sip of water. "Please remind me again how you convinced me to submit to weekly barbarism?"

"A wise, brilliant woman once rallied me into battle, and I simply reminded her what she said. Set an example for your grandchildren—fight."

"Oh, yes." Audrey gazed out the window toward the kids. "That's how you blackmailed me, by twisting my own words against me."

Kate held up her glass.

With a slight rolling of her eyes, Audrey lifted her glass of water and clinked it against Kate's.

The two stood in silence, watching the party. As the children laughed and enjoyed themselves outside, Andy opened another present: a football. He tossed it high into the air and caught it with one hand. The other children cheered.

Audrey's expression hardened. "The police have built a solid case against Scott." She turned to stare into Kate's eyes. "I still don't understand why you retained my own lawyers to represent him?"

Kate swallowed. They had tried to have this conversation before and it never ended well. She had thought Scott's mother would have taken a sympathetic stance, but this was an issue on which Audrey and Kate disagreed.

"He's the father of my children and he's your son," said Kate. "That's reason enough."

"He tried to kill you and threatened to harm my grandbabies. I heard the recording."

Audrey's admission that she'd listened to Scott's confession didn't surprise Kate. It was evidence so, of course her lawyers had it.

"Scott's pleading guilty to all charges. The lawyers are only there to make sure the death penalty is taken off the table and he's sent to a prison where he's relatively safe. He'll still spend the rest of his life behind bars."

From the way Audrey knitted her brow, Kate wasn't sure she agreed with her decision. Audrey looked as if she were about to say something else, but then her eyes traveled back to the children's party. "I suppose it will be Andy and Ava's choice if they wish to speak to their father in the future."

Kate nodded. "They may want to know why he did what he did."

"When they find out the answer, perhaps they can explain it to me." Audrey took a sip of water, her hand trembling.

Andy broke free from the crowd of kids and raced over to the table of birthday gifts. He went down the line of presents until he found a huge bright-blue box covered with rockets and stars.

"I wonder who that one's from?" Kate said.

"It's from Grammie!" Andy shouted, shredding the paper. In a matter of seconds, Andy was clutching the box to his chest, and all the children cheered.

"A video game system?" Kate asked.

"No." An impish grin spread across Audrey's face. "A drone."

The ringing doorbell cut off Kate's laugh.

Audrey turned to get it, but Kate touched her shoulder. "I'll answer it," she said.

As Kate turned to go, Audrey seized her hand. The older woman stood there, staring at her. Kate was used to the way Audrey controlled the silence of a conversation, she was even using the trick herself now, but this was different. For the first time, she suspected that Audrey was at a loss for words. Audrey gently squeezed Kate's hand and nodded her head ever so slightly. Kate wasn't looking for thanks, but she expected that was the closest she'd come to getting it.

Her heels clicked on the floor as she passed through the living room. On the wall hung the photograph of Kate and Emma. Lately, she'd been telling the kids about her sister. Ryan had been right. It hurt at first, but the more stories she told, the better she felt.

Kate stopped at the front door. She gazed out the peephole and smiled. She had hoped he'd respond to her invitation.

Ryan Daley waited on the front steps, a brightly wrapped package under his arm.

Kate inhaled through her nose, and as she let out the breath, she imagined a string running straight through her body and being lifted up. Another of Audrey's magic tricks—the queen's pose, as Audrey referred to it.

She opened the door.

Ryan stepped back and gave her a polite nod.

Kate strode out regally. She felt a pang in her chest at seeing him, but this time the feeling was different. Before, she'd thought she needed a man. Now she wanted Ryan in her life. Audrey had told her to retain her composure, insisting that remaining aloof and distant would draw Ryan in. But Kate was her own woman now and distance from Ryan was the last thing she wanted.

She rushed forward and embraced him. She wrapped her arms around his waist, one hand traveling up his broad back and holding him closer. "I was so worried about you."

Ryan embraced her. His strong arms held her firm for a moment, then he pulled back.

Kate stared up into his chocolate eyes and lost herself in their warmth.

He leaned forward and kissed her. There was a tenderness there along with the fire of need. His strong arms pulled her to him and she felt herself lifted into his embrace. She kissed him back, a muffled moan escaping her lips.

Then, leaning away, she said, "I've been officially cleared of all charges."

"You know that I've only stayed away because I didn't want you to violate the terms of your bail, right?"

Kate nodded. "I'm so glad you came."

Ryan stared into her eyes. "Thank you for inviting me." He held up the present. "I got Andy a baseball mitt and ball. I was hoping he'd like to play catch."

"He'd love that!" *And so would I.*

Kate checked Ryan's face to see if she had said her thought aloud, but she was certain she hadn't. She was back on her regular antianxiety medicine, and all the side effects seemed to have been from the pills Scott had been drugging her with.

"Maybe you two could throw the ball back and forth after the party? I was wondering if you'd stay for that dinner I promised."

Ryan broke into a wide grin. "I'd really like that."

What should she say? *Great? Terrific?* She smiled. "Magnificent."

She held the door open for him. As she turned to follow him into the house, she looked down. The welcome mat sat perfectly square against the front step. Kate bumped it with her heel, knocking it slightly askew. She laughed out loud as she passed over the doormat beneath her feet.

EPILOGUE

Surrounded by books piled high on the desk, Scott sat in the prison library poring over case files. He ran his hands over his head and ground his teeth. All this was Kate's fault. Everything. From the moment he'd married her, his life had spiraled downward.

He blinked rapidly, rubbed his eyes, and stared at the open law book before him. He had to read over the law a couple of times before it fully sank in, but there it was—in black and white.

Scott leaned back in his chair and began snapping his fingers as a smile widened across his face.

He didn't have to dig a tunnel or hide in the laundry to escape. The law would set him free. And he'd take back everything that was rightfully his.

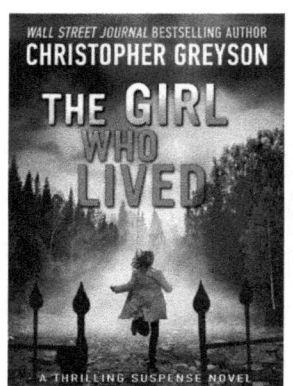

THE GIRL WHO LIVED

Ten years ago, four people were brutally murdered. One girl lived. As the anniversary of the murders approaches, Faith Winters is released from the psychiatric hospital and yanked back to the last spot on earth she wants to be— her hometown where the slayings took place. Wracked by the lingering echoes of survivor's guilt, Faith spirals into a black hole of alcoholism and wanton self-destruction. Finding no solace at the bottom of a bottle, Faith decides to track down her sister's killer— and then discovers that she's the one being hunted.

Best Mystery-Thriller eBook of the Year — *IPB Awards*
Winner Best Thriller — *National Indie Excellence Awards*
Winner Best Thriller — *Silver Falchion Award*
Finalist eBook Fiction — *Indie Book Awards*
Silver Medal Suspense — *Reader's Favorite Book Awards*

How can one woman uncover the truth
when everyone's a suspect—including herself?

The Girl Who Lived should come with a warning label: once you start reading, you won't be able to stop. Not since *Girl On The Train* and *Gone Girl* has a psychological thriller kept readers so addicted—and guessing right until the last page.

IF YOU LIKED ONE LITTLE LIE YOU'LL LOVE JACK!

The Detective Jack Stratton Mystery-Thriller Series, authored by *Wall Street Journal* bestselling writer Christopher Greyson, has 5,000+ five-star reviews and over a million readers and counting. If you'd love to read another page-turning thriller with mystery, humor, and a dash of romance, pick up the next book in the highly acclaimed series today:

And Then She Was GONE

A hometown hero with a heart of gold, Jack Stratton was raised in a whorehouse by his prostitute mother. When his foster mother asks him to look into a missing girl's disappearance, Jack quickly gets drawn into a baffling mystery. As Jack digs deeper, everyone becomes a suspect—including himself. Caught between the criminals and the cops, can Jack discover the truth in time to save the girl? Or will he become the next victim?

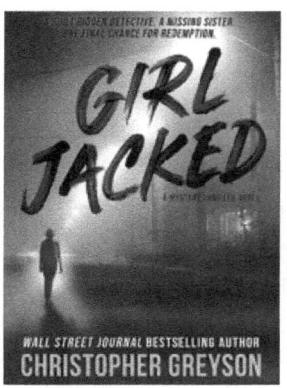

GIRL JACKED

Guilt has driven a wedge between Jack and the family he loves. When Jack, now a police officer, hears the news that his foster sister Michelle is missing, it cuts straight to his core. Forced to confront the demons from his past, Jack must take action, find Michelle, and bring her home... or die trying.

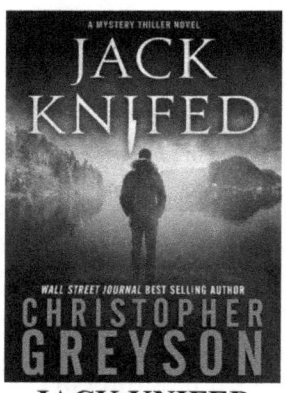

JACK KNIFED

Constant nightmares have forced Jack to seek answers about his rough childhood and the dark secrets hidden there. The mystery surrounding Jack's birth father leads Jack to investigate the twenty-seven-year-old murder case in Hope Falls.

JACKS ARE WILD

When Jack's sexy old flame disappears, no one thinks it's suspicious except Jack and one unbalanced witness. He knows that Marisa has a past, and if it ever caught up with her—it would be deadly. The trail leads him into all sorts of trouble—landing him smack in the middle of an all-out mob war between the Italian Mafia and the Japanese Yakuza.

JACK AND THE GIANT KILLER

While recovering from a gunshot wound, Jack gets a seemingly harmless private investigation job—locate the owner of a lost dog—Jack begrudgingly assists. Little does he know it will place him directly in the crosshairs of a merciless serial killer.

DATA JACK

When Replacement gets a job setting up a computer network for a jet-setting software tycoon things turn deadly for her and Jack. Can Jack and Alice stop a pack of ruthless criminals before they can Data Jack?

JACK OF HEARTS

Jack Stratton is heading south for some fun in the sun. Already nervous about introducing his girlfriend, Jack is still waiting for Alice's answer to his marriage proposal. Now, Jack finds it's up to him to stop a crazed killer, save his parents, and win the hand of the girl he loves—but if he survives, will it be Jack who ends up with a broken heart?

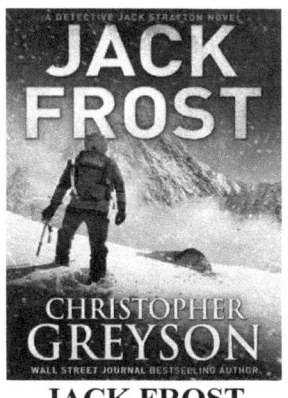

JACK FROST

Jack has a new assignment: to investigate the suspicious death of a soundman on the hit TV show *Planet Survival*. What started out as a game is now a deadly competition for survival. As the temperature drops and the body count rises, what will get them first? The mountain or the killer?

JACK OF DIAMONDS

All Jack Stratton wants to do is get married to the woman he loves—and make it through the wedding. As Jack and Alice fight a deadly killer, their long, happy future together seems like it's just inches from slipping away. This time, "till death do us part" might just be a bit too accurate.

Also available:

Epic Fantasy

PURE OF HEART

Orphaned and alone, rogue-teen Dean Walker has learned how to take care of himself on the rough city streets. Unjustly wanted by the police, he takes refuge within the shadows of the city. When Dean stumbles upon an old man being mugged, he tries to help— only to discover that the victim is anything but helpless and far more than he appears. Together with three friends, he sets out on an epic quest where only the pure of heart will prevail.

Hear your favorite characters come to life in audio versions.
Audio Books now available on Audible!
You could win a brand new HD KINDLE FIRE TABLET
when you go to **ChristopherGreyson.com**
No purchase necessary. It's my way of thanking readers.

INTRODUCING
THE ADVENTURES OF FINN AND ANNIE

Finnian Church chased his boyhood dream of following in his father's law-enforcing footsteps by way of the United States Armed Forces. As soon as he finished his tour of duty, Finn planned to report to the police academy. But the winds of war have a way of changing a man's plans. Finn returned home a decorated war hero, but without a leg. Disillusioned but undaunted, it wasn't long before he discovered a way to keep his ambitions alive and earn a living as an insurance investigator.

Finn finds himself in need of a videographer to document the accident scenes. Into his orderly business and simple life walks Annie Summers. A lovely free spirit and single mother of two, Annie has a physical challenge of her own—she's been completely deaf since childhood.

Finn and Annie find themselves tested and growing in ways they never imagined. Join this unlikely duo as they investigate their way through murder, arson, theft, embezzlement, and maybe even love, seeking to distinguish between truth and lies, scammers and victims.

Don't miss out, pickup the whole collection on Amazon today!

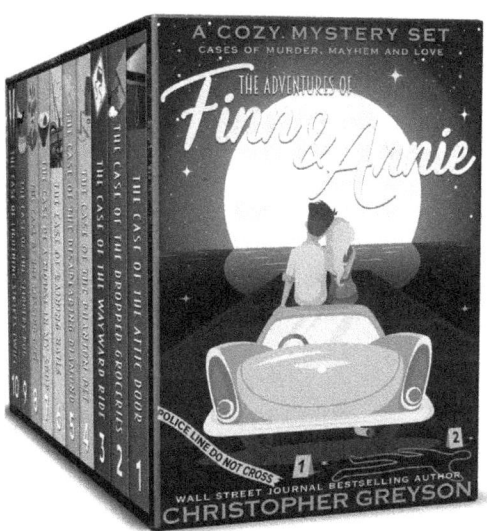

ACKNOWLEDGMENTS

I would like to thank all the wonderful readers out there. It is you who make the literary world what it is today—a place of dreams filled with tales of adventure! To all of you who have spread word of my novels via social media (Facebook and Twitter) and who have taken the time to go back and write a great review, I say THANK YOU! Your efforts keep the characters alive and give me the encouragement and time to keep writing. I can't thank YOU enough.

Word of mouth is crucial for any author to succeed. If you enjoyed the novel, please consider leaving a review at Amazon, even if it is only a line or two; it would make all the difference and I would appreciate it very much.

I would also like to thank my amazing wife for standing beside me every step of the way on this journey. My thanks also go out to my two awesome kids—Laura and Christopher, my dear mother and the rest of my family. Finally, thank you to my wonderful team, Anne Cherry, Maia McViney, Michael Mishoe, my fantastic editors—David Gatewood of Lone Trout Editing, Charlie Wilson of Landmark Editorial, and the unbelievably helpful beta readers!

ABOUT THE AUTHOR

My name is Christopher Greyson, and I am a storyteller.

Since I was a little boy, I have dreamt of what mystery was around the next corner, or what quest lay over the hill. If I couldn't find an adventure, one usually found me, and now I weave those tales into my stories. I am blessed to have written the bestselling Detective Jack Stratton Mystery-Thriller Series. The collection includes *And Then She Was GONE*, *Girl Jacked*, *Jack Knifed*, *Jacks Are Wild*, *Jack and the Giant Killer*, *Data Jack*, *Jack of Hearts*, *Jack Frost*, *Jack of Diamonds*, and coming soon *Captain Jack*. I have also penned the bestselling psychological thriller, *The Girl Who Lived* and a special collection of mysteries, *The Adventures of Finn and Annie*.

My love for tales of mystery and adventure began with my grandfather, a decorated World War I hero. I will never forget being introduced to his friend, a WWI pilot who flew across the skies at the same time as the feared, legendary Red Baron. My love of reading and storytelling eventually led me to write *Pure of Heart*, a young adult fantasy that I released in 2014.

I love to hear from my readers. Please visit ChristopherGreyson.com, where you can become a preferred reader and enjoy advanced notifications of book releases and more! Thank you for reading my novels. I hope my stories have brightened your day.

Sincerely,

CPSIA information can be obtained
at www.ICGtesting.com
Printed in the USA
BVHW081248201222
654627BV00015B/635/J